Song of the Beloved

The Gospel According to Mary Magdalene

Book One – The Jesus Years

Lauri Ann Lumby

Authentic Freedom Press
Published in the United States of America
by Authentic Freedom Press
Oshkosh, Wisconsin
http://yourspiritualtruth.com

Interior design and composition by Sandi Carpenter
Cover design by Gretchen Herrmann, Primary Colors
Cover art "Magdalene" by Toni Carmine Salerno, used with
permission.

ISBN-13: 978-0615775203
ISBN-10: 0615775209

Manufactured in the United States of America

A Note to the Reader

Midrash: (from "to study" or "to investigate") designates an exegesis which, going more deeply than the mere literal sense, attempts to penetrate into the spirit of the Scriptures, to examine the text from all sides, and thereby to derive interpretations which are not immediately obvious.

www.jewishencyclopedia.com

Parable: signifies in general a comparison, or a parallel, by which one thing is used to illustrate another. It is a likeness taken from the sphere of real, or sensible, or earthly incidents, in order to convey an ideal, or spiritual, or heavenly meaning. Parable indicates a deliberate "making up" of a story in which some lesson is at once given and concealed.

Catholic Encyclopedia

As one of my teachers, Jeff VandenHeuvel used to say, "Every story is true, some of them actually happened." This is certainly the case with **Song of the Beloved –The Gospel According to Mary Magdalene.** While inspired by scripture, historical documents and other sacred texts, this story is a work of fiction – period. If I were to define its literary genre, I would suggest that it falls somewhere between midrash and parable. As such, many readers will find within this novel things that resonate with them as deeply true. For others, this book will provoke, confront and challenge. My invitation to you, the reader, is to approach this book with an open heart and an open mind, embracing that which speaks to you as truth, while disregarding the rest. If you get hung up on the details, it may help you to know that my intention is not to present a historically accurate, or scientifically verifiable document, but to express what it may have been like for Mary Magdalene to have been in the presence of and walked in the footsteps of Jesus. This perspective was born completely out of my own imagination while being true to the personal relationship that I have found with Jesus and the Magdalene through meditation and prayer. I hold the spirit of this novel to be true, regardless of whether any of it actually happened.

Lauri Ann Lumby, author

Acknowledgments

To the authors who have gone before me on the path of the Magdalene: Jean Yves- Leloup, Tau Malachi, Susan Haskins, Karen L. King, Roger J. Hooper, Joanna Prentiss and her partner Stuart Wilson, Kathleen McGowan, Dan Brown and Richard Reed, and the one who brought them all together, Cynthia Bourgeault.

Neil Douglas-Klotz for bringing the Aramaic Jesus to light and to Paramahansa Yogananda, Paul Ferrini, Andrew Harvey and Jim Marion for writing about the Jesus I had already come to know in my heart.

Swami Vivekananda and Prem Prakash who through their teachings on Bhakti yoga gave a name to the devotional practice I had come to in my relationship with Christ.

My writing teachers and mentors: Julie Tallard Johnson, Prudence Tippins and Jay Ramsay.

My editor, Sara Eliasen, proofreaders Theresa Lumby Gibson and Sarah Sauer.

The artistic geniuses who made this book so lovely – Gretchen Herrmann, Sandi Carpenter and Toni Carmine Salerno.

My children, Maggie and Wil Schmidt and my spiritual family (you know who you are), along with the writers in my ancestry: Wayne and Mildred Evans and my mother, Connie Evans Lumby.

Without your inspiration, guidance, love and support, none of this would have been possible. Thank you!

Hark! My lover, here he comes,
Springing across the mountains,
Leaping across the hills.
My lover is like a gazelle or a young stag.
Here he stands behind our wall,
gazing through the window,
Peering through the lattice.
My lover speaks, he says to me,
"Arise, my beloved, my beautiful one and come!
For see, the winter is past, the rains are over and gone.
The flowers appear on the earth,
The time of pruning the vines has come,
And the song of the dove is heard in our land.
The fig tree puts forth its figs, and the vines, in bloom,
give forth fragrance.
Arise, my beloved, my beautiful one, and come!
O my dove in the cleft of the rock,
in the secret recesses of the cliff,
Let me see you, let me hear your voice,
for your voice is sweet, and you are lovely."
My lover belongs to me and I to him…

Song of Songs

PROLOGUE

As I face the twilight of my life, I find myself drawn to thoughts of the past. Although I am grateful for the hospitality of the sisters of the holy isle of Avalon who have provided a home and a sanctuary for me in my dying years, and have found a great joy in their presence and our shared work, my heart still aches for the life I have known, and those I have loved. It is of one life and one love that the holy sisters have asked me to write so that they may preserve these stories for the generations to come. Sixty years have passed since that time but the experiences remain etched in my heart.

The life and love of which I speak belongs to the time I shared with my beloved, Jesus bar Joseph. It was through Jesus that I was healed of the demons that destroyed the innocence and wonder I had enjoyed as a child and it was through Jesus that I was restored to my original nature, remembering my Oneness with God in love. It was also through Jesus that I discovered the calling of my soul to be a vessel of God's love in the world, to bring healing and comfort to many and to share the Good News of God's unconditional love. And it was with Jesus that I first lived out this calling. Jesus became not only my teacher, but my closest friend and companion, my partner in ministry, my beloved and my husband.

The love that Jesus offers, however, was never just for me alone. The love that Jesus embodied was for everyone and was intended to bring freedom and liberation to a world trapped in fear. Through his words, his touch, his very presence, he acts as a mirror, showing those with eyes to see, the truth of their Divine and loving nature. In Jesus' presence, we are empowered to remember our truest nature as beloved sons and daughters of Abwoon – the name by which Jesus calls God. This awareness of our truest nature brings the peace and joy for which every man, woman and child hungers, and then compels us to go out into the world to be that awakening love for others as Jesus has done for us.

This is the true wonder of Jesus – not the miracles he accomplished, the stories he told or even the courage that allowed him to face death on the cross. Neither was it the resurrection. Instead, the miracle of Jesus bar Joseph is that his love transcends all fear, for all time. It is this love that beckoned me to boldly stand beside him in being an example of God's love in the world and to courageously continue this mission despite the sword that pierced my heart on the day of his death. It is the transforming power of his love that has raised many from suffering and darkness to discover new life. I cherish the words he offered as comfort to me in my own times of darkness, *"Do not be afraid. I am with you always, even until the end of time,"* and now understand these words are meant for all of us.

Although the loss of Jesus' physical presence has caused me great sorrow, I am filled each day with the joy of experiencing and sharing the fullness of his love. Jesus' presence has healed me, given me comfort, guided my steps and led me to truth. It is for this reason that he has come, not to me alone, but for the whole world – that we may all know peace and so that we may come to know the God that dwells within us and who seeks to be known in the world through our own unique giftedness and call. Much has been and will be written about Jesus' life and teachings, but the limitations of words and perceptions prevent the fullness of Jesus' message from being understood. It is for the sake of this message that I bare my heart and soul, and proclaim the song of my beloved.

Mary, of the House of Lazarus, "The Magdalene"

CHAPTER ONE

Proclaiming the song of my beloved would not be complete without describing the circumstances of my life that brought Jesus into my presence in the first place. Specifically, it was the combination of the family in which I was raised, the experiences of my childhood and the day of darkness that prepared me for the transformation that I would receive through his healing and loving presence. As you will learn, it was through Jesus that the day (and subsequent years) of darkness gave way to the life that had originally been born in me and it was through Jesus' guidance and teachings that I have been able to bring this life into its fullness, in spite of cultural conditions that sometimes frowned on the prophetic and healing gifts of women.

I am the youngest daughter of Levi bar Levi, a middle-class merchant in the province of Judea. Situated along a well-trafficked trade route, our village was a frequent stop for travelers and tradesmen from far-off lands, facilitated by the village well which was strategically placed just outside the village gates. This common well was the center of our existence. It was here that we shared the intimate details of our everyday lives, fostered business relationships and encountered travelers from the outside world.

Our home was located in the center of the village, amidst homes owned by other merchants and craftsmen –

carpenters, weavers, metalworkers, potters and tradesmen. Humbly built of timber and clay, our home consisted of a common living area with an adjoining sleeping quarter that was shared by the entire family. Blankets hung between our parent's bed and the space I shared with my sister, and that shared between my older brothers. While our home was humble, our mother made it warm and inviting.

My father, Levi bar Levi of the tribe of Levi, was a merchant employed in the trade of olive oil and wine. He contracted with the local farmers to sell and transport their products to the merchants who would sell them in lands to the East and to the West. In exchange for this service, my father received a percentage of the sale. My father was not wealthy in his work, but provided for the needs of our family and in this, I felt safe and secure.

Because of his work, my father interacted with merchants from all over the Roman Empire and had an opportunity to meet and experience people from differing cultures, traditions and belief systems. Despite this cross-cultural experience, my father remained a staunch adherent to Hebrew law and found his own comfort and peace in a literal interpretation of the Law of Moses. This preference for literalism led my father to align with the Pharisees of the temple. I had heard that there were other ways of interpreting the Law, but in our household, there was no room for debate. My father had found a measure of peace in believing that all of life's questions could be answered by turning toward the Law and believed that it was through the Law that he could earn God's love. "To strictly follow the Law is the only possible hope of earning God's favorable judgment," Father was often heard to say. I later came to understand that it was fear that had hardened my father's heart to any other interpretation of the Law and from seeing God's higher law of love. As a child, I struggled to understand my father's hardness of heart, especially when my own temperament and that of my brother's were markedly different. As I came to more fully embrace my own original nature in love however, I found a place of compassion within me for my father and the unhealed wounds that caused him to be so rigid.

Now, seeing my father through the eyes of love, I am saddened by the fears within him and the way in which he lived out these fears that came to create in him a harsh and critical nature that then created an atmosphere of palpable tension in our childhood home. Motivated by his vigorous attention to detail, specifically related to the Law, he scrutinized our every action, from the way we arose from bed in the morning to the way we retired at night. Prescribed prayers and rituals, festivals and holy days were faithfully observed, as were the dietary, cleansing and clothing requirements. On the Sabbath, every movement was counted for fear that we might inadvertently infringe upon the Law. If our father perceived that we had strayed from his interpretation of the Law, his own fear of being judged, cause him to react with frightening vengeance. When other tensions were pulling at him, his rage became even more violent. Not wanting to stir his anger, I took to tiptoeing around our father, watching for signs of tension so that I could protect myself from his erratic moods. If I walked into our home and found our father to be in "one of his moods," I was sure to quickly retreat, seeking refuge in the company of our neighbors or under the shade of the olive tree that stood sentinel at the entrance to our village.

My siblings chose their own ways of responding to our father's moods and strict adherence to the Law. Martha, ever seeking our father's approval, would rush to his side and ask how she could help. Levi, obedient to our father's ways, joined him in admonishing "those with careless disregard of the Law." Lazarus, often choosing the role of challenger, would confront our father on his judgmental and fearful nature, which always led to an argument. I feared that one day this approach would lead to Lazarus' demise.

Within me, my father's approach to the Law created a tremendous conflict. Although I took comfort in the prayers and rituals of our Hebrew tradition, I thought the details of the Law to be tedious. I enjoyed the stories of our ancestors and found inspiration and hope in the poetry and songs of our people. In these stories and prayers, I experienced a sense of peace and love that I equated with God – a peace that was far beyond what I could see in the Law. I wondered how the constant fear and anxiety, stimulated by the Law, helped to bring us closer to God, when to me, it made God feel very far away and I wasn't sure this god was someone I *wanted* to know. I much preferred a God that could give me hope and lead me to peace. From my father's perspective, God felt cruel, judgmental and angry. I did not know how to reconcile the God I felt in my prayer or the God I experienced in the Psalms with the fearful and judgmental God my father championed.

In particular, I found myself troubled by requirements of the Law related to my mother during her *niddah* period. When she had her woman-time each month, my father shunned her. He refused to sit near her at table, to sleep in their bed or to touch her. At my father's insistence, these rules also applied to my brothers as they reached thirteen – the age of male adulthood. As a young girl, I felt sorry for my mother – to be treated as if she were diseased simply because of something that occurs in every woman during their childbearing years. God must have created these cycles of bleeding for a reason and who were we to determine that it was bad or unclean? When I inquired of my mother about this, her response was, "We are not to question God's laws, and we are most certainly not to question your father's interpretation of the Law." I listened to her words, but hidden behind the strict tone of her reproach, I sensed that my mother, too, wondered about these teachings. Sadly, in a Hebrew home, it was not the woman's place to question.

Having lived in lands beyond the boundaries of Judea, where the feminine divine is honored along with the masculine, I now know that it was mostly cultural conditioning that kept my mother, Hannah, from asking the kinds of questions that frequently plagued my curious mind. As would be expected from an obedient Jewish wife and mother, she assumed the care and feeding of the children, maintained the day to day needs of the household and presided over the Sabbath meal. She did what my father asked of her and what was expected of any woman of Hebrew descent in Judea. In her role as wife and mother, she would never have dared longing for anything more. Her duty was to raise healthy and dutiful sons and to prepare her daughters to be wives and mothers. It seemed that thoughts beyond dutiful obedience never crossed my mother's mind, but when I listened closely, I sensed that she too questioned the Pharisaic way. As a child, I did not understand her harsh response to my questioning, but as an adult, I now see within her reproach my mother's own mountain of unspoken questions. It grieves me that she never felt the inner freedom to live the truths that may have burned within her. But then again, perhaps the life my mother lived was peace enough for her. The freedom that I craved as a child and embraced as an adult was certainly not for everyone.

My mother, Hannah, born of the tribe of Benjamin, was betrothed to our father when she was but seven years of age. The purpose of their marriage contract was to fulfill the business goals of our father. Several business alliances were passed on to our father from our mother's father as part of their betrothal contract which would be made complete on the day of their marriage. Our father, Levi, waited six years for the contract to be made complete. After the onset of her women's cycles at 13 years of age, our mother was brought to the home of my father, a man twenty years her senior, and made to marry him. It was at the raising of the wedding veil that my mother first beheld the face of the man who would be her husband and her ruler. By all appearances, our mother was grateful and happy to be wedded to a man who promised to be a good provider.

Our mother fulfilled the first obligation of a Hebrew wife by bearing our father a son as his firstborn child. She went on to bear three more children, another son and two daughters. She lived the Hebrew faith to the letter of the Law as my father and his Pharisaic adherents interpreted it, but what I appreciated in my mother, was not her strict adherence to the Law, but the attentive love that seemed to pour out of everything she did. To every act, my mother brought a grace and kindness that communicated her love of God – from the setting and lighting of the Sabbath candles to the specific requirements of food preservation and preparation, to the way she guided us in the Law. Our mother created a way to know the love of God in spite of the rigid standards to which she was being held. I remember, in particular, the way in which our mother carefully and lovingly assisted our father and my brothers in laying *teffilin* and donning the *tallit* for their morning prayers. She performed this action as if it were her own form of prayer and worship and not something reserved for the men alone. Her service to the Law and to her family became her own form of worship and prayer. I regarded her accommodations with awe and knew that unlike our father, whose actions seemed to be motivated by judgment and fear, our mother's actions were motivated by love.

As for my brothers and sister, first there was Levi, the beloved firstborn son. Ten years my senior, he had little interest in either of his sisters. As the firstborn son, he was the rightful heir to our father's estate and the likely beneficiary of whatever success our father might earn. Intent on guaranteeing his position of power and status, Levi was woefully obedient to our father. I often wondered at the great efforts he put forth to please our father, for in truth, Levi could do no wrong in our father's eyes.

Following Levi by three years was Lazarus, the second-born son. He was as different from Levi as a camel is from a palm tree, causing my mother to refer to them as "her Cain and Abel." Arising from the expected competition between first and second-born, Levi and Lazarus' relationship eventually escalated to fierce rivalry. Levi wielded his firstborn status over Lazarus, reminding him of his role as subservient younger brother. Levi bragged about the riches he would inherit from our father and taunted Lazarus about his fate as Levi's servant. Fiercely independent, Lazarus rejected these ideas and proposed that someday he would be more successful than even our father had been, and that his success would put Levi to shame.

It was not the rivalry between my brothers, however, that got Lazarus in trouble. It was his fiercely independent nature coupled with the gift of seeing the world through many perspectives. Lazarus, unlike Levi, only seemed to interact with our father through conflict. He constantly challenged our father with more efficient and better ways of running the family business and managing the household. But the true source of conflict between Lazarus and our father was the Law. Lazarus had an insatiable desire to know and to live the truth, and for Lazarus, that truth had to be grounded in reason. If there was no reason to back up the Law, he quickly set it aside. This became a constant source of tension between Lazarus and our father.

My sister Martha followed Lazarus by three years, which made her four years my elder. Martha was Levi's twin in obedience if not by birth. As the eldest daughter, she sought only to please our parents, most especially our father.   She readily took to a daughter's duty: silent and unseen, she assisted our mother in accomplishing the work that was a woman's to perform. She eagerly assisted our mother in the cooking, cleaning, weaving and mending, and in the care of her younger siblings – namely, me. Her motivation for eagerly participating in these tasks was to gain the attention of our father, enthusiastically showing him every completed task, hoping to earn even a small percentage of the favor our father bestowed upon Levi. Sadly, our father had no eyes for his daughters, so Martha's efforts went largely unnoticed. When she showed him the fruits of her labors, he merely grunted and walked away as if to say, "Of course, this is what is expected of a woman."

While the four years between us created an arm's length distance, I never doubted Martha's love for me. She was a quiet girl who matured into a quiet woman – clear proof of the saying, "still waters run deep." Once Martha allowed you into her heart, she kept you there for an eternity with unwavering loyalty and devotion. I often thought this was a trait that was uniquely her own. Somehow, in spite of our differences in temperament, I had found my way into Martha's heart, for even in the moments of greatest conflict, when my restlessness and impatience got the best of her, her reproaches were wrapped in love and concern. I felt her love most profoundly when, in the darkness of night my restless mind kept me awake, or when night terrors startled me from my sleep, Martha was there to quiet and comfort me. She provided me with the loving support that was unavailable from our mother who was tending to the needs of her husband and sons.

Last of all, there was me, *Little Mary*, as my mother called me in those moments of private tenderness. My father and Levi simply ignored me, so I spent my time with Martha and Lazarus. As the younger sister, I too, was expected to perform the work required of a daughter. What else could a girl of Hebrew descent be doing besides tending to the home and preparing the meals for the men? Although I assisted my mother and Martha in these tasks, I found them mostly tedious. My restless spirit longed for something more – I just didn't know what that something else might be. Plagued by this nagging restlessness, I lacked the motivation to tend to my work with the passion and attention to detail that Martha and my mother expected. Luckily for me, when their frustration with my inefficiencies became too much, Lazarus provided a ready escape.

Lazarus was an inquisitive and adventurous soul who, more than anyone in our household, understood the curiosity that plagued my mind and the restlessness that drove my spirit. He was the perfect guardian for me when my wandering mind or uncoordinated fingers became too much for my mother or Martha. Seven years my senior, I looked up to Lazarus like the father I never felt I had. Even better than that, as brother and sister we shared a freedom that I could not have enjoyed with my father.

Lazarus allowed me to accompany him on errands for our father's business. When we walked to the neighboring orchards and vineyards, he patiently slowed his gait so that my little legs could keep up. While in his care, I explored the rocks, canyons and groves between our village and the farms with which Father did business. Lazarus and I shared an affinity for the land. Restless and discontented with mundane tasks, we both found peace in the open air with the earth beneath our feet.   I remember the times when Lazarus and I shared a moment of wonder over a butterfly emerging from its chrysalis or the ways in which bees made honey from the pollen they had gathered from the flowering trees. We wondered how anyone could deny the presence of God in the midst of these everyday miracles. We felt the presence of God more acutely in the wonders of nature than even in the synagogue or the temple. Lazarus was not only a wonderful brother but became a beloved companion and friend, and it was in his presence and company that I felt comfortable being my truest self. With Lazarus, I found support for my truest nature which found delight in creation and wonder in the workings of God's hand. I also found with Lazarus the freedom to laugh and to play. He holds a very large place in my heart and it was because of him that my memories of early childhood are mostly joyful.

This joy, however, came to an abrupt end the day that my brother's fierce independence finally became too much for our father (or rather, our father's limited vision

became too much for Lazarus). Engaged in his morning ritual prayers, Father uttered the typical formula, "Thank God I was not born a woman, a dog or a gentile." Just as I felt my own heart recoiling at these words Lazarus exploded, "Father, how can you say something so hateful in your prayer?" My father looked upon Lazarus with great disdain, "You should know why I say this prayer. It is because of woman that sin has come into the world. They are the source of all suffering! They are unclean and would be undeserving of being in the presence of God if it weren't for the grace of temple practice." For a split second, I thought I heard my father's heart speak a deeper truth, but just as quickly as it was there, it was replaced by what he had been instructed to believe in the Pharisaic way. I wondered for a moment if this was what my father really believed. With these ponderings in my mind, I sat in rapt attention, waiting to see how this would unfold. The tension between my father and Lazarus was palpable as I felt them both gather up their defensive armor. My father stood in one corner of the room with arms folded hard across his chest. Lazarus stood in the other corner, at first a mirror image of our father's righteousness, but then I saw him purposefully uncross his arms and take a deep breath as if to calm himself.

Then, Lazarus pleaded with the words that had for years been gathering in his heart, "Father, have you not eyes to see? Women are the very reason we are here. It is from their womb that we come into this world. It is to them that the Lord has given the gift of procreation. Without woman, there would be no man. If God saw fit to create women and through them the miracle of birth, should they not be valued as sacred and holy and afforded the same rights as men? I would go so far as to suggest that women should be allowed at temple, to study the Torah and to lead the worship."

At first, my heart leapt in recognition of the way that Lazarus' words spoke truth to my soul, but before I was able to entertain such hopes, a cool shiver of fear crept up my spine. I looked to my father with his fists tightly clenched, as a cold stony silence came over him. I knew that Lazarus had gone too far. Father's body became rigid and in a strained voice he whispered, "Lazarus, you have spoken blasphemy in our home and in the eyes of the Lord." I felt Lazarus gather his defenses around him in anticipation of a strike as our father proclaimed the dreaded words of banishment, "Lazarus, I withdraw from you the name of Levi. From this moment, you are no longer my son." Levi bar Levi turned his back on my brother and silently walked away.

I felt my heart drop to my feet knowing the severity of this curse. Levi would no longer be my father's son. He would no longer be my mother's son. He would no longer be our brother. He would no longer be *my* brother. His name, his right to the name, his right to anything of Levi bar Levi's was permanently severed from this moment forward. I looked to our mother, who had been listening at a distance and begged her with my eyes to intervene. Mother simply looked at me with sadness in her eyes and shook her head in silence. Then with the weight of a stone being rolled across the entrance to a tomb, my mother hung her head in sorrow, turned and silently walked away.

Lazarus stood there stunned and immobile. My heart dropped to my feet in panic. I ran to Lazarus, threw my arms around him and began to plead, "Please tell Father you were wrong. Take back what you said! Please don't let him send you away." Then I began to cry. Lazarus, the one person with whom I experienced the freedom to be my truest self, would be cast out into the wilderness to find his own way. I would never be allowed to see him again, to enjoy the company of his presence or to enjoy the delight and wonder I shared with him in nature. Lazarus, the only one with whom I could laugh and experience joy would be gone. Lazarus could not leave. Lazarus could not be banished.

Lazarus placed his hands on my shoulders and listened to my tearful pleading. I felt in his touch the deep sorrow that now burdened his heart and within that sorrow, I saw a glimmer of regret, but before the regret could take hold, I felt Lazarus, once again, gather his defenses around him. He knelt before me and with a deep love in his voice, gently explained, "Mary, it is because of my love for you, for Mother and for Martha that I cannot take back what I said. How can it not be true that you are worthy and sacred in God's eyes? How can you not be deserving of the same rights as men?" I then felt him gather his resolve around him as he boldly proclaimed, "Mary, it is for you that I accept this sentence of banishment."

Lazarus hugged me tightly, kissed me lightly on the cheek, and lingered for awhile holding his cheek to mine. "Mary, I love you," he whispered as tears choked his voice. "When you are of age, I will take you away from this place of imprisonment and help you find a life where all women are free."

He stood up, gathered his pride and walked out the door. I was roughly seven suns when Lazarus left to find his own way in the world. He was fourteen.

CHAPTER TWO

Without Lazarus, I found myself even more restless than before. I could not sit still. My mind raced. My fingers grew more clumsy and my unresolved grief left me feeling angry and impatient. I missed him terribly and the only way I could find comfort was by spending time outside our village exploring the world. Revisiting the wonder of nature, watching blossoms unfurl, and regarding the cycles of the seasons helped me to feel connected with him. I imagined that with God's help, I was not alone in my outside explorations and that Lazarus was always at my side. With my parents occupied with my other two siblings, and because of my mother and sister's impatience with my restlessness, it was easy for me to slip from their view and disappear into the wilderness that surrounded our village. I never strayed too far from the village gates, always remaining close enough that they could be seen, but just being outside the gates of what was feeling more and more like a prison was sometimes comfort enough.

I must confess that it was not only curiosity or restlessness that drove me to wander out alone. An inner rebellion compelled me to go out despite my father's warnings and prohibitions – "a righteous and respectful woman would not dare set foot outside the village gates without a proper chaperone." The reserved distance I had held for my father previous to Lazarus' banishment had now turned to seething resentment. I hated my father for driving Lazarus from our home. And in my hatred, I was no longer open to seeing or hearing the fleeting glimpses of tenderness or regret that he might unwittingly show. Banishing Lazarus had sealed the door that may have been open for any level of trust or respect and while I did not want to do anything that might hurt my mother or sister, going out alone was the one thing that I could do to symbolically refuse the constrictions of my father's rules. I believe that Martha and my mother knew full well what I was doing, but chose to look the other way. I often wondered if this was perhaps my mother's way of absolving her guilt over allowing Lazarus' banishment as I frequently observed regret on her face when Martha or I mentioned his name.

As long as I was home for prayer and to assist Martha in the preparation of the meals, nobody seemed to care and I was free to entertain my own form of rebellion.

After seven years of exploring beyond the village gates without reprisal, I had grown accustomed to these wanderings. Unfortunately, this unfettered freedom left me unsuspecting of the dangers that might lurk right outside my door. I had no idea that my father's protestations were indeed valid warnings of the perils that might greet an unsuspecting girl who was bold enough to seek beyond the village gate. A child might have escaped danger at the well that morning, but I was no longer a child. I had unknowingly grown into a beautiful woman of fourteen. While it should not have been so, my waist-length, curling dark hair and blossoming figure left me even more vulnerable to the potential evils of men.

On that morning in my fourteenth year, I was awakened out of a deep sleep by a fearful dream. In the dream, the moon shone a brilliant orange and began to spin and whirl as if it were about to explode. I had the sensation in the dream of the world coming to an end and woke up with my heart pounding in my chest and sweat dripping from my brow. There was no way I was going to fall back to sleep. Instead, I decided to clear my mind by going out early to the village well to draw water for the morning *mitzvahs*. As I departed my father's home, I heard his protestations echoing in my mind and I was reminded that it was inappropriate for me to go to the well without either a male escort or a larger group of women. But since I had grown accustomed to exploring outside our compound by myself, I thought "what could be the harm in going to the well this one time alone?"

As I quietly slipped beyond the village gate, my gut tightened with a creeping sense of foreboding and the hairs on the back of my neck stood on end. I hastily brushed these sensations aside as the workings of my overactive imagination and boldly continued toward the well. By the time I saw the seven drunken men it was too late. I turned to run, but they quickly descended upon me like a flock of hungry vultures. As the men took their turn with me, one, and then another, and then another part of my soul was violently torn from within me. Eventually, seven pieces of my soul were devoured as if plucked clean from my bones. All that remained was an empty carcass where my soul had once been, and I was left there, presumably to die.

The women of our village found me at daybreak covered in dirt – the shreds of my robe tattered, my body beaten and bruised, the inside of my thighs covered in

19

blood. The mothers covered their daughters' eyes and drew them away as the older women of the village wrapped their shawls around my exposed body. They gently picked me up and rushed me to my father's house in silent haste, not wanting to be seen by any of the village men. They carried me in secret to my mother and Martha who, panic stricken, led me to the bed that Martha and I shared.

Placed gently upon the bed, my mother and Martha began tending my broken body. They removed the tattered shreds of my robe, and with gentle and loving hands, cleansed my battered body with a mixture of water and healing herbs. What was left of my soul had retreated to the darkest corners of my mind and I lay there paralyzed and numb. Only a silent witness, I watched my mother and sister care for my broken body as if viewing it from above.

In the midst of their care, my brother Levi, burst through the front door of the house. In two strides he reached the linen cloth that hung down guarding our privacy, tore it down and cast it aside. Filled with righteousness he stood at the foot of the bed and directing his accusing gaze toward our mother, pointed in fury toward me. "This Mary has brought shame upon the House of Levi and you have dared to bring this unclean woman into our home! I will send word to Father and inform him of the sin that you have brought upon this house."

My mother took a deep breath and set aside the cloth she was using to wash me. With measured breath she brushed off her robe and slowly stood to face my brother and placed her hands upon his shoulders. "Levi, I am your mother. I have watched you grow from a boy to a man and in that journey, I have not been unaware of your own sinfulness. I have kept my silence even though I know what you have done in secret. I urge you to be merciful toward your sister as I have been merciful with you. She could not have known the danger that awaited her at the well."

"Mother, no respectable Hebrew mother allows her daughter to roam free. It is your indulgence of Mary that is the ultimate cause of the shame that now threatens the House of Levi." Puffed up with self-righteousness, Levi violently shoved our mother's hands aside and stormed out the door.

Mother returned and knelt beside me. Choking back tears, she confessed, "Mary, I am afraid this will not go well for you. We both know your father's adherence to the Law. I wish it were not so, but I cannot protect you from his judgment. I am only a wife and a mother in your father's home. Let us pray that the Lord will find a way of mercy for all of us." My mother clutched my hands to her heart as she prayed. I could only pretend to join her in prayer as my mind remained paralyzed with shock. After her prayer, Mother left me in Martha's care as she went to prepare herself for our father's return – or so I assumed.

Hours, or perhaps days later, Father returned home in a rage. He stormed into the house, his venomous anger preceding his physical presence. He came to my bed, grabbed me by the arm and dragged me from our house through the village, shouting for our neighbors to join him while I stumbled along in stunned silence; for his anger was not at the injustice or hurt that had been done to me but at the shame it had brought to our family. Once we reached the center of the village, he shoved me backwards toward the judgment pole. As my back struck the pole, my consciousness returned and my feelings abruptly re-awakened. I looked around me into the faces of my accusers. These were the men and women that I had grown to love. They had tended my scraped knees, fashioned trinkets for me with their own hands, accompanied me to worship, and dried my tears when Lazarus faced banishment. These people were in many ways more family to me than my own father had been. And yet now they stood before me, aligned with my father, in judgment. I suddenly felt shame for what I had done and what had been done to me; but, even more so, I felt betrayed. How could those I had come to love now stand as my accusers? A chill crept through my body as my father began to speak.

"This girl is guilty of the sin of adultery," my father proclaimed. "According to the law, I sentence her to death by stoning." My mother, who had been following close at our heels and who now stood directly facing me, sucked in her breath in shock as the color drained from her face. I saw her look upon me with deep sorrow in her eyes and I felt her heart break at the realization of her helplessness in this situation. There was nothing she could do to save me. My heart cried out and my eyes pleaded with her to rescue me from Father's vengeful judgment. My mother looked back at me with eyes filled with despair. She hung her shoulders as she silently drew her veil across her face in resignation while she turned and walked away. This final glimpse of my mother forsaking me is forever etched in my mind. At that moment I knew that my fate was now in my father's hands.

For a moment, I ignored the grief and shame that wracked my body and gathered what I had left of my courage and rebellious spirit. I wrapped this counterfeit strength around me and looked straight into my father's eyes, daring him to throw the first stone. My father glared back at me, his eyes seething with hatred. He reached down to grab the first stone which he would have happily cast when Lazarus suddenly broke through the crowd. "Stop this!" he shouted. "She has done nothing wrong." Lazarus, now a man of twenty-one, towered over our father and his unexpected presence startled our father just long enough for Lazarus to step between us. "You will not harm her. I will take her into my charge." With that, Lazarus draped his own cloak around me as a show of protection, wrapped his arm around me and gently guided me from the crowd. I glanced back as I saw my father spit on the ground where Lazarus had trod, kick the dust, and shake it from his feet.

As Lazarus led me from the crowd, I kept my head bowed, not wanting to look into the eyes of the villagers who had betrayed me. As we passed through the crowd, I felt the brush of a loving hand and looked up to see my sister Martha with tears in her eyes. We locked eyes for a moment when Martha cried out for the whole village to hear, "You Levi bar Levi, are no longer my father. I go with Lazarus to care for him and for my sister, Mary, where I too might be valued." With gratitude and wonder in his eyes, Lazarus reached for Martha and drew her into his embrace. Together, the three of us made our way through the throng and toward the departure gate.

In this bold act of defiance, Martha and I had left behind all our familial ties, including our dowries and any hopes of betrothal or marriage. In defying our father and leaving his home, we had sealed our fates and would never fulfill the expectation to marry and bear children. Martha and I would be the wards of Lazarus and would, from this point on, cease belonging to the House of Levi. We were now Martha and Mary of the House of Lazarus as we began the ten mile journey east to Lazarus' home just outside the village of Bethany. As I looked up at the moonless sky, a strange shiver of foreboding came over me and wondered if indeed the world had come to an end.

CHAPTER THREE

In the silence of the journey, my mind once again retreated into the cover of darkness and I surrendered to my brother's lead. Martha followed, furtively gazing back at our village as it disappeared behind us. I guessed she was pondering all she had left behind and wondering about her choice. By choosing to go with Lazarus, Martha left behind not only her familial ties, but any hopes of betrothal. She would forever be labeled the *sister of a whore*.

Knowing what I now know about trauma, I should have been trembling and terrified as we walked those ten miles without much more than Lazarus' cloak to cover me. Instead, shock had slammed the doors on my feelings and to my awareness of anything but my brother, my sister, and the empty road before us. Eventually Lazarus' anger broke the silence.

"I hate that man! What Father did to you Mary, and what he would have eventually done to you, Martha, and what he has done to me, is unforgivable. The best day of my life was the day our father banished me from his home. He had no right to treat you as he did Mary. And Martha, you deserve better than what Father allowed you. He has proven himself to be a small and evil man and he will pay for his actions. In fact, I will make sure that he does."

Lazarus went on to boast about the success he had built for himself in the seven years since being banished from our father's house. He proudly explained how, after leaving Father's home, he had secured employment with one of the farmers Father had shunned because of his religious beliefs. Lazarus took advantage of this knowledge and offered his services as a laborer. As the years passed, Lazarus proved his worth and was elevated to manager of the estate. Lazarus gloated over the victory he felt in this achievement, and I wondered if it was indeed victory in the achievement that he felt, or his own vindication. Lazarus went on to brag about how he had purposefully chosen a humble existence, setting aside every possible wage until he could become a landowner and businessman in his own right.

As Lazarus described it, he eventually acquired enough money to purchase a small olive orchard of his own. He built a press and set about perfecting the extraction of only the finest oils from the fruits in his small grove. What began as a small venture quickly grew into a thriving enterprise. With pride in his voice, he explained how he had come to produce some of the most highly coveted oils in the district and how he had developed trade with many of the most successful and well-known local and traveling merchants. He boasted that his oils were now in demand as far away as Persia and the Far East. His business, he explained, put our father's meager trade to shame. I could hear the sense of vindication in his voice as he proclaimed his hard-won success. I understood his desire to outdo our father and in a sense it seemed deserved, but the Lazarus that I remembered was motivated by kindness not by the righteous indignation that I was now observing in him. I was confused by the changes I was seeing in my brother.

After many hours, we arrived at the well that stood along the trade road and just outside the perimeter of Lazarus' compound. We paused to fill our water skins and turned north toward the low wall that marked the boundaries of Lazarus' property. I stood, mouth agape, as I took in the testament that Lazarus had built to his success.

We arrived at the household gate and gazed in awe at the eight foot high door of solid cedar and the smoothly polished timber and limestone walls that enclosed Lazarus' home. Lazarus unbolted the gate and showed us inside. With nothing but the clothes on our backs, Martha and I had no trouble entering the gate; but, we could not help stumbling as we beheld the grandeur of what Lazarus now called home. By the standards of the day, Lazarus' home was exceptionally well-appointed.

After Lazarus gave us a brief tour of his home, he invited Martha and me to bathe and cleanse ourselves from the long journey and afterward, to join him in breaking our fast. With no appetite, I excused myself from the invitation to dine and went straight to the bath. To my surprise, I found clean robes waiting there for me. I later learned that Mother had included them when she sent for Lazarus, anticipating that at least I would eventually find my way into Lazarus' home. I eagerly shed the cloak that Lazarus had so generously given me to cover me in my shame, but felt a stranger in the robes that belonged to another Mary from another time. I was no longer Mary of the House of Levi. I was cast out – an *anawim*.

After bathing, I found the room that Lazarus had designated as mine and went directly to the bed. I was never more grateful for a place to rest my weary body. As my head hit the linens, the events of the day began to unfurl in my mind. The shock that had shielded my mind through the assault, the discovery, the judgment, the death sentence, the rescue and the escape now gave way to an acute remembering. Suddenly alone with my own thoughts and feelings, I began to grasp the horror of what those men had done to me. A tremor of humiliation and shame spread through my body as I remembered how the men fell upon me like wild animals on fresh prey, how I struggled for escape, how I screamed in terror behind the hand that was clasped over my mouth and how tears poured from my eyes as my cloak was torn in two and my legs ripped apart. As the first man forced himself into me, my spirit fled – a candle snuffed out, leaving behind only darkness.

In that moment of violation, my mind had gone blank. But, now alone in my room, every detail of the assault came rushing back – the leering faces of the seven men looming over me; their stale breath reeking of alcohol; the scruff of their beards on my tender skin; the weight of their fumbling hands on my naked body; the pressure of their bodies against mine; the violent thrust of their lust between my legs painfully and shamefully tearing my womanhood to shreds. As the details raced through my mind, I grew sick with revulsion and was overcome with nausea. Too stricken to move, I leaned over the side of my bed and vomited on the floor beside me.

I could not stop the images racing through my mind which turned from the assault to the moment of discovery. When the women came at daybreak, a collective gasp rose from their lips as they found me naked and all-but unconscious beside the village well. In the darkness of this vision I heard a woman's plaintive wail and felt someone place a cloak over my shameful, naked corpse. Now, lying in the bed that Lazarus had provided for me and freed from the sanctuary of shock, I experienced the fierce humiliation of being discovered like this – naked, violated, sinful, and unclean. Even the memory of the gentle way in which the women carried me home and tended to my battered body was not enough to lift the cloak of shame that grew heavy upon my body.

Next came flooding in the memory of my father's face when he returned home and discovered my sin – his eyes seething with disdain, revulsion, and rage-filled hatred – not for what the men had done to me, but for what I had done to him. By venturing out alone, I had brought this tragedy on myself and had brought sin upon the House of Levi. Gazing into the memory of his accusing eyes, my shame grew thicker. I felt the terror of my father dragging me to the village for judgment and sentencing. Trembling in fear, I tried to avoid the condemning glares of those who ran to witness my shame. My father's judgment ran through me like a spear.

The memories tumbled over each other into my awareness which turned to my mother. Over, over and over she drew her veil across her face and turned her back toward me. Again and again the ground upon which I had based my existence was pulled out from beneath my feet. I reached out in desperation for my mother who in one gesture banished me from her sight. My heart torn in two, I plunged into the void – absent father or mother, alone, abandoned.

My memory now turning toward the villagers, I searched for one friendly face, my heart pleading, "Won't you defend me, take me into your home, offer me the love that I have shown you?" Instead, I found each of them staring back at me in revulsion and disgust, chanting their accusations: "unclean, adulteress, sinner, whore." I grew smaller and smaller as I was obliterated from their lives.

In a single moment, I no longer belonged to the house of Levi, I was no longer Hannah's daughter, and I no longer belonged to the people of our village. My heart shattered in a million pieces as I tumbled deeper into the darkness.

The shame that I felt for myself was excruciating, but it was nothing compared to the guilt I felt over the shame I had brought upon my family. Now Lazarus and Martha too must bear the burden of my shame. Between the threatening voices of guilt and shame, I heard Lazarus' urgent pleadings, "Mary, no matter what the Law says this is not your fault. Those men are to blame for their evil doings. You have done nothing wrong." I struggled to grasp his words, but as the darkness crept in, his words disappeared into the void. The light dimmed, a damp cold engulfed my mind and I became numb as I plunged even deeper into the abyss.

Before surrendering to the depths, however, a low and raspy voice began to taunt me, "Mary, where was your God in this? Where was your God when those seven men fell upon you? Where was your God when your innocence was stolen from you? God could have saved you. God could have prevented this horror. At the very least, God could have allowed you to die in your shame. Instead, God has abandoned you. God has betrayed you. God has left you alone to suffer in your guilt – untouchable, unclean, a whore." I found myself drawn in by these words and as I gave myself to them, a cold shiver of emptiness and fear filled my body. Cold and numb, I surrendered to the darkness where the shame, the guilt and the indelible sense of betrayal began to slip away. Even at the tender age of fourteen, I sensed this darkness would not come without a cost, but if the darkness meant freedom from this pain, it was a price I was more than willing to pay. So

I retreated from the terrors of that day and with open arms welcomed the stone that rolled over the entrance of my self-appointed tomb.

I chose to live in this state, holding at bay, as if behind an immovable stone, the demons of shame, guilt, betrayal, grief, sorrow, loneliness and abandonment. I remained in a constant state of darkness, taking refuge in my room in the beautiful home Lazarus had set up for himself and that he now shared with his unwanted sisters.

For years the darkness remained, while I, for the most part, remained in my room, barely leaving my bed but for the bare essentials of survival – eating a few bites of the food my sister lovingly placed before me, shuffling beside Lazarus in the garden for a few moments to silence his begging, and allowing Martha to bathe me before insects made a permanent home in my hair. Occasionally, the guilt demon would rouse me to offer a vain attempt at helping my sister with the household tasks. Martha feigned appreciation, but the slow plodding cloud of darkness that I had become clashed with her efficient and fastidious nature. Pity and impatience would eventually get the best of her and she would release me from my chores. Grateful to return to my tomb, I quickly retreated into darkness. The great irony was that although this life held no appeal and there was really no reason to go on living, I lacked even the motivation to enter into the simple task of death. I was too depressed to die.

Locked within my chosen tomb of despair, I was blind to the tomb into which my beloved Lazarus had also retreated. In retrospect, I can now see the devastating effects all of these events – especially his own banishment – had on the life of my precious brother. His once enthusiastic, playful nature had soured into bitterness, suspicion and an icy aloofness.

The conflict between Lazarus and our father had wedged itself within Lazarus' heart. He could not reconcile his own beliefs about God with those of our father and he could not make peace with the contrast between father's rigid adherence to the letter of the Law and the prayers and rituals through which Lazarus had found comfort as a child. However, Lazarus later confided to me that, more than anything, he deeply grieved our father's easy banishment of him. For seven years, Lazarus had sustained his fury at a God who could have let this banishment take place. In turning his back on our father, he also turned his back on God. He ceased his observation of the Law, forsaking even the prayers and rituals which, in the past, had given him comfort and guidance. Although Lazarus feigned religious observance when in the company of the farmers and merchants with whom he did business, in the privacy of his home, he neglected all the things that made him Jewish.

When Lazarus saw our father treating me with such revulsion – going so far as to bring me, his own daughter, to death – the fragile remains of his faith turned to dust. With no one to turn to, neither family nor rabbi, nor healer, nor even God, Lazarus was helpless to halt or slow my rapid descent into darkness. In the face of his powerlessness, the dust that remained of Lazarus' faith simply blew away. While tending to the essentials of his business so as to insure the survival of his new-found household, Lazarus retreated into a tomb of his own. Unlike my tomb of darkness and despair, Lazarus' tomb was composed of the bitter bile of rejection and resentment combined with the desire to spite our father by becoming more successful than he. It was from this tomb of bitterness that Lazarus found release at the hands of a man that would prove to be the savior of us all and the man to whom I would eventually give my life and my love.

CHAPTER FOUR

Fourteen years passed since our exodus from the house of Levi. I was now a woman long past the age of betrothal, as was Martha. Lazarus had continued to exist in his tomb of bitterness accompanied by the relentless pursuit of professional success. I remained in my tomb of despair while Martha dove head-first into tending to the needs of the home – masking her own grief-filled heart with menial tasks: gardening, cooking, cleaning, weaving, sewing, etc. etc. etc. She took the typical women's duties onto her capable, but over-burdened shoulders. While time had passed, nothing had really changed for Lazarus, Martha or me.

It was at this time that we began to hear stories of a new preacher that was ministering in the villages around our humble home. Years before, we had heard of the radical prophet, John the Baptizer. Many declared him the "new Elijah." He was described as a rough and rugged man who professed to abide by the austere life modeled by the Essenes. Although, or perhaps because, John the Baptizer had gathered a large following of people looking for a glimmer of hope in the dismal existence of Roman occupation, he had recently been arrested and executed by the House of Herod. It was rumored that Herod's stepdaughter had asked for the Baptizer's head on a platter – a request Herod was all too happy to oblige.

An initiate of the Baptizer's, Jesus bar Joseph, had risen up in his place. Apparently the two differed somewhat because in contrast to John's message of austerity, Jesus' message was one of compassion. He had been traveling from village to village around the province of Judea when Lazarus heard that he was making his way toward Bethany. Considering Lazarus' dismal lack of faith and the skepticism he now harbored toward anything that even dared to speak of a loving God, I'm not exactly sure what drove Lazarus to seek Jesus' presence that day: perhaps he wanted to join the crowd in heckling Jesus or, perhaps he was truly curious; or maybe, he harbored a hidden longing within his heart. Lazarus never confided to me his motivation, but I sense it was the latter. What I learned later, while in the company of Jesus, was that God works in mysterious ways and opens the hearts of even the most hard-hearted individuals if that is their deepest longing. As such, I give Lazarus' longing credit for driving him into the village that day to get a glimpse of this man, Jesus.

As Lazarus told it, he entered the village and was drawn by the sounds of a gathering crowd. He followed the noise until he came upon the synagogue's courtyard, where he discovered a crowd of people listening intently to the preaching of what Lazarus originally determined to be "an unremarkable man." Lazarus approached the crowd and upon seeing this "unremarkable man," dismissed him as just another preacher. He turned to walk away, but just as he made his way toward leaving, Jesus caught Lazarus' eye, smiled and began to tell a story. Something in Jesus' countenance and the tone of his voice compelled Lazarus to stay.

"A man had two sons…" This man called Jesus began to tell the story that is now known as "The Parable of the

Lost Son." As Jesus unfolded this story to the crowd, he slowly approached Lazarus. Jesus came to stand before my brother and reached out to place one hand on the top of Lazarus' head and reaching around, placed one hand in the center of Lazarus' back just between his shoulder blades. Jesus looked deeply into Lazarus' eyes and uttered these words, "So the young man got up and went back to his father. While he was still a long way off, his father caught sight of him and was filled with compassion and joy. He ran to his son, embraced him and kissed him." At that moment, Lazarus fell into Jesus' arms and wept. Jesus held my brother in his arms as Lazarus' heart released the grief he had been carrying for so long and stroked his hair as he continued the story to the crowd.

When the tale was finished, the crowd generously departed so that Jesus and Lazarus could talk privately. In the presence of this holy man, Lazarus unburdened his grief, his bitterness and his sorrow, shedding the tears of loss that he had stubbornly held within his heart for all those many years. He told Jesus about the tension he felt between the God he had come to know in the rituals and prayers and the judgmental and vengeful God that Father had preached. He explained to Jesus how he had left his faith behind because he could not reconcile these contrasting images of God. He also shared with Jesus how he was sure that even if he wanted to return to God, that God would not want him back. My brother also unburdened himself of the guilt of having left God behind. Jesus listened intently and told Lazarus of the God that he had come to know – a God that was unconditionally loving and merciful, a God that did not judge but only loved and a God that was awaiting Lazarus' return with open arms.

Lazarus often described how, in those moments while first listening to Jesus describe his beliefs about God, it felt as if the boulder that had been sitting atop his head, separating him from God, was slowly rolling away. Jesus' compassionate words, accepting presence and loving touch had healed my brother and restored his belief in a kind and loving God. In Lazarus' words, he felt as if he was raised from the dead, his broken spirit restored and his hope and belief in God renewed. Lazarus immediately invited Jesus to come and stay with us, offering all we had by way of food, hospitality and shelter. Jesus graciously accepted. Jesus accompanied Lazarus home that evening and it was through his loving presence that another miracle was accomplished. The miracle was me.

CHAPTER FIVE

W hat I remember from that day was that I was lying curled up in bed, immersed in the pit of darkness that had become my tomb, while Martha was in the dining area preparing the evening meal. I had attempted earlier in the day to lend some assistance, but my mournful brooding became too much for Martha and she dismissed me from my chores. As I lay in the darkness of my mind, a noise came from the outer room. I heard the door open and my sister Martha scurrying from her usual place at the cooking pit to welcome whomever had arrived. I heard Lazarus' voice as he introduced someone to Martha.

Lost in my place of darkness, I wasn't really listening for details and began to drift deeper into the cavern in my mind when I heard clearly and plainly, as if the man were standing beside me, "Where is Mary, your other sister? Doesn't she live here too?" I heard the hushed whispers of my brother, presumably reciting to this stranger the story of my shame. I crawled deeper into myself as I tried to ignore the taunting demon in my head, "See, you are a shame to your brother as well. Listen to the shame in his voice as he tells this man of how you gave your innocence away."

Just as I was about to slide over the precipice into the deepest pit of this darkness, I heard a light rap on my door. Knowing I would never get up to answer, Lazarus slowly opened the door and peeked in, "Mary, there is someone here I want you to meet." I turned to face the wall and grunted as if to say, "Go away!" Apparently this guest was hard of hearing or did not realize when he was not welcome because I soon heard footsteps and the scraping of the stool as he pulled it up to sit beside my bed. I gathered my knees and shoulders around me as this man gently placed his hand on my shoulder. I recall feeling startled that, rather than the creeping fear of violation that I had come to expect in a man's touch, I felt an overwhelming sensation of peace and warmth fill my body. Against my own will, I felt my shoulders retreat from their usual place around my ears and for the first time in years, my chest opened to receive what felt like my first breath of air. It seemed that the darkness that had overtaken my mind began to retreat. Curious, but not yet willing to look this man in the face, I kept my eyes toward the wall, resting in wonder over this very unfamiliar sensation of calm. I felt the man's hand slightly shift in pressure as he leaned in closer and whispered, "Mary, it wasn't your fault."

The peaceful calm immediately retreated as I felt the constriction of betrayal. How could Lazarus have told this stranger my secret shame? As if in response to my thoughts, I heard Lazarus gasp, "Mary, I did not tell him." And yet this man I did not know…Of course, Lazarus met him in town. Everyone knew the story of Mary who brazenly went unaccompanied to the well and gave her innocence away to a band of drunken men. I silently drew my invisible armor around me to shield myself from this man's prying eyes and greedy hands. Perhaps Lazarus had finally had enough of me and was hoping to give me away in service to this man. I guessed it could be worse. Just as I began to slip into the darkness and lock the door behind me, I heard the man whisper again, "Mary, it was not your fault. The sin was theirs, not yours. In you there is nothing to be ashamed of – nothing to forgive."

I struggled to ignore him, to remain within my tomb, but there was a quality to his voice that drew me in – almost against my will. He spoke with a gentle authority that immediately invited my trust. Listening to his voice, a rich baritone that seemed to tug at some long-lost place within my heart, was like being enfolded in a rich bath of goat's milk and rose petals or tasting the first, unadulterated spoonful of honey from a newly harvested comb. After he spoke, the space around me held the heady aroma of the air after the first spring rain. In short, his voice was heaven.

As I began to get lost in the reverie of his voice, he said again, "Mary, it was not your fault." Slowly letting down my guard, I rolled over to gaze upon this man. As I turned to face him, he gently took my hand in his. I cautiously lifted my gaze to meet his eyes. What I beheld took my breath away. My heart skipped a beat. Never had I seen eyes such as these: kind, almond shaped, of a color beyond description – sometimes blue, sometimes green, from some angles a deep amber and from others, the darkest brown. It was as if his eyes reflected the very world. But for all their intricate beauty and impact, it was not the color that was the most remarkable; but that like his voice, his eyes possessed a quality that drew you in. His eyes conveyed a peace and compassion that were rare in human beings. In those eyes I saw no defensiveness, no fear, no anxiety, no pride, no need to control. When he gazed upon me, instead of the judgment or lust I had come to expect from men, I saw only acceptance, understanding and love. Beyond that, I felt something completely foreign – a feeling I can only describe as adoration. In his gaze, I felt not only loved, but truly and completely adored. That moment, when I first experienced the refuge of Jesus' eyes, is permanently etched in my mind and forever upon my heart.

Although the demon-filled part of me struggled against it, I allowed myself to receive his adoring gaze. As I allowed his adoration to sink into me, I felt the curtain that hung in the temple of my mind ripping apart and falling away, revealing the tabernacle of Elohim, which cast a light that penetrated that which had previously been only darkness. As the darkness dispersed and the light of God filled my being, the stone that had entombed my heart, rolled away. As my heart softened, and without that stone to staunch its flow, a tide of grief flooded my throat, broke through the noose of silence that had bound my voice and burst through my lips.

My grief had finally found its release, and there seemed to be no end to my tears. I cried and I moaned, sobbing and wailing from the depths of my soul as I let go of all those years of shame, sorrow, betrayal, isolation and pain. It felt like hours that I grieved and all the while, Jesus gently held me in his arms. The dam collapsed as I poured out my grief in the arms of a complete stranger. When I thought I had not one tear left, I would catch my breath a bit, and the tidal wave of grief would begin all over again. With each passing moment I felt the sensation of more and more being released. The clenched feeling in the center of my belly that held my shame along with the deep sense of violation gave way to expansiveness and freedom. The dark places in my mind where I hid from

40

the pain filled with light and I no longer felt the heavy weight of confusion or immobility. The temptation to wonder if life was worth living or if I even had a right to be here after what I had allowed fell from the chains that had bound my hips and legs and I suddenly felt alive and as if I had a right to be here and maybe even to take joy in life. My self-doubt began to flee, and I sensed an inner compass that would direct me to places of safety and to a life of fulfillment. Finally, I felt the flame of resentment, anger and hurt that I had harbored towards all of those men, including my father, burn itself out, leaving behind a smoky haze through which I glimpsed a sliver of the sun, heralding the dawn of a new day.

Feeling refreshed, renewed and cleansed of all that had held me bound from foot to crown, I drew in a deep breath and slowly turned to gaze into Jesus' kind, chameleon-colored eyes. As my eyes met his, I half expected to feel the tight clenching of my gut that I had previously experienced in the company of men. Instead, I felt a deep sense of safety. I knew that I could trust this man. But when I looked into his eyes, I felt something more than just safety and trust. As our gaze met, my heart skipped a beat and I gasped for my breath. The keenest adoration and an overwhelming respect and love for this man completely possessed me. I steadied myself, guessing that anyone who had experienced the healing miracle that I had, would harbor intense gratitude and adoration for their healer. But as I slid my eyes to sneak another peek at him, this possession overtook me again! In the space of that moment, our eyes locked and something unexpected passed between us. I held my breath and saw that Jesus, too, felt that same *something.* Instead of the compassionate concern with which he had initially greeted me, he now appeared startled. He quickly recovered as his eyes softened and the look of shock was replaced with awe-filled wonder. A gentle smile soon graced his lips and with what sounded like relief and wonder, he whispered, "Mary, it is you." I frowned back at him in confusion, but as I looked into his eyes, I felt something that could only be described as recognition. It seemed as if I had known this man before. I experienced an ease and a comfort with him that one does not usually feel with one just met. This ease was more even than what one feels with someone gifted in rapport as Jesus surely was. I can only describe it like this: he felt familiar, but in an ancient sort of way. As I surrendered to this knowing, strange images began moving through my mind. Like glimpses of dreams, I caught fleeting images of Jesus and me together, hand in hand walking through the desert or sitting beside each other at table. I observed us in different times and distant lands – in clothing and settings much different from our own – in wooded and mountainous lands, amid marble-columned temples near the great sea, in faraway lands frozen with ice and snow. As I witnessed these images, feelings of adoration, longing, desire, and even loss danced in and out of my heart. It was as if I were recalling all of the dreams that had lay dormant in my mind, hidden within the darkness of my tomb. I was confused by these images and sensations, but at the same time, there was something about all of this that felt like truth.

As I accepted whatever truth these images held for me, I relaxed under Jesus' touch and melted into the feeling of his body as he moved from the stool to sit beside me on the bed. As Jesus took my hand in his, I wanted nothing more than to be with this man, to spend time with him and to be in his presence so that I could understand more

of what he meant by "it is you." Instead, the energy spent in releasing fourteen years of grief had exhausted me and won over my desires. I was suddenly tired beyond imagining. "Mary," Jesus said, "There will be time enough for understanding, but now you must sleep." He gently squeezed my hand and smiled at me in reassurance and I immediately fell into a deep and dreamless sleep.

On the third night, just before dawn, the dreamlessness ceased and I enjoyed the beauty of a magnificent dream. In the dream, Jesus stood before me clothed in brilliant white. Surrounding me was a company of celestial beings, dressed not in clothing, but in light. They seemed to be presenting me to Jesus. Jesus came before me, placing one hand on the center of my belly and the other between my shoulder blades, and he began to pray. Looking toward the heavens, he began to sing in a language I did not know, in tones that sounded discordant and unfamiliar. He seemed to be singing in a language not of this world. As he sang, my body began to convulse between his hands and while his singing rose and fell to my movement. Jesus held me tightly as I trembled and shook. And then, Jesus began to scream – not a scream of terror, rather, a scream of command. As he commanded, I saw seven smoky figures emerge out of me. As these figures emerged, they looked at me with demon eyes and screamed in agony as they were being cast out. I realized that these were the demons who had overtaken me that morning at the well. As Jesus continued to command them, they departed from me and disappeared into the light. Then, from deep within me, I saw an image of seven lights shining, the light that had gone out of me with the demon's attack. The tone of Jesus' song responded to this light by shifting from one of command to invitation.

43

He gently sang to these lights in encouragement as they gathered strength and began to grow. The seven lights expanded within me and began to weave themselves into each other, creating within me a place of strength, stability, courage and empowerment. I realized that in the weaving of the light, I was becoming whole. And in the moment I felt as if I was filled, I joined my voice with Jesus' and began to sing. My song, I discovered, reflected the joy-filled songs of delight and wonder that I had shared with Lazarus on our childhood walks. I sang to the flowers and the sky, the birds and the crawling things, the mountains and the fields. I sang in joyful celebration of all that God had made, most especially, me.

As I gently awoke from the dream, I realized that for the first time in fourteen years, I was excited to greet the day. I got up from my bed, bathed and cleansed myself, brushed my hair and put on a clean robe. I saw for the first time how beautiful my surroundings truly were. My bedroom, while simple, was well appointed. Instead of a simple bedroll I had a raised bed in the Roman style with a mattress stuffed with down and wool. At the foot of the bed was a wooden chest for storing linens, robes and an outer cloak for cooler weather. Beside my bed was a table with an oil lamp. And along the far wall and below a window which looked out on Lazarus' lush gardens was a low bench for sitting or reclining. I took all this in with a sense of great wonder and delight, grateful for the life God had led me to and to my brother's generous caring.

In the fourteen years I had lived in this remarkable home, I had never appreciated the lush, private garden adjacent to my bedroom. As if seeing it for the first time, I was filled with wonder and delight and decided it was time to enjoy it. I left my private chambers, turned down the hallway that led to the private garden sanctuary, found the garden door, opened it and entered into the magnificent sanctuary that Lazarus had so carefully cultivated. I started along the stone pathway that slowly meandered through the olive trees and flowering bushes, taking in every leaf, flower, branch, stone and petal as I made my way. I rounded a low stone wall around which I remembered a bench, the perfect place for sitting while delighting in the rising of the morning light.

As I rounded the stone wall, I was shocked to see Jesus sitting on the bench. I quickly turned to leave, knowing it would not be appropriate for me to be alone with a man in the garden, even if it were Jesus. Jesus stood up, "Mary, don't go. Lazarus has already given me permission to share this garden retreat with you. He had hoped that you would recall your childhood love of the time before dawn and that you would find this garden satisfactory to that need. Please join me."

With a mixture of hesitation and elation, I sat beside Jesus on the stone bench. He crossed his legs beneath his robes, set his hands upon his knees, closed his eyes and began to intone *"Abwoon d'bwashmaya. Abwoon d'bwashmaya,"* the beginning lines of the Kaddish. Instead of the traditional Hebrew, however, Jesus used Aramaic, the language of the common people. I closed my eyes and allowed Jesus' rich baritone voice, the very voice I had heard just moments before in my dream, to carry me, again, beyond place and time. I soon found myself sinking into a deep and peaceful state and found my body filling with light. My breathing slowed and calm entered my entire body. As I rested in that state of peace, time slipped away as I realized that Jesus had ceased his chant and we both simply rested in the silence. As I enjoyed this peaceful repose, I found my heart beginning to expand with feelings of deep compassion and my spirit with exuberant joy. Abwoon had not abandoned me. God had not betrayed me or been punishing me for my sin. God had been here all along wrapped in the light and love I had pushed away as I retreated into my tomb of darkness. As I reclaimed the awareness of God's infinite presence, a smile began to play on my lips. I felt the touch of Jesus' hand on mine and looked over to see that he too was smiling in joy. I once again closed my eyes and allowed myself to simply enjoy the love of Abwoon that I now knew had always lived within me; that I had seen within Jesus and that now seemed to want to play between us.

As the sun broke over the horizon, the cock crowed and Jesus gently squeezed my hand. It would be time to go about the work of the day and Martha would need my help in preparing the morning meal. I began to rise when Jesus spoke. "Mary, I am called to depart from the house of Lazarus and return to my companions in Galilee." My heart sank in disappointment but Jesus reassured me, "Mary, do not be afraid. I am with you always, even unto the end of time, and be assured, I will be returning to the house of Lazarus as Abwoon has ordained it to be so." I wondered at the strangeness of Jesus' words. First "it is you" and now "I am with you always." What could he mean by this? As if in response to my thoughts, Jesus answered, "Mary, I do not yet fully understand these words myself, but I trust that in time, we will both understand the words that Abwoon now speaks to my heart." More words that I did not yet comprehend, but there was something in the way that Jesus spoke that assured me that what he said would prove true. Together, Jesus and I left our garden sanctuary to greet the day before us – he to inform Lazarus of his imminent departure and me to assist Martha in preparing the morning meal. Together, we broke our fast and Jesus departed soon after but not before the house of Lazarus offered our deep gratitude to him for raising not just one, but two of us from the dead.

CHAPTER SIX

After Jesus' departure from our home, life at the house of Lazarus began to change. Because I was no longer trapped within the paralysis of depression I could finally embrace my role of service to the household, assisting my sister in the daily tasks of household management and Lazarus with his business, which had grown to the point that it was operational all day, every day. Consequently, workers were present at all times and our responsibilities to them had expanded. It had fallen to Martha to manage the operation of the orchards and vineyards when Lazarus was away trading his wine and oils. I believe that Martha was grateful for my help, yet I had the feeling that, as my assistance lifted her burden, restlessness began growing within her.

Martha had sacrificed much in leaving our father's home. She had left behind her dowry, along with any chance of marriage. More damaging than even that, however, was the loss of our parent's love. Martha had put great stock in her efforts to secure our father's approval and when she was forced to face the truth that Father only had eyes for his sons, Martha's heart was broken. It was the knowledge of our mother's love that had sustained Martha in those years of trying to appease our father, and now even Mother's love, it seemed, had been denied her. I suspect that being overly burdened by the

48

household chores gave Martha an opportunity to ignore the significance of these losses. I often wondered when the dam behind which she had hidden her losses would burst.

Inspired by my morning in the garden with Jesus and by memories of the way I had felt the presence of God in the silent time just before the dawn, I began to rise before Lazarus or even Martha and retire to the garden to simply rest in the peace of that silent presence. Sometimes I spoke to the invisible God, offering my prayers of gratitude for healing and for having met Jesus. At other times I intoned the Aramaic chant that Jesus had shared with me that morning in the garden. But mostly, I sat in the silence and listened. As I sat and listened, I found a place of quiet growing within my heart and in this quiet I found peace.

Ironically, this peace was often interrupted by thoughts of Jesus. As hard as I tried to keep my mind still and focused on prayer or on the daily tasks of running a home, I found myself drawn to the memory of that moment when Jesus first looked into my eyes. Reveling in that moment, my heart would beat faster, sparking heated excitement throughout my entire being – first tickling the ends of my toes, then moving up through my entire body as I recalled his look of adoration, replaying the memory of the moment he rested his hand on my shoulder and whispered, "Mary, it was not your fault."

My breath quickened as I recalled his surprised proclamation, "Mary, it is you." What did he mean by these words? And what of the strange images that seemed to pour from my imagination of life spent with Jesus in places and times so different from our own? Why couldn't I just be quiet, remaining in peaceful contemplation and in awareness of this present moment? Instead, I found myself daydreaming of the next time I would gaze upon

Jesus' face and feel the warmth of his hand on mine. Then the doubts would begin to filter in. What if he wasn't really planning a return? Was he having any of these feelings for me? Was I just a foolish woman grasping after impossible dreams? Surely Jesus has his choice of women, so why on earth would he choose me, a woman unclean and a sinner? It was while I wrestled with these sorts of doubts that I would be overcome by a keen sense of Jesus either sitting beside me or gently touching my arm, and once again I would be restored to peace.

The peace that I had begun to cultivate within myself and the God that I had reclaimed seemed to spill out into our home and all around us. Part of me always knew that Martha had never forsaken God and still found Elohim in the day to day tasks that were the center of her life. Lazarus, who had forsaken God when banished from the house of Levi, began arising early in the morning to commune with the God that he had come to know through the bounty of nature in his orchards and vineyards. Although I had suspected Lazarus' return to spiritual contemplation, I was surprised when he announced one day that he would like to resume our observation of the Hebrew traditions and rituals of our childhood. I had found contentment in the quiet moments before dawn; thus it mattered not to me how we communed with Adonai, but Martha responded with such great enthusiasm that it was difficult for me to not be excited as well. I think that she had secretly longed for the rituals and prayers through which we had found comfort in our childhood home.

Despite our father's forbidding our mother to interact with us, and that for all intents and purposes, we were no longer her children, our mother had managed one parting act of love. With the help of one of the widows from the village our mother had covertly managed to send to the house of Lazarus a chest filled with several personal and precious belongings.   Martha had kept this chest safely hidden under her bed until the time was right to reveal its contents. Both Lazarus and I knew that the contents of the chest were under Martha's keeping and we dared not even take a peek. So when Lazarus announced that he would like to resume some of our Hebrew rites and rituals, Martha quickly rushed up the stairs to her room. We heard the scraping of the heavy chest as it was pulled out from beneath her bed, and the bang of the heavy lid as it hit the top of Martha's mattress. We soon heard the sounds of rummaging and the rustling of fabrics and parchments as Martha searched.

Into the sanctuary of Lazarus' beautiful dining room, Martha quickly returned with a bundle of objects in her arms. She placed the bundle atop the enormous cedar wood dining table – large enough to seat twenty – and began to reveal what lie within. She drew forth two earthenware candle holders and two beeswax candles wrapped in parchment. She placed the candlestick holders on the table and placed the beeswax candles into them. These were the two Sabbath candles which represented the two commandments: *zakhor* which represents the commandment that we are to *remember* the Sabbath and keep it holy; and *shamore* which reminds us to *observe* the Sabbath and keep it holy. Martha, as the woman of the house, would usher in our Sabbath observance by lighting these candles. After lighting the candles, she would extend her hands over them, draw the light toward her three times in a circular motion, and cover her eyes. With her eyes covered, she would recite the Sabbath prayer:

*Baruch ata Adonay Eloheinu melech haolam asher
kideeshanu bimitzvotav vitzivanoo lihadleek ner
shel Shabbat kodesh.*

Blessed are you, Lord our God, King of the universe,
who has sanctified us with His commandments,
and commanded us to kindle the
light of the Holy Shabbat.

After presenting the Sabbath candles, Martha brought
forth from her bundle a hand-fashioned and polished
bronze container which I knew contained *mezuzah*. She
handed the bronze container to Lazarus who removed the
metal stopper and pulled forth the mezuzah, the sacred
scroll. He unwrapped the scroll and began to read in
Hebrew the first part of the *Shema* – the sacred prayer of
the Hebrew people:

*Sh'ma Yis'ra'eil Adonai Eloheinu Adonai echad
Barukh sheim k'vod malkhuto l'olam va'ed
V'ahav'ta eit Adonai Elohekha b'khol l'vav'kha uv'khol
naf'sh'kha uv'khol m'odekha
V'hayu had'varim ha'eileh asher anokhi m'tzav'kha
hayom al l'vavekha
V'shinan'tam l'vanekha v'dibar'ta bam
b'shiv't'kha b'veitekha uv'lekh't'kha vaderekh
uv'shakh'b'kha uv'kumekha
Uk'shar'tam l'ot al yadekha v'hayu l'totafot bein einekha
Ukh'tav'tam al m'zuzot beitekha uvish'arekha*

Hear oh Israel, the Lord is your God, the Lord alone!
Therefore you shall love the Lord,
your God with all your heart,
and with all your soul,

and with all your strength.
Take to heart these words which I enjoin on you today.
Drill them into your children.
Speak of them at home and abroad,
whether you are busy or at rest.
Bind them at your wrists as a sign and
let them be as a pendant on your forehead.
Write them on the doorposts of your houses
and on your gates.

After Lazarus read the scroll, he rolled it up and returned it to its container. He brought the bronze container to his lips and, as he lightly kissed it, I watched a tear fall from his eye.

He offered it to each of us as we offered our own prayer of reverence and thanksgiving. Martha returned to her bundle and brought forth the *tallit* and *tefillin* that Lazarus had left behind at the house of Levi. I heard Lazarus gasp in wonder as Martha came behind him and placed the hand-woven prayer shawl across his shoulders while reciting the *tallit* blessing:

Baruch atta Ado-noy Elo-hai-nu Melech ha'olam asher kid-sha-nu b'mitz-vo-tav v'tzi-vanu l'hit-atef b'tzitzit.

Blessed are you, Lord our God, King of the universe, who has sanctified us with His commandments, and commanded us to enwrap ourselves with *tzitzit*.

Martha returned to her bundle one final time and removed the *tefillin*. She handed Lazarus this leather pouch and straps containing the hand-written scrolls of the Torah, and Lazarus began the sacred ritual of laying

53

the tefillin. First he placed the pouch across his forehead, brought the straps behind his head and tied a knot. He let one strap fall on his right side across his chest, the other he wrapped around his left arm where the final binding was accomplished around the middle and fourth fingers of his left hand. By placing the tefillin in this manner, Lazarus, like all Hebrew men performing this ritual, was honoring God's command that we shall bind God's word upon our arms and as an ornament between our eyes. As he laid the tefillin, he recited the ancient blessing:

Barukh atah Adonai, Eloheinu, melekh ha'olam
Asher kidishanu b'mitz'votav v'tzivanu
L'hani'ach t'filin

Blessed are you, Lord, our God, sovereign of the universe
Who has sanctified us with His commandments
and commanded us to put on tefillin

As Lazarus completed the blessing, I saw that he wept. He reached out and embraced Martha in gratitude for her loving gesture and for her understanding of his longing to reclaim the parts of his Hebrew upbringing that had once brought him life and joy.

Finally, Martha removed from the bundle its final gift: the scrolls of the Torah – the Psalms and the writings of the prophets which had been intended as a gift to Lazarus at his betrothal. It was the custom in our family that the father gifted to each of his sons copies of these sacred writings. Lazarus grabbed the scrolls and hugged them to his chest as he began chanting what he recalled from the Psalms of praise. It was a joyous day for our brother and Martha, and I shared in their joy.

While we had freely chosen to reclaim some of the

remnants of our Hebrew youth, there were some aspects of our faith that we did not feel called to reinstate in our spiritual practice. In particular, we found no call to literal interpretation of the Law or to the strict methods of adherence that had been required in the house of Levi. We agreed to honor the Sabbath and to keep some of the traditional prayers, blessings and rituals. We were elated to discover that the reading and study of the Torah, along with other scriptures supported the private prayer that Jesus had modeled for us and that we now embraced as our own. While scripture often posed a challenge in its representation of God as sometimes vengeful and jealous, Jesus' brief stay had enlightened Martha and Lazarus to another perspective. Jesus had used the three days in which I had slept to pray with Lazarus and Martha and to instruct them in The Way of Love.

Jesus showed Martha and Lazarus that Elohim was unconditionally loving and kind and that there is in fact, no separation between us and Adonai; that in truth, we are One with God and that our human journey is about remembering that love. Now, when we approached the scriptures, we looked upon them through this lens and found them to be much more loving and inspiring than how we had received them as children. We also found in this new perspective, the gauge for measuring all of our decisions about prayer, belief and observance. We chose to embrace those which reflected this life-giving presence, and to set aside those which proved not to be life-giving or reflective of this love. This approach made the house of Lazarus an anomaly, but thankfully we were far enough away from Jerusalem – or so we thought – to escape the scrupulous gaze of the Pharisees who would have found this perspective heretical.

Chapter Seven

Two full cycles of the moon passed and we began hearing that Jesus was again journeying toward Bethany. From his last visit, he had returned to his home in Capernaum and had ministered to the people of Galilee who lived along the shores of the inland sea. As we heard of his imminent return, our household flew into anxious preparation. I watched in amusement as Lazarus began hasty repairs to our home while Martha busily cleaned and swept the house, tidied the gardens and began food preparations. You would have thought that Caesar himself was coming.

I, too, found myself anxious with anticipation, but not about the appearance of our home or whether there would be enough of the right foodstuffs to eat. Instead, I found myself drawn again to my memories of the sensation of Jesus' touch, the movement of his body from the stool to his place beside me on my bed and how the bed sank under his weight, the closeness of his presence as we sat together in the garden for prayer, and the soft timbre of his voice that at once brought peace along with the shivers of gooseflesh. Mostly, I found myself imagining the depths of his chameleon colored eyes where I saw only the reflection of love and felt nothing but contentment. I should have thought myself silly for entertaining these thoughts, but decided that being well past the age of

56

betrothal, there could be no harm in a twenty-eight year old woman entertaining the long-forgotten dreams of childhood. Besides, Jesus, well past the age of betrothal himself, had most certainly chosen the Essene vow of celibacy and there was little chance of any of these thoughts coming to fruition, so what was the harm in a little daydreaming?

On the day after the Sabbath, a messenger arrived from the village to tell my brother that Jesus had asked to dine with us and that he would like to bring along several of his companions. Of course, my brother's answer was yes, throwing Martha into a tizzy. "Several men?" she asked. It is one thing to host a single man – but him and all his companions too? Who does he think he is – and how are we to feed all these people?!" Lazarus took Martha's hands in his and looked into her eyes, "Sister, all will be well. On many an occasion, we have fed our entire staff. Certainly we can handle a few Galilean fishermen. You will see." Martha responded with a snort, tossed off his hands and stomped away in silence. As she stalked away, I'm sure I saw smoke shooting out of her ears. I scurried after her, reached out to place my hand on her shoulder and assured her, "Martha, I will help you." She touched my hand and turned to glance at me in acknowledgement, and for just a moment, her usually furrowed brow softened enough to offer me a look of gratitude.

We busily set about preparing the meal while Lazarus made his way toward town to meet our expected guests. It was not long before we heard the clamor of voices in the yard, and in a cloud of dust, Lazarus burst through the door to usher in our guests. As was customary, I hung back in the shadows with my sister and watched as Lazarus welcomed into our home the most rag-tag group of men I had ever set my eyes upon. These were not the men of leisure or the merchant trades. They were working men – browned by the sun with deep lines etched into their faces and well-calloused hands – the fishermen, farmers, metal workers and shepherds of our culture. These were men hardened in body and mind by day upon day, year upon year, generation upon generation of hard physical labor – men of the thankless trades which rewarded them with little but the clothes on their backs.

One man in particular stood out. Swarthy and strong with broad shoulders, coarse hair and beard and a deeply lined complexion, the intensity of his eyes told the tale of a man who had fought long and hard to seek out a meager existence and wasn't about to let anyone take that away from him. "Stubborn-arrogance" was the name I would have given him, for he seemed like a two-ton boulder standing in the way of the world, unwilling to move. I later discovered his name was Simon.

Lazarus ushered in this motley crew while Martha and I stood in rapt attention. Jesus brought up the rear. As he gracefully stepped over the threshold, I gasped in wonder at this man. My heart began to pound, my palms began to sweat and the pitcher of water I held in my hands nearly fell to the ground as my hands began to tremble. Martha hissed in my ear, "Mary, get ahold of yourself!" Attentive to my nervousness, Jesus caught my gaze and smiled lovingly. Against custom, I looked directly into his eyes and returned the smile. As I met his gaze, the earth returned beneath my feet and my heart was restored to peace.

As the men settled around the table, Martha and I prepared the ritual washing. Lazarus took the basin, the pitcher of clean water and the towel and washed the feet and hands of each of our guests. As Lazarus approached him, Jesus smiled and turned his gaze toward me. "Mary, would you do the honors?" A collective gasp was uttered around the room. Women, especially unmarried women, most especially unclean women were not allowed to touch a man, let alone perform the ceremonial washing. As the master of the house, this honor was reserved for Lazarus. I held back and shook my head in reluctant refusal, as my heart prayed for the miracle that would allow me the honor of performing the ritual washing, if nothing else but for the pleasure of feeling the touch of Jesus' skin upon mine. In response to my reluctance, Jesus began to teach, "In the Kingdom of God, there is no male or female, slave or free, Jew or Gentile, clean or unclean. All are one in the Kingdom of God. Let Mary come forth." Lazarus bowed his head in acknowledgment of this truth. While a single tear escaped his eye, he beckoned me forward.

I could not believe what I was hearing. Jesus had just confirmed what Lazarus had believed and what I could only hope to believe. Jesus had just affirmed the very beliefs for which my brother had been driven from our father's house and for which he had taken both of his sisters into his home. In teaching in this way, Jesus had also answered the silent questions in my own heart about women's place in God's kingdom. It was more than I could possibly take in. With no more thought for my own selfish desires to feel the touch of Jesus' skin on mine, I rushed forward and fell before Jesus feet overcome with tears of joy. With my own tears I washed his feet and, at the risk of appearing foolish, smothered his feet with my kisses – kisses not of lust, but of sheer gratitude. I unbound my hair and dried his feet with my veil. My heart was filled with joy and I felt like a caged bird suddenly set free upon the wind.

In my joyful abandon, I had forgotten my sister Martha. I suddenly became aware of how my brazen behavior would be an affront to her traditional sensibilities. Martha still held tightly to the traditional role of women as vehicles for breeding and tending the home – forever in the shadows with downcast eyes. I slowly rose from my place at Jesus' feet, repositioned my veil and returned to my rightful place beside Martha for the task of serving the afternoon meal.

We began the busy work of serving the usual courses of a celebratory meal – for that is what it was. I should have been focusing on the task at hand, leaving the men to their talk, but I kept finding myself drawn to Jesus' words. I found myself frozen in place first, simply by the sound of his voice which warmed my heart and filled me with a buoyant sense of joy, and then by his words. Floating on words like mercy, forgiveness and compassion, I was startled out of my reverie by my impatient sister's elbow to the ribs. I quickly set aside my reverie and resumed my womanly work. After the fourth elbow jab, I shifted my awareness from the specific words to the overall sounds of the men in discussion. What struck me most was the dramatic contrast between the sound of Jesus' voice and that of the man named Simon. While Jesus' voice was warm and soothing like honey lovingly applied to a wound, Simon's voice was like walking into a patch of stinging nettle – raw, red, angry and impatient. His was a voice that gnawed in irritation while Jesus' voice elicited a soothing calm. I wondered at this strange man that seemed to admire Jesus, yet vehemently questioned and challenged everything he said. It seemed he searched for

60

a logical explanation for those things of which Jesus spoke that could only be known in the heart. I made a mental note to observe this man Simon carefully.

What began as a celebratory afternoon meal soon drew into the evening and late night. As the sun set, the lamps were lit and I found myself, once again, admiring the home my brother made for himself. In addition to the dining table and benches that comfortably sat twenty, there was a central clay oven surrounded by high tables for preparing food. Drying bunches of herbs hung overhead and there were low cabinets beneath the tables for storing cookware. In the style of the Romans, Lazarus had large cedar wood cabinets adjacent to the preparation tables where plates and bowls were stored, along with serving platters and cooking tools. The limestone walls were decorated with hand-painted designs of flowering vines in colors of ochre, red, violet and green. I was proud of my brother for the thought and attention to detail that went into making this home. I was awakened out of my reverie when the casks of wine were brought out. This was the signal for Martha and me to retire to our private chambers to leave the men to what would eventually prove to be loud and raucous talk. Unable to sleep amid the noise and distracted by romantic daydreaming, I shifted my attention to listening. While I could not make out the individual voices, I found I was able to tune my ears to the gentle rise and fall of Jesus' soothing voice and it was there I found rest for the next thing I knew, I awoke to the morning star shining through my window.

CHAPTER EIGHT

With the men camped outside the orchard walls, I knew it would be safe to continue my morning routine, so I hastily dressed, brushed my hair and, unlike most mornings when only in the company of family, I quickly donned my veil. I eagerly went to the garden to enjoy a few moments of repose before another busy day began. I rounded the low wall just beyond the ancient olive tree and sought my favorite bench, the one Jesus and I had shared two moons ago. I was startled to find that Jesus too had sought this pre-dawn retreat.

Jesus sat in silent prayer wearing a course mantle of rough hewn linen over which was draped a lighter weight, more finely woven woolen cloak of a deep true red. The over cloak provided a striking contrast to the muted pallet of the pre-dawn morn. I started to turn back toward the house so as not to disturb him, but more importantly to avoid risking the accusation of impropriety from among his companions. In truth, I wanted nothing more than to rest there in his presence and my heart pounded its urgent request. Just as I turned to leave, his honey-warm voice broke the silence, "Mary, there is no need for you to leave. You have just as much right as I to enjoy this time of communion with God. Please sit and we can honor this sacred time together." My head knew that I should refuse, but my heart wanted only this – to rest in prayer with this man of peace and to feel his warmth beside me. So I sat beside him in sacred silence as we had done on the third day after he had raised me from the dead, and I was overwhelmed with joy. We enjoyed what felt like a lifetime of silence before Jesus spoke, "Mary, what do you seek?"

"What do I seek?" What did he mean by this question? Had he heard the silent daydreaming of my heart or was his question about something else? As I struggled to decide his meaning in this question, he asked again. "Mary, what do you seek in this life?" I silenced my heart and determined that his question must pertain more to life in general, rather than specifically to the fanciful romantic daydreams of a woman considered to be sinful and unclean. But still, no one had ever asked me what I would seek. In our culture, it was men who sought, not women. Oh, I supposed we dared to dream of a marriage to a kind man that produced healthy children. But there were no desires allowed beyond that. A woman's path was pretty much laid out for her. As I sat in shocked confusion, Jesus took my hands, looked deep into my eyes and asked again, "Mary, what do you seek?"

Perhaps I had stopped breathing because a slight grin played upon Jesus' lips and a twinkle entered his eyes as he laughingly whispered, "Mary, breathe!" I laughed, took a deep breath and considered his question. *What did I seek? What did I seek?* As I pondered this question, the tightness in my belly that I had long ago accepted as permanent, suddenly released and a soft warmth began to rise up from my belly and spread throughout my being. As this soft warmth reached my forehead I found myself weeping – not the wretched sobbing of grief, but the gentle tears of

63

release. Through these tears, I found the answer to Jesus' inquiry. Release was what I sought. But release from what? Did I dare to share with Jesus my secret dream? "Mary, what do you seek?" he whispered a fourth time. I looked deeply into his chameleon eyes and whispered my one-word response, "Freedom."

As I shared this secret – the secret known only in the deepest parts of my being, I felt as if a huge weight was being lifted from my shoulders. My shoulders relaxed. I sat a little taller and I could breathe – deep, long, nourishing breaths. Jesus smiled, and with wonder in his voice responded, "Mary, in the kingdom of God there is freedom – freedom beyond imagining."

"Yes, I know that this is what the prophets tell us, but, and I'm ashamed to admit this, I don't want to wait. I want freedom in my life now," I pleaded.

"Mary, the kingdom of God is *now*."

"So the Messiah *has* come?"

"Mary, the kingdom of God is *within* you." And he gently placed his hand over my heart.

The kingdom of God is within me? I remember how I could not make sense of this, at first. This was not what the Law taught. The Law taught that the kingdom of God is outside of us and can only be obtained by those free of sin – those who obediently lived according to the letter of the Law. But, something in his words spoke truth to me and I had experienced something like this in my time of repose alone in the garden and when I had shared this time with Jesus. The kingdom of God is within. I sat in silence allowing this new awareness to take root within me. Buoyed by Jesus' encouragement, I grew increasingly bold. "Do you know what I really want? I want the same freedom that the men have. I want to sit at the foot of the Master and learn about God. I want to study the Law and the prophets and have the opportunity to discuss and debate as men do. I want the freedom to sleep outdoors and to travel to hear the words of learned men. I want to be free from the tedium of women's work – rather, I want to choose it freely, not be forced into it simply because I am a woman. I want to know God as men know God, through the Law and the prophets."

"Mary," he asked, "is knowledge of God obtained through the Law?"

"Of course," I started to say, but something told me this was not the whole truth.

Jesus smiled and nodded, "Go on."

"Well, I know that God is in the Law, but sometimes the Law feels restrictive and not very freeing. So if what you say about the kingdom of God is true, something isn't quite right."

"Mary," he asked, "What gives you peace? What fills you with joy? Where do you know that you are good? Where do you know love?"

"This gives me peace," I answered, gesturing toward the pre-dawn sky and the garden which was our sanctuary. "This gives me joy," I waved my hand between us. "And, when I imagine your presence, Rabbi, I know that I am good and that I am loved."

"Mary, it is here that you know God." As he uttered these words, a large space seemed to open in my heart like arms spread wide to take in the morning sun. The cock crowed, signaling the coming of the dawn. Jolted back to my social conditioning, I hastily dropped Jesus' hands and turned and ran toward the house to assist my sister in the morning preparations.

With all these men about, there was much to prepare

for breaking our fast, and in the midst of it all, it almost seemed as if my time with Jesus had only been a dream. But when I stopped for a moment to breathe, I felt the brilliant warmth of a new day – or perhaps, a new life, dawning.

As Martha and I finished clearing the table after the morning meal, the men began settling into their postures for discussion and debate. I filled a fresh pitcher of water and went to place it on the table before our honored guest. Just as I did this, Jesus gently placed his hand upon mine. "Was there something else he needed?" I asked him with my eyes. "Yes Mary," he replied aloud, "I would like you to join us for the discussion." An audible gasp of shock filled the room and I could feel the lightning bolt of my sister's rage as she turned and stomped from the room. The blazing heat of embarrassment began creeping up my back and rising to my hairline. More than anything, I wanted to accept this generous, though admittedly scandalous, invitation. I did not, however, want to bring more scandal upon my family nor did I wish to hurt my sister. It was one thing to share the Torah among siblings, but to study and to be taught in the company of men? That was unspeakable! While I stood there aghast, Jesus addressed those at table, "In the kingdom of God, there is no male or female, slave or free, Jew or gentile. We are all one in the kingdom of God. This woman has the same right as each and every one of you to sit at this table and partake in the knowledge of God." I heard the whispered grumbles and from the voice of Simon I heard, "But teacher…" Jesus promptly held his hand up to silence him and gestured to the empty cushion beside him and invited me to recline. With downcast eyes, I hesitatingly sat beside Jesus as he had invited. While I felt incredibly self-conscious, I also felt an overwhelming sense of freedom in being invited to absorb the teachings of this amazing man along with the titillation of knowing I would be just a hairbreadth away from the man with whom I would love to spend the rest of my days.

I sat in rapt silence as I listened to Jesus teach about the kingdom of God. After living under my father's roof and hearing his warnings of God's wrath, Jesus' teachings shocked my ears. Whereas I had found my father's teachings to cause me anxiety, Jesus' words brought me great peace. On a very deep level, I embraced his explanation of a God that was loving, kind and merciful – a God free of jealousy, spite, judgment or wrath. Indeed the word Jesus used to describe the God that he knew was *Abwoon.* This was a familiar term usually reserved for the intimate connection with one's own loving father (a word I never dared use with my own). And yet, as Jesus told us, even this familiar term was insufficient in describing the vast, infinite nature of our loving God. This God, Jesus taught us, was beyond gender, race or even religious affiliation. This proved to become a sticking point for the *chosen people* with whom Jesus found himself sharing his message.

Listening to Jesus' heartwarming message, I completely lost track of time. I was startled out of my blissful, single-minded awareness by the stomping, huffing and crashing about of my dear sister. "Good grief, was it time for the afternoon meal already?" I started to rise when Jesus grabbed my hand. Shivers ran up and down my spine as he gently urged me to stay. Jesus himself rose and went to Martha in the preparation area. He gently placed his hand on her shoulder and led her away from the group. While out of earshot, it seems I was still able to hear their conversation.

"Martha, what troubles you so?"

"Lord, I do not wish to be disrespectful, but does no one care that my sister has left me to myself to do the serving? There is too much work here for only one and I don't even know how we are going to feed and care for all of these men you have brought. I need help. There is not enough of me to go around. Tell Mary to help me, she will listen to you."

"Martha, do you not see that Mary has chosen the better part?

"The better part??!! Are you mad???" I sensed Martha's faltering efforts to conceal her frustration. "Someone needs to do the work around here. Someone needs to cook and clean, prepare the garden, care for the home and all those who live in it! What do you think would have happened if I had sat around all day looking at the stars while Mary and Lazarus each fell apart and retreated into their tombs of darkness? We would all have perished! It has always been me. I have been the one to do the work, to make sure the finances are taken care of and to make sure that during the lean times all are fed. There is not enough time in the day and it is a constant struggle to make sure every mouth is fed and though Lazarus does the work to provide, it has always been up to me to make sure there is enough to go around and that all the work is done to run a household and a business."

I saw an image in my mind of Jesus taking Martha's hand, looking deep into her eyes and asking for the third time, "Martha, what troubles you so?"

I felt the sensation of Martha's heart melting and I saw her in my mind's eye collapse into Jesus' arms as she poured out her grief. For the first time I heard her describe the burden her life had been.

"My heart was terrified and broken when I saw what those animals had done to my dear sister. A sweet, innocent child destroyed in one terrible moment by the evil actions of men. But even more devastating than that was our father's reaction. While I expected him to react strongly, I had no idea he would adhere so stringently to the Law as to choose death for our beloved Mary. How could he kill his own daughter? How could he kill his own flesh and blood? And by his own hand? I was devastated, because I figured it out: if Father could do this to Mary, he could most certainly do this to me. The foundation and hope upon which I had built my life – a life built on seeking my father's approval – was suddenly pulled out from beneath me. I know this was not Mary's fault, but I could not help but resent her for having been so brazen. If she had just waited for the women, like a good girl, none of this would have happened. Except if this had not happened to her, I'd still be seeking my father's approval in vain. In the end, I was forced to leave behind the only life I had known to be servant for Mary and Lazarus. Now she is healed and for the first time in years, I am not alone. But as she sits at table with you, again I find myself abandoned and left to do the work and the worry on my own. As I listened to my sister's words, my heart sank in support of her struggle.

"Martha, are you ever really alone?"

"No, my Lord. I know I am not truly alone, I have Mary and Lazarus. And we have God. God provided for us a home and the means to survive and most generously, God has sent you so that my sister – the one I was afraid we had lost – could once again be found. For this I offer prayers of thanksgiving."

Martha took Jesus' hands in hers, kissed them, and

69

held them to her cheek.

"Martha, your earthly father is wounded and afraid and can never take the place of the God that knows what you need even before you do and provides for that need. Never forget this – your heavenly Father, is with you always, holding you, guiding you, providing for your every need. You are never alone. When you are feeling alone and afraid, remember this! Also know that while your earthly mother is unable to be present to you as she could be, God can also be Mother to you, providing the nurturing and support that your mother had once been able to freely share with you. As to your worries about money, time, food and shelter, does not God provide for the birds of the air and the fish of the sea? Are you less worthy than those? Abwoon gives you everything that you need in abundance. Trust in God and in this you shall find peace. And finally, when you feel burdened and unappreciated for all the responsibilities you bear, know this once again: you are not alone. Your talents at making a home and running a business are a gift from God, who supplies you with all the love, patience and forbearance you need at any given moment so that you can share these gifts joyfully and without burden."

With these words, I felt the sensation of my sister letting go of her worries and fears that she was alone and that there was never enough of the things she felt she needed: food, clothing, shelter, support. I felt her relax into a state of peaceful contentment and faith, knowing that what Jesus said was true and that when she felt afraid, she need only turn to Abwoon for comfort.

Jesus called my name, "Mary, would you come here please?" I quickly got up and rushed to them. Martha looked up at me, embraced and wept silent tears of joy. What happened next proved Jesus' sincerity and demonstrated the love for each other that he urged us to live by: he went out toward the men and invited them all to get up and help prepare the afternoon meal. There were grumbles of protest, to be sure, especially from the man called Simon, but in the end, they obeyed. As the men, including Jesus, prepared the meal, Jesus reminded us again that, "In the kingdom of God there is no male or female, slave or free, Gentile or Jew. All are one in the kingdom of God."

Jesus and the men remained with us for a fortnight, each day following the same routine which included Jesus and me rising before dawn and sharing our sacred time of prayer in the garden, departing at cockcrow to meet the others in the house to prepare to break our fast. Between meals, we reclined at table.

Martha now joined us to listen to Jesus teach. Initially, Martha and I remained silent as we listened to the men discuss and debate. After a few days, however, Jesus began to ask, "Mary, what do you think? Martha, what are your thoughts?" Martha, still in shock over the turn of events that permitted her to even sit at table, vigorously shook her head in refusal. I however, had become emboldened by my time with Jesus in the garden and began to respond with enthusiasm. It seemed the men were shocked by my contribution, although I wasn't sure if it was due to the intelligence of my replies, or their offense at a woman permitted to speak. For Simon at least, I believe it was the latter.

As the word of Jesus' visit filtered into the village, other men began to join our gathering, first from among Lazarus' staff, then from the nearby village. Since there were only so many spaces at the table, people took to sitting on the ground and as the crowds grew, they spilled out into the courtyard beyond the dining room where another large table sat, and an outdoor clay oven and a hand-pump which provided the water for our daily use. The woven canopy that hung above the courtyard protected our visitors from the afternoon sun. As the crowds filled our home and courtyard to overflowing, we still provided the meals for all these visitors, providing not only nourishment for the heart through Jesus' words, but nourishment for the body through the generosity of the House of Lazarus. I often wondered how all would be fed – but somehow, there was always enough.

At the close of the second Sabbath, Jesus announced that it was time for them to return once again to Capernaum and that they would be departing after breaking fast the following morning. Upon hearing this news, my heart stopped and I began to feel the sadness of loss well up within me, choking my throat and filling my eyes. Jesus reached over and took my hand in his (for he still invited me always to the seat at his left) and in my head I heard Jesus' soothing voice, "Be not sad Mary, I am with you always, even unto the end of time." At this, I felt my heart resume its beating and my sorrow lifted.

The next morning as I went to the garden, I assumed that Jesus would be too busy preparing for his journey to join me in prayer. But there he was in the same place he had been every day since his arrival. Forgetting propriety, I rushed to embrace him, "Rabbi, do not leave, stay and continue to teach us. We….I…have so much I want to learn!" Jesus looked deep into my eyes and began to teach in a way reserved for me alone. "Mary, do not cling to me. I must be about the work of Abwoon. And, while I go to those who call out to me, so, also, shall I remain in you."

At first I was puzzled by these words but gazing into those eyes, etched forever upon my soul, I remembered... and understood. I remembered the weeks after his first visit when I would come to the garden for prayer and – behold – he was there. When I brought him to mind he seemed to be as present to me as he had been the day I poured out my sin. I also remembered the times at table when he spoke to me in silence, in that sacred place within where only I could hear him; and there was the conversation between him and Martha that I heard and felt as if I'd been there, not just a silent witness sitting a room away surrounded by loudly debating men. I knew we could not hold Jesus captive as our own private teacher, for his message was destined for all corners of the world. I realized that I need only open to my awareness of him and I would be able to keenly feel his presence. I resolved to try to be content with this, but knew in my heart how much I would miss him – the strength of his body beside me as we reclined at table or shared the garden bench, the soothing timbre of his voice as it warmed not only my soul but my body as well, and the tingling shivers that rushed up and down my spine when we touched. I would try to be content in his absence, but my heart suggested that this might not be so.

Continuing this private instruction, Jesus began to instruct me in what to expect in the coming weeks and months: "Mary, the love of Abwoon cannot be contained. Once it ignites in the heart of one who believes, it spreads like wild fire. Lazarus will be called into the village to share the message of this love to those who have ears to hear. But to you and Martha, the women will come, and they will come to hear the love of Abwoon that transcends gender, social status, position, married or unmarried, widowed or barren. They will come to hear the message of God's freedom, and you and Martha will be the vehicles through which this freedom shall be revealed."

"Jesus, how is it that you know these things?" I asked. "I know these things in the same way that I knew to leave my home in Capernaum to travel to Bethany to the house of Lazarus, or the same way that I knew the moment that I saw you that it was you," he responded with a bashful glimmer in his eye. My heart skipped a beat and I lowered my eyes, daring to ask more. Shyly I asked, "Jesus, what do you mean by these words?" Jesus took my hands in his, "Mary, Abwoon speaks to me deep within the silent places of my heart. I have learned to trust this voice and to strictly adhere to what it tells me and what it shows me. It is through this voice that I knew not to accept the many marriage proposals that my parents so lovingly sought to enter into on my behalf. It is the voice that instructed me at age sixteen to join my cousin John in his studies with the Essenes. It was this voice that advised me to depart from those studies to travel first to the West and later to the East in search of learning beyond what Judaism had to offer. It was also this voice that invited me to forego the customary vows of celibacy taken by so many of my teachers, both here and abroad."

At the mention of celibacy, my heart began to race and my hands shook in nervous anticipation. "Yes Mary, it is through this voice and through the visions provided by our loving Abwoon that I came to know you, long before I came to the house of Lazarus two moons hence. And when you first looked into my eyes on the day that you were healed, the light of recognition was ignited within me and I had the strong sense of the same light being lit within you." Jesus looked deep into my eyes with an imploring gaze that seemed to say, "please tell me what I sensed is indeed true."

As I returned his gaze, a wall collapsed in the center of my mind and a flood of memories that had been held at bay came flooding in. The visions that, before now, had come in fleeting glimpses began to take shape and I clearly saw childhood dreams and musings of a man much like Jesus and the life we shared and would share together. I saw two people as balanced equals sharing a deeply passionate love as well as a common mission, and in that mission bringing forth and modeling a new love in the world. I also saw that in coming together, not only were we one, but that we grew even more complete within ourselves because of the other's presence in our lives and that out of this coupling would arise a third experience – a new being that was part of us, yet beyond us – an experience that would become a beacon not only of the love that we were as individuals, but an even greater love that arises when we come together as one. Most striking, however, were not the specific images, but the feelings of peaceful fulfillment that accompanied them. As I dwelt on these images, I had the sense of a firm foundation being laid beneath my feet – a strength that moved from the soles of my feet through my body to the top of my head. In the awareness of this newly emerging love, I felt strong, courageous, content and whole. As I breathed in these visions and their accompanying sensations, I felt a tear tracing its way down my cheek. I turned my gaze upward to look into Jesus' eyes and saw that he too was weeping. In unison, we reached up to wipe the tear from each other's eye. Jesus gently laid his hand on my cheek as we sat in this wonder-filled silence.

"Jesus," I asked, "What does this all mean?" "I'm

not completely sure," he said, "but I trust that in time, Abwoon will reveal the meaning in its fullness. Until then, we must trust this knowledge to be true and have faith that in this, we shall never be apart. While Abwoon's work will require me to be separated from you, we shall never really be apart. The visions that we share have shown that we are one and are destined to remain as one. I also know that in you a significant portion of Abwoon's plan will be made manifest and for this I am profoundly grateful. It is a relief beyond explanation to find one such as you who is not only open but fully able to receive the truth of our Oneness in Abwoon. To know that we will share in the revelation of this truth brings me a joy that is beyond description."

I sat in awe-filled wonder as Jesus lay our immediate future before me. I should have felt frightened, or at least overwhelmed, but instead I felt a profound sense of readiness and I knew that this was exactly as it should be. We spent our final moments together in silence as we watched the brilliant morning star and prepared for the work before us.

Jesus and his companions departed shortly after breaking fast and after the table had been cleared and the house tidied. After their departure, Lazarus, Martha and I retired to our private rooms to absorb all that had taken place in these few short weeks that felt more like a lifetime. As I entered into the silence, I heard Jesus' sweet voice in my head, "Remember Mary, I am with you always, even unto the end of time."

CHAPTER NINE

The next morning, apparently overcome by the happenings of the fortnight, I awoke to the sun blazing through my window. I must have needed the rest! I arose fully expecting to find Martha hard at work. Instead, I found my brother and sister needed the rest more than I. I quietly stole outside to gather water from the well to begin the morning work. Instead of going toward the well within our compound, I felt strangely called to go to the well outside our compound that sat along the trade route. This well was about 100 yards beyond the outer gates and accessible to all passers-by. I was not surprised to see from a distance that someone was at the well, presumably a traveler seeking refreshment.

I thought about turning back toward the house but, instead, prodded by an inner voice that reassured me that this situation was safe and that the traveler needed help, I approached with caution and was relieved to discover the traveler was a woman. While I let go a sigh of relief, I also felt shock. Why would a woman be traveling alone? From a distance she seemed to be attired in traditional travel wear, but as I drew closer, I saw the travel-wear to be a disguise. The rough-hewn robes of woven hemp were not enough to hide the brilliant silks of the temple prostitutes. The kohl-lined eyes, dyed lips and golden jewels betrayed the truth of who this woman was. Now

I understood the need to travel alone. No woman of respectable status would travel without the company of a male chaperone – preferably her father, husband or elder brother. This woman clearly fell under the category of questionable status. But, who was I to judge?

I nodded a greeting and offered her a kind smile. Warily, she nodded back. "Peace to you," I offered by way of welcome.

"Lady," she inquired, "Forgive my boldness, but does the man called Jesus reside with you?"

"For a fortnight we enjoyed the blessing of his company, but just yesterday, he departed for his home in Capernaum. Are you seeking him?" I asked.

Her shoulders sank in disappointment. "I heard this man Jesus promised freedom. I was hoping he could free me." She then gingerly pulled down the shoulder of her gown to reveal the signs of her imprisonment. She had obviously taken a great risk in journeying in search of Jesus.

Without a moment's hesitation, I spoke, "I'm sorry he is no longer here. Though he promised to return, I cannot say how long it might be. You are welcome to join my sister, brother and me as we break our fast." I know Martha and Lazarus might question my generosity, but, she obviously needed help and who was I to refuse – especially after Jesus' prediction that women would seek Martha and me for help in discovering the healing compassion and peace of our loving God?

I invited the woman to join me in our home. As we walked toward our private compound, I suddenly realized that I had neglected to offer a proper introduction. "I'm sorry, I am Mary and I reside here with my sister Martha, in the home of our brother Lazarus."

"I am Salome. I am the property of Asher, one of the priests of the temple." So my suspicions were correct. If the religious officials got wind that we were sheltering one of their goods, they would not be happy.

As we approached the compound and opened the gate, Martha and Lazarus came out to greet us. "Salome, I am Martha, sister of Lazarus and I welcome you into our home. You are free to remain here as long as you wish." Lazarus and I exchanged stunned looks. How did Martha know we were coming, more importantly, how did she know Salome's name? Martha silently ushered Salome into our home and invited her to sit at the seat of honor. We quickly joined her and it was here that we listened to the story of Salome.

As Salome told it, she was born among a nomadic tribe that traveled throughout the East. They were a beautiful people of darkened skin, luxurious blue-black hair and eyes black as onyx. They were typically shepherds and merchants, seeking grasslands for their sheep and goats while transporting for sale the riches of the Orient. She described the life of freedom and travel that I had secretly longed for. She had come from the land of the many-armed gods of the East, traversed the magnificent slopes of the Himalayas and witnessed the ancient ruins of Babylon.

While still a young girl – of six or seven suns – her family had pitched their tents just outside the holy city of Jerusalem. Her father and brother were herding the flocks to graze while she and her mother prepared a cart of silks and spices to take to the market. As she and her mother readied for departure, a gust of wind fell upon them and picked up one of the silks she had neglected to secure. The priceless, brilliant orange silk was lifted into the air and began to be carried swiftly away. Knowing the price this silk would bring, Salome instinctively ran after it. Only fifty yards from her mother's watchful eye, Salome crossed the path of a man on horseback, who, struck by her beauty reached down, scooped her up, and raced off with her on horseback, deaf to the piercing wail of her mother and her own plaintive cries for mercy.

What happened next was a blur. The man took her to a house of women where she was bathed, dressed and painted, and given a drink that made her feel like she was drifting away on the clouds. She was placed in a line of women who followed one another into a room gloriously colored in brilliant purple, fuchsia and tangerine. Jeweled tables surrounded the place where they stood and soon began to fill with men who appeared to be dressed in sacred garb. Were these the high priests of Jerusalem? She had heard stories of them with their long beards, fringed robes and striped shawls. Under the influence of the cloud drink, the men who surrounded them soon turned a blur of ecru and indigo stripes. Then the music began.

Forgetting where she was, and perhaps due to influence of the cloud drink, she lost herself in the music. The women around her began gyrating their hips and swaying their arms in rhythm to the music. Reminiscent of the sacred songs of her homeland, she forgot herself and began to join in their dance. After the dance was finished, the men applauded. The horseman came out and began to auction off the women, one-by-one, to the highest bidder from among the temple priests. Soon enough he came to Salome and there was but one man who offered a bid for her. Looking upon this man, she abruptly awoke from her cloudy haze for a chill shivered down her spine and the hair on the back of her neck stood up. The lecherous look of this man repulsed her. The woman who had bathed and clothed her earlier took note of her look of horror and quickly intervened with another cup of the cloud drink.

The next thing she remembered was waking in the women's room surrounded by other snoring women. Her body ached and her head hurt but the most disconcerting sensation was the dull ache between her legs that seemed to reach up somewhere deep inside her and the dried blood that she found in her undergarments when she later went to relieve herself. She ran to the woman who served as mistress of the house and shared her concern with her, in alarm; but her only response was, "Pay no mind to that little one, the drink will help you to forget."

From this day on, Salome was the private entertainment of the high priest called Asher. She soon learned that he fancied little girls. The cloud drink, if not able to make her forget, at least allowed her to remain numb. As her menarche began, she found Asher's treatment of her suddenly changing. Whereas he had been somewhat gentle to her in the past, she now found him violent. His play became rough and he frequently struck her. Something in her rebelled and she became determined to step out of her numbness. She decided to refrain from taking the cloud drink with the hope of realizing the truth of her condition. She wanted to feel the impact of every strike of Asher's palm, every punch of his fist, every pull of her hair, every insult and every abusive word. She wanted to taste the revulsion and hatred she felt for this man. And so she did. She felt it all. And, when she found herself pregnant with his child (apparently the cloud drink also served to prevent such tragedies), he beat her until the babe in her womb was expelled in a bloody pulp. She nearly died in a heap at his feet, but when her mistress got word, she sent her ladies to tend to Salome's broken body.

Thankfully, Asher wanted nothing to do with her until she healed, and so she was rushed to the ladies' house to be nursed. While recovering from her injuries, the rumors of Jesus began to reach her ears. The ladies talked and giggled as they dreamed of Jesus coming to rescue them like King David, himself, riding in on a white horse to take them away. Salome knew these to be the frivolous daydreams of women who would never have the courage to leave with him even if he did come. It was at that moment that Salome decided she would go looking for Jesus herself.

This search was what brought her to Bethany. Under cover of darkness, she managed to escape the women's house. She thought she saw the mistress wake to witness her departure, but no alarms were sounded, so perhaps she had imagined it. But, as she approached the usually guarded door, she found the guard sound asleep. She was sure that between his snores she smelled the tangy-sweet aroma of the cloud drink. And lying beside his sleeping body was draped the outer cloak of the Hebrew women who sometimes came seeking women's potions from the head mistress. She quickly donned the cloak and headed outdoors to freedom – or sure death. She traveled in haste along the road from Jerusalem to Bethany not caring that this journey could kill her. She'd already lived in hell. Death could not be worse.

She arrived in Bethany before dawn and waited by the village well, hoping to get news of Jesus there. When the first women arrived she inquired, "Do you know where Jesus bar Joseph might be staying?" "At the house of Lazarus to be sure," one woman replied, "One mile into the country along the old well road." This is what had brought her to our well.

As she finished her tale, Martha and I shook our heads with the sad familiarity of the desperate plight of women. As we turned to our dear brother Lazarus, we saw him weeping. Without discussion, we nodded our mutual agreement to offer refuge to this woman – this prostitute of the temple priests.

After the meal, Martha and I left Lazarus to clean up as we went about our unspoken plan to assist in the protection of our new-found sister, Salome. Martha knew of a plant that would change the appearance of Salome's blue-black hair to a deep auburn and went out to search among her secret stores its powered compound. I prepared a healing bath of hyssop, cedar and salt from the Dead Sea to soothe her aching body and ease her troubled mind. From the sacred earth of the Dead Sea, I formed a paste to scrub the kohl from her eyes and paint from her lips. After bathing, we applied the sacred henna to her hair and let it do its work. Salome emerged a new woman – her skin remained the deep olive of the people of her tribe, but free of the markings of slavery, and her hair now glowed a deep, brilliant, auburn. We exchanged her temple wear with one of my rough-hewn robes and bound her hair in one of my veils. She could easily pass for any of our Hebrew sisters. Unless examined closely, she no longer bore the appearance of the Salome of old, property of Asher, priest of the temple. She was now Salome, sister to Martha and Mary of the House of Lazarus.

After enjoying a few days of healing baths and restful sleep, Salome quickly fell into our daily routine. Accustomed to late nights and equally late mornings, I never had to worry that Salome would interrupt my

sacred morning prayer, though I would have welcomed
her company if this was what she had desired. I had
come to cherish this sacred time in which I could be one
with Jesus. I had only to draw him into my awareness
and there he would be, sitting at my side in silent prayer
– or so it seemed. At times I was tempted to discount
these visits as the imaginings of my foolish mind, but
I remembered what Jesus had said about the voice
of Abwoon that resided within his heart, and when I
consulted that place of compassion and love within, I
knew that Jesus had in fact been with me in prayer.

Indeed, it all felt too real to simply be my imagination,
for as I imagined him sitting beside me, I could feel
the warmth of his body next to mine, I could feel the
sensation of his fingers resting on the bench and gently
reaching over to touch my hand or the side of my leg. I
felt the rise and fall of his body as he breathed and heard
the gentle sound of his breath as he relaxed into prayer.
Even the most active imagination could not produce the
very real physical sensations of Jesus sitting beside me
in prayer. And certainly, imagination alone could not
produce the shivers of pleasure that overtook my body as
I felt the touch of his fingers reaching towards mine or
the dancing beat of my heart as he inched his body closer
to mine, or the warmth that spread through my belly in
response to the rise and fall of his breath. Even if this
was only my imagination, these thoughts gave me such
pleasure that I continued to indulge them and bask in the
wonder of them. I only dared to dream that Jesus might be
feeling the same.

It was shortly after Salome settled into our routine
that the other women began to come. Perhaps fueled
by Lazarus' visits to their men, these women seemed

compelled to speak to the women that Jesus had invited to sit at table. We readily welcomed these women into our home where we heard their stories of love, loss, joy and sorrow, pleasure and pain. In the sanctity of our home, these women unburdened their souls and we provided comfort through compassionate listening. We also shared with them Jesus' teachings on the kingdom. Some women heard these words and found comfort, others asked to learn more and some stomped off in indignation. These women, I came to learn, were either not ready for the kind of freedom promised by our Lord or were simply content in the traditional role that Judaism had laid out for them. I sensed that neither path was right or wrong, simply differing according to the unique needs of the individual.

As our little "ministry" began to grow, we continued to hear word of Jesus and the fervor he was creating in the Jewish world. For the poor, the sick and the outcast, Jesus' message provided a much needed healing balm to their wounded hearts. In his message they found a renewed sense of hope. There were countless stories of men and women who, like I, had experienced miraculous healing in the loving touch of this man.

The rich and powerful found Jesus' message for the most part uninteresting. Yes, there were a few whose hearts were open, but most were quite simply too content with their wealth and status to consider anything new. These were the ones who in the end suffered the most when Jerusalem eventually fell.

Initially, the religious authorities simply ignored Jesus, discounting his presence as just another passing fancy. Lazarus however, predicted that this freedom from attention would not last. Jesus' message, he speculated, would threaten those who earned their power by making

God something to be feared. I sensed truth in Lazarus'
words and I worried for Jesus' safety. I offered an anxious
prayer to Abwoon and willed that the feelings I had for
Jesus, which grew stronger each day, could reach out to
him and enfold him in a blanket of safety. I could not
bear the thought of any harm coming to him or that in
this we might somehow be separated. As the anxiety
within me grew, I once again heard Jesus' voice, "Mary, do
not be afraid. I will be with you always, even unto the end
of time."

86

CHAPTER TEN

Several months had passed and our household was now packed to overflowing with women seeking to hear Jesus' message of freedom. Lazarus' home, the testament to his success, motivated by his desire to have revenge upon our father and oldest brother; had been transformed into a center of healing and comfort to those who found their way into our home. Our gatherings would begin around the dining table inside the house but would eventually spill out into the outer courtyard. During the times we set aside for personal reflection, the women who came wandered the magnificent gardens that surrounded our home. Many found their connection with God through the beauty that had been cultivated here. Others found God in the hospitality that we, the House of Lazarus, offered without condition to anyone who came. The majority found comfort in a time away from the day to day stress of their lives and in the opportunity to enjoy a few moments of silence in the company of other women who also desired this time alone.

While I had introduced and successfully incorporated silent contemplation into our gathering of women and had found fulfillment and solace in communal contemplation, I looked forward in anxious anticipation to my private time with Jesus. I could not wait for the morning when I could arise from my bed, dress, and go alone to the garden

to be with Jesus, alone, in prayer. While I enjoyed the miracle of his presence in my prayer, I found that even this was not enough. I longed to feel his body beside mine, to feel the warmth of his breath as it brushed the side of my cheek when we talked, to feel the skin of his fingers as they gently caressed the back of my hand. I grew restless and frustrated with a God that would keep me apart from the man with whom I wanted to spend every waking moment. In this, I sometimes thought God was cruel. I prayed to Abwoon that if I could not find peace in this, that at least I might find wisdom.

Four turnings of the moon had passed since Salome's arrival. It was now the first morning of the new moon, and as I settled into prayer beneath her silvery crown, I drew my attention to Jesus. As usual, there he was at my side in prayer, but instead of sitting in silence, he began to converse with me, "Mary, I am well pleased with the healing ministry you, Martha and Lazarus have provided to the people of Bethany. Abwoon has shown me that much healing has taken place and wounded hearts mended as through your word, their hope in a loving God has been restored. I will be returning to the house of Lazarus soon to continue teaching the house of Lazarus and to proclaim the Kingdom of God to the men and women of Bethany."

A thrill of excitement ran up my spine. Jesus was soon to return! Oh, how I longed to hear his voice…to look into his eyes and to feel the touch of his hand on mine. My heart began to pound as anticipation filled my body and my mind began to race with ideas of all the things we would do while he was here: the conversations…the stolen glances…the kisses I only dared to wish that we might share… But, I listened again to his words, "to

continue teaching the house of Lazarus and the men and women of Bethany," and that in my selfish imaginings, I had forgotten the reason for Jesus' return. I quickly set aside my own selfish desires and drew my thoughts to the men and women of Bethany who had only learned of Jesus through our teachings and who would soon see him face to face and experience the life-altering grace of his presence. I thought also of our beloved Salome who might find healing for the hardness that still imprisoned her heart, for although Salome had risked her very life in search of Jesus and his healing message, she still carried within a stoniness that all our listening, words of comfort and healing measures could not fully penetrate. She still doubted that a loving God could have allowed her to be taken from her mother and father's loving arms and to be sold into cruel sexual slavery to the temple priests. "What kind of God allows that fate upon a child?" She often wondered. In all my prayer, I could find no answer to her quandary and wondered upon it myself.

I awoke the next morning with a profound sense of anticipation. I had the acute feeling of Jesus' imminent arrival. I was tempted to abandon my prayer to awaken Martha so that we could begin our preparations, but recalling Jesus' teaching about the abundant nature of God, I decided there would be time enough for both prayer and preparation.

As I stole out the door toward the garden, I glimpsed a figure in the dark darting through the sliding front doors that separated the inner from the outer dining rooms and toward the gate that separated our compound from the outside world. Could Martha already be up and going for water at the outside well? And if so, why would she be going there unaccompanied? Had Lazarus sensed that

Jesus was soon to come? I suddenly knew – of course – it was Salome! What could be her business this time of day? I heard Jesus' comforting words, "Mary, leave her be. This is her path to travel." At this gentle reminder, I continued toward the garden to enjoy our morning repose.

I had grown accustomed to the peace of Jesus' presence beside me and of his occasional sweet voice. This morning, I was startled by something altogether different. Just as I sat down and closed my eyes, a vivid scene unfolded in my mind. It seemed as if I were viewing this scene through someone else's eyes. The scene I beheld was that of one approaching our home on the road. I suddenly realized the vision I was beholding was through Jesus' eyes as he showed me the crowd that now traveled with him. I was so excited to know it was Jesus that I began to rise from my bench to run and greet them. "Mary, wait. There is something you need to witness from where you are," I heard him say.

I saw what Jesus meant. As he approached our home, his attention was drawn to the traveler's well. There, sitting at the well was Salome. I suddenly felt a blast of anger and hatred that seemed to be radiating from her, directed at Jesus. With the exception of my father, I had never felt such emotion erupting out of another human being. As the blast of Salome's rage hit me, my inclination was to run. I witnessed Jesus, however, had another response. Instead of running from Salome's anger, he moved toward it, drawing it into his heart and as he did this, the rage was transformed into compassion and love. Salome sat at the well, her whole body rigid and her eyes ablaze with indignation. Jesus approached the well, "Woman, get me a drink." Salome quickly covered her shock and surprise at Jesus' command with rage. "Get it yourself, prophet! If you can work miracles, surely you can get your own water!" Nonplussed, Jesus approached the well, lowered the bucket and drew himself a drink. After drinking his fill, he offered Salome a drink.

"I don't want your water! I want answers," Salome retorted as she pushed away the water he offered to her.

"Salome," he replied gently as he again offered her the cup, "The water I have to give is the water of life. She who drinks this water will thirst no longer."

"Don't speak to me in riddles prophet," she spat back. "I want to know how your god, this god that you say is all-loving could take me from my beloved family and cast me into the pits of hell! What did I do to deserve this from your supposedly loving god?"

"Salome, please have a drink. Then we shall talk."

Reluctantly, Salome accepted the cup he offered and took a tiny sip. There was a look of surprise on her face and she blinked as if she was trying to see something far on the horizon.   She gently wrapped her hands around the cup and took a long draught of the water, finishing the cup. She held it out to Jesus, asking for more. She drank fully of the second cup and then sat with the cup in her hands upon her lap and closed her eyes. Her body relaxed, her breathing slowed and a smile slowly illuminated her face. When she could no longer contain her joy, a sob burst forth from her chest, "Oh my Lord!" she exclaimed. She fell to Jesus' feet, kissing them while shedding tears of relief. When her tears had been spent, she rose up and like a giddy child, grabbed Jesus' hand, dragging him behind her toward our front gate shouting with excitement, "Lazarus, Mary, Martha, Jesus is here! He is here! He has saved me! He showed me everything that happened to me! Hurry let us make ready the feast!"

I sprang up from the bench and ran from my garden through the house and to the gate to welcome them with Lazarus and Martha close at my heels. I attempted a proper greeting, but Salome rushed right past me with Jesus. He turned and gave me a wink and a quick smile, enjoying the youthful enthusiasm that now filled my adopted sister's heart. Salome ushered him in and sat him at the place of honor at table. She rushed around gathering all he would need to break his fast. We followed close behind along with the men and women who had accompanied Jesus to our welcoming home on this early morning. We bid them to recline and completed the task of setting the table with dried nuts and fruits, cheeses and breads for all present to enjoy an early morning feast. Once everyone was gathered at table, Salome excitedly relayed what had transpired at the well:

"As I have shared with my adoptive family, it was Jesus' message of freedom that empowered me to leave behind my former life of slavery. I was excited and happy to meet this man, but the more I learned of his God, the angrier I became. How could a loving God rip me from my family's love and throw me into the hell in which I have been living? How could a loving God make a little girl of seven have to lie with a cruel and hateful man? How could God destroy my innocence and life in this way? I died the day the man on horseback kidnapped me in plain sight of my loving mother. Her cries of pain have haunted me all these long years. Today, however, I have come back to life. I took a drink of the water Jesus gave me and my eyes were suddenly opened! For the first time, I beheld the light. I saw all the ways in which God's love had broken through my tragedy to soothe my pain. I saw how God had provided a path of freedom for me from this hell in which I had been living. To begin, the Lord God made me born of female form. Drinking the water, I saw the evil priest Asher and his wicked taste, not only for little girls, but also for little boys, especially those whose parents had innocently and faithfully dedicated their sons and offered them in service to the temple. Little did they know the fate that would befall them if they were placed in service to Asher. The things Asher did to me were terrible, but what I endured was nothing compared to what the boys endured – unspeakable acts of violation and torture. It was a wonder these boys survived at all. And Asher, while visiting the women's house but once or twice a week, had access to these boys 24 hours a day, seven days a week. I do not know how the other priests never knew – for even the sins of Sodom and Gomorrah were nothing compared to Asher's sins."

"Then I saw our head-mistress, Chuza. Although hardened by her years as mistress of the women's house, there was something in my childish ways that warmed her heart. God revealed to me how she saw me as the daughter she could never have. While she had no choice in my fate, she took pity on me. From the first day of auction when she stepped in with the second cup of cloud drink, to selecting the herbs with which she prepared my foods, hoping to prevent the usually addictive nature of the drink, Chuza seemed to be easing my pain. And her final act of mercy: making sure that Jesus' message reached my ears, drugging the guard and providing a Hebrew robe for my escape.

Upon drinking the water, my eyes were opened, but much more than that. I was released of the rage I had felt toward a God I thought had abandoned me to powerlessness. I saw instead the way God had given me the courage to endure, the ingenuity to hatch a plan of escape and the motivation to follow through with that plan. I am now free of the shame brought on by years of violation and torture. I am no longer filled with the bitter bile of resentment or plagued with thoughts of revenge. Before drinking the cup, I had thoughts of going back to Jerusalem and taking my revenge on Asher, but now I only feel pity for him. God has saved me. My eyes are open and again I have life. This man Jesus has given me the water of life and raised me from the dead!"

And then our dear Salome wept silent tears of gratitude.

At that Jesus took a deep breath and was about to speak when Simon brusquely interrupted, "Lord, who sinned, this woman or her parents that this wicked fate has befallen her?" In unison, Salome, Martha, Lazarus and I, along with several of the other men and women, recoiled at Simon's intrusive words. I wanted to jump in and admonish him for this cruelty toward Salome. But, more than that, I wondered if he had learned anything in his many months of travel with our Lord. Thankfully, Jesus handled it better than I would have.

"Neither she nor her parents sinned. Has not the glory of God been revealed in her survival, escape and return to life? Abwoon is a loving and compassionate God whose love is without condition. There is nothing we can ever do to separate ourselves from the love of God. No punishment is given except that which we inflict upon ourselves. God waits with open arms for us to open our eyes to see the presence and action of God in our lives. Salome's experience presents a perfect example. It was not due to her sin but to the realities of the human condition that caused these tragedies to befall her. Yet even in the

deepest pits of hell, God was still there. Salome was simply unable to see the glory of God that shone in her midst. Opening her eyes to God has raised her from the dead. This is the promise in the tragedies that we all suffer."

"But Lord," Simon argued, "this is not what the Pharisees say in their interpretation of the Law."

"Simon, they are entitled to their opinion. The question remains, what speaks truth to you?"

"What speaks truth to me? Isn't the truth in the Law?"

"Mary, what are your thoughts on this?" Jesus asked of me.

My heart jumped at his inquiry and without thought to Simon's response, I readily answered, "It seems to me that there is truth in the Law, but at the same time, if we truly believe that God's way is the way of freedom, it invites us to examine the Law more carefully. We should be asking: 'Where is the Law supportive of freedom in our lives? How does it help to bring us closer to God? Where does the Law only stand as an obstacle to full communion with God?'"

"Well said Mary." At this, Simon cast me a scornful glare. Jesus continued, "Let me give you an example. If you are journeying a short way from home on the Sabbath and come upon a man who has been beaten and robbed and in need of assistance, and offering that assistance would require you to take more steps than are legally allowed on the Sabbath, would you help him or leave him to die? Simon, what do you say?"

"I would help him of course!"

"Of course you would. So it is with the rest of the Law." Now Mary, would you respond to the question about Salome's sin or lack thereof?"

I glanced over at Simon before proceeding. He offered a harrumph of disgust, crossed his arms over his chest and looked away. I now felt unsure as to whether I should respond, but Jesus interrupted my discomfort, "Mary, don't indulge your fears. Simply honor the truth within you."

I took a deep breath and offered my thoughts. "The Law seems to suggest that the suffering we experience is a punishment for our sins or those of our parents. And yet, how does one explain the suffering of those who are: loving, kind, and God-fearing? There must be another way to look at it. What if the truth is simply that our human condition includes suffering – not because of something we did wrong, but just because. The question of sin is less about the suffering and more about what we do with it. We sin when we allow suffering to close our eyes to God's presence and activity or close our hearts to God's love. The invitation is to keep our eyes fixed on God and our heart open to God's love – even in the midst of the greatest suffering."

"Well said Mary – to which I would add" remarked Jesus, "Even in closing our eyes and our hearts there is still no sin."

At this, Simon stood up and pounded his hand on the table in challenge. With his teeth gritted and the veins bulging on his forehead, he confronted our Lord, "Do you mean to say there is no sin?"

"There is no sin except that which you make to exist when you act according to the habits of your fearful nature. This is where sin lies," Jesus explained.

As he said this a great expanse filled my heart and I felt my being open to a whole new level of peace.

"Do you mean to say, Lord, that what we have called sin is in fact merely a symptom of a deeper fear?" I inquired.

"Yes Mary. That is exactly it!"

At this, Simon stood up and stormed out the door. Jesus took his behavior as a cue, inviting us to spend some time in quiet reflection as we absorbed the deeper meaning of this discussion. After a few moments, Simon returned to his place at table and joined us in prayer. I breathed a sigh of relief an offered a silent prayer of thanks that Simon's heart had been opened, or so I thought.

Apparently my prayer was premature as I witnessed Simon's actions the rest of the day. While Jesus continued to offer to me the seat of honor at his left, he insisted the seat of honor at his right remain vacant. I gave this no heed, believing that Jesus meant no special designation in the seat that had been chosen for me or for the seat at his right. Simon, however, seemed bothered. "How can he offer the first seat of honor to a woman and leave the other seat vacant? Is there not one among us worthy of sitting at his right hand?" As he muttered his thoughts to those nearest him, I saw Jesus give Simon a quick glance of rebuke, followed by a barely noticeable look of profound sadness. Simon pretended to ignore Jesus' rebuke, but I saw his face take on a slightly redder hue. Later while we took a break to relieve and refresh ourselves in the outdoor air, I happened upon Simon in the courtyard with another group of disciples. I heard him ask again, "Is there not one among us worthy to sit at his right hand?" beginning a heated discussion among those present as to what it meant to be worthy to sit at Jesus' right hand. "I was the first one chosen…I've contributed most to his ministry…Jesus speaks to me alone…I am the eldest among us…I've left the most behind to follow Jesus…" Each seemed to believe he had the most right to sit in the coveted seat of honor. As we returned for the afternoon meal and lessons, the arguing continued. Simon had stirred a hornets' nest and the entire company was now arguing about who should be first among them. As the men argued, Jesus looked upon them with great sadness, a sadness that tugged at my own heart. And Jesus began to pray. He took a deep breath and taught us in this way:

"You know that in the human world those who are recognized as rulers lord it over their subjects and make their authority felt through the use of power and control. If you are to follow in God's way, it shall not be so among you. Rather, whoever wishes to be the greatest among you must become the servant. Abwoon has not sent us to be served but to serve, for in the Kingdom of God, the first shall be last and the last shall be first. As to who shall sit at my right or left hand, that is not mine to give, but is for those for whom it has been prepared and will be revealed by Abwoon. Mary sits at my left because Abwoon has ordained it. He or she who is to sit at my right has not yet been revealed, and so the seat remains vacant."

The men hung their heads in shame and began to eat in silence. Simon joined in the silence, but glowered as the resentment within him took deeper root.

After we finished our meal, men and women alike cleared the table, washed the dishes and tidied up our home after which Jesus announced there would be no more lessons that day for he had need of prayer. The group disbanded. Lazarus, Martha and Salome remained in our home while the men returned to their encampment beyond our garden wall. As everyone departed to their repose, Jesus gently reached for my hand, "Mary, would you come and pray with me?"

"Of course Rabbi," I responded, trying not to appear overly excited, even though I could barely contain the beating of my heart in anticipation of sharing this sacred time with him. Hand in hand, Jesus led me to our usual place of prayer in the center of the garden.

Chapter Eleven

Side by side on the garden bench, with our feet firmly on the ground and our hands resting in our laps, we journeyed to the silence in the center of our hearts where Abwoon dwells. My mind was spinning with all that had transpired that day and inner silence eluded me. I turned my attention to my breath, hoping that my mind would find rest there. In time it did and I was startled out of a deep inner peace when I felt Jesus move to rest his hand upon mine. With his touch, my skin grew hot. I breathed deeply, opened my eyes, and looked over at Jesus who remained in the silent serenity of prayer, or so I thought. Just as I looked upon him, he gently smiled. He gently squeezed my hand and turned his body toward mine. "Mary," he began, "I cannot tell you what it means to be able to share this time with you. The house of Lazarus has become a sacred refuge for me, a place to be away from the crowds and a place where I have found a kindred brother in Lazarus and sisters in you, Martha and Salome. It is so good to be in the company of those whose hearts are open."

He bowed his head and I saw a single tear escape from the corner of his eye. "What is it?" I asked.

"Mary, the work of Abwoon is never easy. I know the peace and joy that all can know if they would but open their hearts to God, and I am saddened when that task seems impossible. I know nothing is impossible with God and I know God is at work even in those whose hearts have turned to stone – but I grieve for each moment that fear is chosen over love, and it is a great source of frustration when those closest to me do not yet seem opened to embracing God's love."

"Rabbi, do you speak of Simon?"

"Yes, of him and others like him. Simon is such a good man – loyal, hard-working, and readily willing to lend a hand to any man who needs it. At the same time, he is stubborn, prideful and limited in his vision. He cannot see the Kingdom beyond that which he thinks he knows and understands. And he cannot see that women are God's children. He believes women are only here to serve and it was for this reason he asked me to heal his mother-in-law. She had come to live with Simon and his own beloved wife, Leah, after her husband had died, and she was all that remained when Leah and their unborn child perished during childbirth. After Leah's death, Simon's heart grew even colder than before and he armored himself against the loving affections of another. His mother-in-law became a constant reminder to him of the loss of his beloved and he built a wall of detachment between them. His request for her to be healed was not so that the glory of God could be revealed, but so that she could fulfill her role as servant – what she had become for him in his life. In healing her, I hoped that Simon would see not only the glory of God, but be healed of his hardened heart, but sadly, none of this came to pass. Instead of taking her rightful place as disciple alongside the rest of the Galilean brethren, Simon's mother-in-law sits at Capernaum awaiting our return so that she can resume her role as servant."

"Can't you heal Simon's stony heart and darkened vision?" I inquired.

"No Mary," he replied with sadness in his eyes, "not until he desires to be healed. And, it is more than a stony heart and darkened vision that plague Simon. He lusts for power, stirs quickly to anger, envies others, and refuses to take time to listen and hear the truth that Abwoon would reveal to him. Additionally, his pride keeps him from embracing the humility that must be embraced if one is to do God's work, and in his arrogance, he refuses to trust in God. There is much Simon will need to release in order to receive a healing in any way similar to the healing you have experienced."

I felt the sadness in Jesus' heart and breaking with protocol, I reached toward him, wrapped my arms around him and tried to comfort him in his sorrow. I pictured the love of God in my own heart reaching deeply into Jesus' heart providing healing and comfort. As his breathing slowed, I could feel Jesus relaxing into my loving comfort, and his grief slowly lifted. Jesus gently pulled away from my embrace, placed his hand upon my cheek and looking deeply into my eyes, "Mary, thank you. I cannot tell you what it means to me to have a companion in this work who understands the joys and also the frustrations that come with sharing God's way of love. You are a blessing to me and while I trust in the providence of what Abwoon has revealed to me, these four months apart have challenged me. I cherish our sacred time together in prayer where we can connect in that place of Oneness, but I cannot help longing to be with you in this way, face to face, hand to hand and hopefully heart to heart."

With his words, the deep place within me where I had carefully contained the longing that I, too, had felt in

102

Jesus' absence, burst open and tears began streaming down my face. I had tried to be courageous, trusting and strong in Jesus' absence, surrendering to Abwoon's guidance and wisdom, but it had been difficult work. After Jesus had shared his visions with me and after the wall collapsed behind which my own visions had lay hidden, all I wanted was for these visions to be made manifest. I longed to be in Jesus' presence, to stand beside him, to hold his hand, to feel his body next to mine. I wanted to be worthy of ministering by his side, to heal as he healed, to bring comfort to those who longed to know love, to be his companion as together we performed Abwoon's work in the world. And in a very human way, I wanted to feel his arms around me, to feel the touch of his lips against mine, to lay my head on his chest and feel the beat of his heart against my cheek. With brimming eyes, I looked deeply into Jesus' eyes, baring all the longing that I had contained for those past four months. Jesus laid his hand along the side of my face, leaned in, and in response to all of my desires, gently kissed me. I returned his kiss as the strangest combination of fiery excitement and contentment filled my being, and I felt like I was home.

After we kissed, Jesus put his arm around me as I snuggled beside him and together we watched the moon rise in the east and the stars take their places in the sky. I would have been content to sit beside him through the night, but knew it must not be so. As the crickets began their evening chant, Jesus drew me closer to him, bent his face toward mine and we kissed a second time. Without need for words, together we rose and hand in hand left the garden to return to our places of repose – I to my private quarters and Jesus to the encampment beyond the garden walls where he rejoined his Galilean companions.

As I drew the covers around me I replayed these delicious moments in my mind – the sensation of Jesus' soft lips upon mine and the fire that was alight within me as we kissed, the warmth of his arms around me and the sensation of being home. I hoped that these thoughts would become the dreams that would carry me through the night. I was not to be disappointed.

CHAPTER TWELVE

B y the next day, the town's people had heard of Jesus'
arrival. At first they trickled in, one at a time; but
soon they came in droves to sit in Jesus' presence
and to hear the message of God's love. For the house of
Lazarus, our time to have Jesus to ourselves had come to
an end, but when tempted by thoughts of disappointment,
all I needed to do was to look into the eyes of the people
enlivened with hope and my disappointment was quickly
replaced with joy.

As the days passed, our spacious home became too
small to accommodate the crowds, so our gathering moved
beyond the garden walls. The people sat in friendly
clusters sharing their bread and water while Jesus walked
among them teaching and listening to their stories. He
was frequently seen crouched down delivering a personal
message, holding the withered hand of a widow or kissing
the forehead of an innocent child. His presence spoke of a
deep compassion and acceptance that many of the people
had never before experienced.

As Jesus moved through the crowd, Lazarus, Martha,
Salome and I, along with several of the village women,
went from person to person offering water, a small piece
of dried fruit or goat cheese, as well as oil to anoint their
hands and heads in protection from the sun that shone
overhead. Occasionally, Jesus' eyes would find mine

105

and beckon me over to a woman in need of the sort of help that Jesus knew only I could provide. I needed no instruction, only a look in Jesus' eyes that told me to draw the woman to a private place where she could freely unburden her heavy heart, shed tears of grief or find relief for righteous anger. Martha, Lazarus and Salome were called in similar ways to offer support to the men and women who gathered through gifts that were uniquely their own – Lazarus through instruction on scripture, Martha through attentive listening and Salome through a loving touch. With Jesus' guidance and support, we had found the unique ways in which God had individually gifted us to be God's love in the world.

In contrast, the many of men who came with Jesus from Galilee, instead of being drawn to serve, seemed to stay very close to Jesus – seemingly hanging on his every word. Simon, especially, seemed bent on memorizing Jesus' stories and teachings, which I thought rather fruitless since Jesus' parables changed with each telling, depending on who was listening. It was not the words themselves that were important, but the deeper truths behind the words. Simon placed great importance on knowing and recalling the exact wording and was frequently heard correcting Jesus when the stories differed in the telling. Jesus' patience with Simon left me awestruck. I wanted to strangle Simon for his constant interruptions, a feeling which revealed my own intolerance and judgment. Just because I had been healed of the seven demons did not mean that I was suddenly free from the inner fears and attachments that we all face.

After several days of ministering to the people of Bethany, I noticed a new couple in the crowd, an older gentleman and a female companion that I could only assume was his wife. Both bore the marks of wisdom with softly lined faces, graying hair and for him, a graying beard. Both the man and the woman's attire were rather non-descript which failed to betray their tribe, their heritage or social status. The only thing that gave him away as a man of learning was that his hands bore none of the calluses or imbedded grime of the laboring classes. In truth, I would not have given the couple a second glance had it not been for their eyes. Both had eyes of the most brilliant blue I had ever seen – not the azure of the sea, but a deep indigo like the lapis stones so popular among the Egyptian Jews. As a very young girl, I had seen such a stone when our family made a pilgrimage to the great temple in Jerusalem. I had seen a group of what looked like Hebrew women, but their eyes were lined with kohl and their robes were adorned with these deep blue stones. My mother caught my curious stare and told me these were descendents of the Jews that had chosen to remain in Egypt rather than depart across the Red Sea with Moses and his followers.

Along with their brilliant indigo eyes, the man and the woman bore a look of kindness similar to what I saw in the eyes of my brother. In them there appeared to be no malice, pride or deceit, only pure gentleness and compassion. I sought out Lazarus to inquire who this couple might be. "I wondered how long before Nicodemus and Joanna would find their way here," was his response.

So, this was Nicodemus, the well-loved rabbi from our village who had been elevated to also serve in the temple precincts in Jerusalem, and his wife, Joanna. Considered "unclean" by law, I had never ventured inside the tiny synagogue where the people of Bethany went to hear the word of God and I had not been to Jerusalem since the

107

childhood visit with my family. Lazarus was not a man of the synagogue, but he had enough business in the village of Bethany and in the great city of Jerusalem to know of the beloved rabbi. Rabbi Nicodemus was known to be a man of great kindness and compassion and was well-loved by the people, and his wife along with him.

"Why does he not wear the robes of his position?" I asked of Lazarus.

"Perhaps not to draw undue attention," Lazarus guessed.

Just as I was about to pry more information out of Lazarus, I saw that Jesus had caught the eye of Nicodemus and was walking toward him. I realized that I did not need to move closer, because the conversation was open to me as had been the discussion at the well between Jesus and Salome. As Jesus approached him, Nicodemus moved to greet him. Jesus bowed deeply in the greeting of honor, "Good day, good Rabbi. We are greatly honored with your presence along with the presence of your beloved wife. Won't you come into the home of Lazarus and share with us your wisdom?"

"Thank you, Jesus bar Joseph. Joanna and I would be greatly honored to partake of your wisdom as well."

Jesus, Nicodemus and Joanna moved toward the house. As they departed the crowd, Jesus looked over to me and signaled for me to join them. I quickly grabbed Salome and Martha so we could adequately prepare to serve our honored guests. Lazarus was already on his way and the crowd, recognizing the teachers' need for solitude, reluctantly departed. The Galilean men stood there in stunned confusion but quickly recovered when they realized a proper meal was at hand.

As Nicodemus and Jesus approached the table, Jesus

offered Nicodemus the seat at his right hand and Joanna took the seat to Nicodemus' right. They both bowed in humble gratitude as Nicodemus accepted Jesus' invitation, "Today I humbly accept this seat of honor, but only for today for I know there is another who is more worthy of this esteemed seat."

I noticed Simon's ears prick up in curiosity over this ominous acceptance. "Who is Jesus waiting for and how does this old man know….or is Jesus simply waiting to offer it to me once he thinks I am ready? What do I need to do to earn that seat? Haven't I done enough for him already?" I imagined him to be thinking. But just as I began to push it out of my imagination, I noticed Jesus shoot Simon a quick glance of rebuke. Apparently Jesus had "heard" it too.

Once everyone had taken their seat, I went to provide the ritual cleansing. But, before I could begin, Jesus rose from table, took off his outer cloak and took the basin, towel and pitcher from my hands. He invited me to sit, and beginning with Nicodemus, he performed the ceremonial foot washing. A grumbled protest went up from the Galilean men. Jesus put up his hand to silence them. They were content to oblige until Jesus reached Simon's seat.

"You will not wash my feet, Lord. It is I who should wash your feet."

"Simon, until you learn the meaning of humility, you are not worthy to wash the feet of anyone here at table."

"Then wash my hands and head as well," Simon boldly proclaimed.

"Simon, your hands and head are already clean. Will you let me wash your feet so that you may be ready to accept the path of humble service?" Jesus asked.

109

"As you wish," was Simon's exasperated reply.

"If we are to follow the path of Abwoon, it is the path of humble service we must walk – never expecting or asking for the seat of honor, performing the tasks traditionally assigned to women and servants, bowing to the poor and outcast, embracing the unclean, visiting the imprisoned, feeding the hungry and clothing the naked. In the Kingdom of God, the first shall be last and the last shall be first."

As Jesus shared these insights, I noticed the rabbi's face lit with a broad smile of recognition as he nodded in excited agreement. "Well-said teacher," he praised.

During the course of the next three days, we remained indoors listening in rapt attention as Jesus and Rabbi Nicodemus excitedly shared, explored and discussed the entirety of the Hebrew scripture. Their focus was on all the ways in which God's magnificent love revealed itself. It was truly a joy to witness these two great teachers breaking open scripture, appreciating in each other, a kindred spirit. It was obvious that Rabbi Nicodemus knew the love of God and was honored and enthused to have found a fellow teacher who also shared this knowledge and point of view. I also took note of the way that Joanna actively participated in the discussion and how Nicodemus and Jesus gave honor and respect to her words. Over the course of those three days, it became obvious that Joanna served quietly alongside Nicodemus as an equal and that he treated her as such. It was inspiring to watch the way they interacted with each other, holding each other's hands, gently touching each other's shoulder or cheek, leaning toward each other as they spoke in intimate whispers and even offering each other a gentle kiss. Clearly a great love existed between them which was

110

rare in Hebrew homes of our time where most marriages were arranged as a legal contract and where there was only hope, but no expectation of love. As I observed the interactions between Nicodemus and Joanna, a glimmer of hope ignited in my heart as to what it might look like if Jesus and I were to marry. I allowed myself to revel for a moment in these fantasies.

As I continued to listen to Jesus and Nicodemus, I also found it refreshing to hear the way they were breaking open scripture. It was as if these two great teachers in their discussion and exploration of the sacred writings were separating the wheat from the chaff before our eyes – peeling away the layers of false human perception and fear to reveal the brilliant light of the seed within.

"What are your thoughts on the story of the fall of man?" questioned the rabbi.

"I have heard some say this is a story of how humans angered God through their disobedience," Jesus began. "If we believe in a loving God, how could this be? What if instead, it is a myth used to make sense of the human condition? On an even deeper level, what if this is a story about the gift of free will? In God's great goodness, God gave us the insight to understand, that in order to really know who God is, we also need to know the absence of God. So even though God knew it would create suffering, God allowed us to choose the perception of God's absence so that we could freely choose to remember and to know God. From that perspective, it is not the story of man's fall, but the story of our choice to grow spiritually and of God's great gift in allowing us to choose. Only in having this choice can we grow in wisdom and knowledge as God so graciously intended."

"Rabbi, these insights have clearly come to you

through God. What a gift to see the light that we so often overlook," observed Nicodemus.

"I believe it to be as the Psalmist wrote," continued Jesus,

> **'Darkness is not dark for you,**
> **And night shines as the day.**
> **Darkness and light are but one.'**

In our human condition, we can choose to see things through the veil of darkness, or we can open our eyes and see the light within. Darkness, suffering, evil and sin exist only because we choose to see through the lens of judgment. God sees beyond our judgment to perceive the light within. In this way, everything becomes a sacred opportunity for healing and growth. For those that have eyes to see...let them see."

"Amen Rabbi, Amen!" And Rabbi Nicodemus bowed his head in silent prayer.

As I took in the conversations between these holy men, it seemed as if another layer of hardness had fallen from my heart. Because I was considered unclean, neither the temple nor the synagogue was open to me. I had only my father's rigid, fearful perspective on the law to guide my understanding. While Martha, Lazarus and I had begun to explore the scripture from the lens of love, I found comfort in knowing that our father's perspective was not universally accepted. As I listened to Rabbi Nicodemus reflect upon and affirm Jesus' teachings, and observed Joanna agreeing with these perspectives, my own judgments and limited perspectives on Judaism fell away. As these judgments fell away, a place within me, already loosened, was now opening and allowing me to see our faith in a new light which permitted me to honor and

112

appreciate that which was of God, while allowing me the freedom to set aside that which had been tainted by man's limited perspective.

Then I remembered the words of the Psalmist,

"Darkness and light are but one",

And I was given pause to reflect further. Who am I to judge what is "of God" and what is not? Do not all things come forth from the mouth of the Most High? If so, I reasoned, even those things colored by man's perceptions must be of God. I grasped the notion that perhaps the invitation for me was to look deeper into those things I perceive to be of fear so that I can see the light of God in its midst. As I sat with that thought, Jesus' voice, the one I heard only in my mind, offered this additional thought: "It is all ordered so that the Glory of God may be revealed. Mary, for those who have eyes to see in this way, let them see." I glanced up at him and saw he was smiling at me. He now spoke aloud so the whole room could hear, "Mary, don't you ever doubt the voice you hear within. Herein dwells the voice of your truth. For those who have ears, let them hear."

CHAPTER THIRTEEN

O n the evening of the third day, Jesus announced
that he and the Galileans must again return to
Capernaum, and that they would depart in three
days time and would be traveling the long way through
Samaria. At this Simon began to protest, "Lord, why
should we waste our time with those heathens? Are you
not the Messiah of the Jews that the prophets foretold?
Did you not come but for the lost children of Israel?"

"Simon!" Jesus shot back in frustration, "you are an
obstacle to me! Get behind me! In the Kingdom of God
there is no Jew or Gentile, slave or free, male or female,
all are One with God. Do you not have ears to hear or a
heart to listen?"

"But Lord, are you not the Messiah about whom the
prophets foretold?" Simon pleaded.

Jesus sighed and placed his hand upon Simon's
shoulder, "Simon, it is you that say I am." At this Simon
placed his head in his hands and silently wept. Jesus
continued to offer comfort to Simon, then he began to
sing,

"Wela tachlan l'enesyuna, Ela patzan min bisha"

I immediately recognized this phrase from the
Kaddish, the ancient prayer of mourning. My mother
and the other women had taught me this prayer as the
song offered in preparation of those who had died. I

114

joined Jesus in singing this prayer. The other women, along with Rabbi Nicodemus soon joined in. It seemed that in offering this prayer, we were inviting Simon to surrender something within him to which he had grown quite attached. Was it his idea of Jesus as the prophesied Messiah? This is what I, too, had come to believe about this man, for he had surely saved me along with every other man and woman under our roof.

"But Mary," Jesus' voice interrupted my thoughts, "How do you define Messiah – as Warrior King?

I had never given this thought. Many of the Hebrew people were seeking a warrior king in the name of David – one who would expel the Romans and restore the kingdom of Jerusalem to its former glory. This felt like one of those man-made ideas. This part of the world has always been at war and I sensed it always would be. Are not our souls more important than worldly power? I would much rather be imprisoned by Rome than return to my former state with an imprisoned spirit.

"Mary, once again you have chosen the better part," Jesus offered to me in silence.

At this I felt deep compassion for Simon for it would be a difficult journey setting aside the idea of Jesus as warrior king, and Simon's attachment to this image of Jesus would surely cause him great suffering. I prayed for his heart to be open to a broader interpretation of Jesus' mission and to let go of his religious and nationalistic pride. Jesus' message of love was universal and certainly could not be contained within the tribal pride of Judaism.

After praying over Simon, Jesus returned to his pending departure. "We will stay here for three more days to continue ministering to the people of the town and countryside. Rabbi Nicodemus and sister, Joanna,

115

we would be much honored if you would join us in our ministry."

"We would be greatly humbled and honored to be God's vessel in this way," Joanna answered for both.

I had completely forgotten about the crowds of people who had come before Rabbi Nicodemus and Joanna had graced our abode. Remarkably, not one had ventured an audience in the days that Jesus and Nicodemus had engaged in discussion. "Should we send word that the people may once again come?" I asked aloud.

"Mary," Jesus responded, "There will be no need, the Spirit will compel them to come and so shall it be." And I trusted in his word.

During the three days that we spent with Nicodemus and Joanna in our company, Jesus and I had continued our time of private prayer in the garden. As Nicodemus and Joanna departed in their final evening with us, and the Galilean men went to their encampment outside the compound walls, Jesus invited me to join him in the garden. We found our bench and sat. I expected that Jesus desired prayer and began to enter into a prayerful posture when Jesus began to speak. "Mary, what did you observe between Nicodemus and Joanna?"

"What do you mean?" I asked.

"Well, what did you see in them that differed from what you have seen in other couples and what did you think of it?"

My heart fluttered in nervous expectation as I entertained the thoughts that had gone through my mind as I had observed Nicodemus and Joanna over the past three days. I was anxious about sharing these thoughts with anyone, let alone Jesus. They felt much like the romantic thoughts of a child who still believed in myth

116

and magic. I took a deep breath to gather my thoughts, and to calm my anxious heart. Did I dare tell Jesus what I really felt about Nicodemus and Joanna?

Privy to the anxiety dancing in my mind, Jesus reached for my hand and gently squeezed it in reassurance. Emboldened by this show of support, I spilled my guts. "I am inspired by what I have seen in Nicodemus and Joanna. Never once did I see my parents share any sort of intimacy and my mother would never have received the kind of honor or respect that Nicodemus shows to Joanna. In our home, there was no love between my parents, only the traditional contractual arrangement. My mother was certainly never treated as an equal or a companion in the way that Nicodemus seems to treat Joanna."

"I agree," said Jesus. "It is rare to see true love blossom between a man and a woman who are only brought together through contract, and even more rare in our culture to see men and women who seem to be comfortable showing the love they feel for each other and rarer still to see them working side by side as a team. What do you think of that?"

Again, I was hesitant to share what I was really feeling. I did not want to appear bold or, worse yet, ridiculous. But so far, Jesus and I seemed to be of the same mind, so I gathered my courage around me and blurted out, "That's what I want!" I was startled by my response as I had not intended to be *that* bold. But Jesus simply smiled. "Mary, that's what I want too." I relaxed as he said these words and sat in silence pondering the idea of a loving partnership built on mutual honor and respect. I had often wondered if there really was such a thing, but as we had witnessed it in Nicodemus and Joanna, I dared to believe it might be possible.

117

Jesus took my hands in his and with longing in his voice confessed, "Mary, I too want the kind of relationship that Nicodemus and Joanna have created. In fact, I have spent my life dreaming that such a love might be possible – love with another who is equal yet unique, with whom I could share not only my mind, my hopes, my dreams, my vision, but also my heart. Mary, I want this kind of relationship with you." At his words, my heart nearly ceased beating and began racing in anticipation. Jesus, looking deeply into my eyes pressed on, "Mary, the day that Lazarus brought me here and our eyes first met, I knew. I knew in the deepest part of my being that you were the one God had intended for me. I saw in you the woman that Abwoon had revealed to me in my prayers and who danced within my dreams. And as I have grown to know you, I am more and more convinced that what I have discerned is indeed truth, and I can only dream that your feelings may be the same. While I know I must continue the work of Abwoon and that means being apart from you, I never feel separate from you. I feel you ministering at my side. I hear your soothing and reassuring voice when I am tempted to doubt my mission. I feel you at my side as we recline in prayer. And yet, while I feel this Oneness, I also long to be near you. To touch your face. To truly hear your voice. To feel the sensation of your breath as it rises and falls in prayer. It would be enough just to love you and to be loved in return, but when I see the gifts that you have, your eager curiosity, the way in which you understand, integrate and embody the way of love, my heart soars for I can think of nothing more fulfilling than to share this life and mission with you. Mary, I love you and want nothing more than to have with you what we have observed in Nicodemus and Joanna."

Song of the Beloved — The Gospel According to Mary Magdalene

At this pronouncement, I was struck silent and could only nod my head in enthusiastic assent as tears of relief and gratitude streamed down my face, Jesus had now spoken the words that I, too, had carried in my heart. Jesus reached his arm around me, took me into his arms and we shared a long and tender kiss in consummation of our mutual love. As we kissed, my heart soared in gratitude and wonder for this miracle that was far beyond anything I ever could have imagined for myself – a woman, unclean and long past the age of betrothal, finding a love such as this. My heart ached with the enormity of this love and I wondered could a love such as this be given freely or was there a cost to this love? I quickly set that thought aside and returned to the wonder of this kiss.

At dawn, they began to come, just as Jesus had promised – men, women, children, the sick and the elderly. Rabbi Nicodemus and Joanna set up an area on the outskirts of the crowd and together, broke open the scriptures for those who had ears to hear. Emboldened by his kindred encounter with Jesus, Rabbi Nicodemus spoke with a new-found confidence of the love of God. Many found themselves deeply moved by this fresh perspective of Adonai.

Reflecting the commitment we had made to each other in the garden, Jesus and I moved about the crowd together, teaching, healing and comforting. My heart blossomed in excitement and awe at how well our teamwork revealed the way of love. Side by side we listened as someone unburdened their story of loss or betrayal, and for those who required more intimate attention, Jesus and I would separate and serve as a source of attentive presence for them in private. We were never

119

far from each other and whenever I searched Jesus out in the crowd, he looked up and returned my glance with a smile. After each private healing, Jesus and I would meet back in the center of the crowd, take each other's hand and look out again into the crowd to see who was next in need of healing or a listening ear.

I was beginning to get a glimpse into what our life together might look like. Working together side by side healing the sick, comforting the hurting, bringing light and hope to those stranded in darkness. I also felt a connection growing between us as our minds, our hands and now our hearts served as one, deepening and widening my sense of fulfillment and contentment. More than anything, it just felt right….as if this is how we were meant to live our lives, Jesus with me and I with him, working together as one, sharing God's love with those who longed for it. I cherished these moments together knowing that in just a few short days, he must return to Capernaum, and I wondered how our love would endure in these required separations. As I pondered these thoughts, I heard Jesus' sweet words of reassurance, "Mary, do not be afraid. I am with you always, even unto the end of time."

On the morning of the third day, a group of lepers brought themselves as near to the crowd as they dared. "Jesus bar Joseph, we seek you!" They shouted over the crowd. In spite of the roar of the crowd, Jesus heard them clearly. He reached out to squeeze my hand and I nodded in understanding as Jesus began moving toward the lepers. From across the crowd, Simon caught sight of Jesus and ran after him, grabbing the sleeve of his robe. "Rabbi, what are you doing?" He pleaded. "These men are unclean! Tell them to go away."

Jesus shook Simon's hand from his robe and rebuked him, "Get behind me Satan!" Simon dropped his head in shame and retreated to the other end of the crowd.

Jesus ran toward the group of lepers, enthusiastically embracing and kissing each one. "Brothers and sisters, we are so glad that you have come! What is it you seek?" He inquired.

"Rabbi, we wish to be made clean."

Jesus glanced in my direction and waved me toward him. "Mary, I want to teach you how to extract the spirits that cause the disease of leprosy," he explained. He invited the lepers to sit. Jesus laid his hands on the first leper, a woman, and began to speak in a language I did not know. As he spoke these words, the body of the leper began to tremble and shake, and then Jesus' utterances became more urgent and grew louder. As the trembling seemed to reach a climax, Jesus shouted toward Abwoon, "Into your hands I commend this spirit." The trembling suddenly stopped and we saw that the leper's skin had been made clean.

Jesus then invited me to follow the same ritual with the next leper who was a man. "But Jesus, I don't know the words that you speak," I argued. "Mary, it is the language of the Holy Spirit, the Shekinah, it will be given to you when you are open to it." Trusting Jesus' words, I laid my hands on the leprous man, as Jesus had done, and offered a prayer to Abwoon. Then, just as Jesus described, I had the sensation of words filling my being and trying to escape through my mouth. I set aside my nervousness over this strange occurrence and simply opened my mouth. Out of my mouth spilled sounds and utterances that seemed to transcend time. As I allowed these words to flow, the man began to tremble and shake, just like the woman before him. I felt the words within me reaching a crescendo as the man's body trembled, and then I heard the words, "Lord, into your hands I commend this spirit," and the trembling stopped and the man was clean. I looked over at Jesus who smiled at me in acknowledgment. Together, we continued this ritual until all the lepers were healed. Then Jesus said to all of them, "You are clean. Your faith has healed you! But, do not tell anyone what has been done."

The men and women who had been healed of leprosy and freed of the shame that often accompanies this affliction, thanked Jesus enthusiastically and joined the rest of the crowd to listen to Jesus' word. All but one, that is. As the men and women reclined, I saw one man slip away from the crowd. At this, I moved closer to Jesus and gestured in the man's direction. Jesus nodded sadly, "It was not enough for him to be made clean, now he must laud it over the chief Priests and Scribes. He goes toward the temple in Jerusalem. At daybreak, I must depart."

My heart sank, but even more than the sinking of my own heart, I feared the hint of foreboding in Jesus' voice. "Jesus, what has Jerusalem got to do with you?" I cautiously inquired.

"Mary, how do you think the Chief Priests and Scribes will respond to the way of love?"

"Oh," I suddenly realized, "If they are like my father, they will feel threatened by the news of God's love. It is through the images of a vengeful God that they are able to manipulate and control people. What would they do with a compassionate, loving God?"

"Exactly, while many are men of open eyes and heart, those in control have eyes only for that which keeps them in power, and the source of their power is fear. A leper

122

who has been made clean will shake them to their core.
As it is not yet my time, I must now certainly depart."

While saddened by this news, I could not cling to him
if it meant he would be in danger. So I offered a silent
prayer that the angels would guard him and keep him safe.
I rushed into his arms and embraced him as silent tears fell
from my eyes.

"Mary, I too am troubled by this. I don't have a good
feeling about this situation or about the Pharisee's reaction
to it. The last thing I want is to be apart from you, but
it feels like that is what is necessary at this time. And, I
do not want to put you into danger by lingering or by
bringing you with us to Capernaum. The best we can do
is hold within our hearts the tension of the unknown and
of being separated from each other and trust that in our
love we will never be parted."

Together we sighed in resignation to what we knew
must be. As we gathered the strength to take this next
step, Jesus continued to hold me, lovingly stroking my
hair. Shivers of desire ran up and down my spine while
a vast space seemed to open up in my soul – a space
that could accept this impending distance, even after (or
perhaps because of) the commitment we had made to
each other and our dream of loving partnership. Jesus
took my face in his hands, kissed me on the lips and gently
wiped the tears from my face.

CHAPTER FOURTEEN

We embraced for a moment longer. Jesus took a deep breath inward, placed his arm around me with his hand resting on my lower back and guided me toward the gate that marked the entrance to our compound. We stood there in silence as we turned and regarded the crowd. As if Jesus had offered a silent command, we were soon joined by Rabbi Nicodemus, Joanna, Lazarus, Martha and Salome. The Galilean men gathered in a group nearby. Jesus held up his hands and a silence fell over the crowd. "Brothers and sisters, I am humbled and grateful for the hospitality shown by the men and women of the House of Lazarus. I shall return, but must be moving on to the community in Capernaum and places in between. While I am about the work of Abwoon in Capernaum, these humble people, Lazarus, Martha, Salome, Rabbi Nicodemus, Joanna and Mary will continue the work of Abwoon right here, for the fine people of Bethany. Let us offer prayers of God's blessing over these men and women today."

Jesus invited us to stand before him. Then, he moved to stand directly in front of me.

"Mary," Jesus said, "You have the vision of one perched upon the highest tower, seeing all truth beyond the illusions and I see that you shall be a tower, providing a beacon of light for those journeying in the darkness. You

124

shall now be called *Mary, the Magdalene* and I commission you as rabbi and teacher in my stead."

As he prayed these words upon me, I had a brilliant vision of Herod's palace and the magnificent tower of Miriam – bedecked in jewels that caught the glistening light of the sun and reflected out so all could see. I saw a humble stone tower of lesser origins surrounded by a small group of men and women, humbly clad, heads bowed in prayer. I felt an energy coming up out of the earth piercing the bottom of my feet and moving up through my body. It seemed to focus at the base of my spine, moving up my spine to the top of my head where it exploded in a rainbow of flame. It felt as if all my insides had been purged of darkness, fear and constriction. I suddenly felt free – so free I think I could have taken flight. I heard a song of praise coming forth from my lips in a language I did not know. Jesus joined me in this song of praise.

Our song was suddenly interrupted by the harsh impatient voice of Simon, who had been skulking around the corner of the garden wall when he heard the prayers Jesus had offered us. He came stomping toward us in righteous indignation. "Rabbi, I have given up everything to follow you and have gone wherever you will, do I not also deserve a new name?"

"Simon, you are as stubborn and unyielding as a two ton boulder. If you wish to have a new name, I will call you Cephas," was Jesus' reply. For the first time, Simon stood there speechless.

Moving quickly from Simon's outburst, Jesus returned to prayer. He raised his hands over us in blessing. "Loving Mystery that we call Abwoon, you have called these men and women, Lazarus, Nicodemus, Joanna, Martha, Salome and Mary to be vessels through which

125

your loving compassion may become manifest in this world. We know that you guide them by the light of your truth and hold them in your loving embrace. I send them forth to proclaim your loving counsel and to heal the sick." At that the crowd erupted in applause. We were quickly swept up into the crowd and welcomed as their teachers in Jesus' stead.

Between enthusiastic hugs, I searched for Jesus and saw that he had drawn Simon, called Cephas, off to a quiet place to listen to him in private. For just a moment, I sensed I knew Simon's thoughts and it seemed all he wanted was to know that Jesus loved him, but that what he hadn't yet realized is that he had to love himself before he could really know the love that Jesus was reflecting back to him. Instead, his envy grew over what he perceived as Jesus' favoritism of the house of Lazarus. I was deeply saddened by whatever wound had caused this envy in Simon's heart. I silently offered a prayer to Abwoon that someday, Simon, called Cephas, would be open to receiving the gift of God's merciful love.

For the remainder of the afternoon, we turned to celebration. There was an air of sadness in the crowd over Jesus' imminent departure, but at the same time, there was much gratitude for the time he had been here, of the teachings received and the healings accomplished that we could not help but celebrate in joy. We dined together as the sun began to set and the crowds reluctantly departed as darkness began to cover the land. The Galilean men went to their tents near the well, Rabbi Nicodemus and Joanna returned to their home in the village and Lazarus, Martha and Salome retired to their private chambers. As the moon began to rise, I found myself alone with Jesus just outside the gate of our compound. We stood there his eye, "is beyond description for it cannot truly be seen – but only felt. The face of God is the heart that skips a beat as it first looks upon the face of one's true love and it is in the last tear shed as a loved one is laid to rest. The face of God is in all of it – the light and the darkness, the joy and the sorrow, the peace and the conflict."

In his words, I began to find new strength and the light of hope and I too longed to know God in this way. I pleaded with Jesus, "Can you teach me to see God in this way?"

"Mary, there is nothing to teach. You need only look for it and there it is."

I knew what he said to be true and I offered a silent reminder to myself, "Look and you shall see."

We sat in silence looking for the face of God when another star blazed across the sky. Jesus said his goodbye, "Mary, the Galileans and I will depart before dawn." I felt my heart leap to my throat. I choked back tears of separation as Jesus reminded me, "Mary, remember, not only are we One with God, we are one with each other. We shall never be separate. When you forget, simply call my name or look for my face, and there I will be." He wrapped his arms around me and we kissed with a new sense of passion as we anticipated the impending time of separation and in recognition of the love that was taking root and blossoming between us. Before saying our goodbye, Jesus prepared me for what would lie ahead.

"Tomorrow morning, the house of Lazarus will be visited upon by the priests of the temple. Remember there is nothing to fear. Treat them as you would treat me and look beyond the illusion for the face of God that shines in each of them. Remember, there is nothing to fear." At that we embraced and departed for our places of rest and repose.

in silence gazing up at the magnificent night sky. As we watched, a shooting star blazed a trail across the sky. I shivered at the specter of this omen and instinctively made the sign against evil. Jesus reached out and took hold of my hand, "Mary, let us not be afraid. Abwoon reminds us that fear is merely an illusion that arises out of our false perception of separation. If we are one with God what is there to be afraid of?" While I wanted Jesus' words to be true, I could not still the anxious sense of foreboding that now haunted my thoughts. Jesus was in danger. He knew it and I knew it. And all the prayers in the world were not going to change the course of human nature. Instead, I prayed to Abwoon for the courage to endure whatever might lie ahead. But still, I had to know:

"Jesus, are you really afraid of nothing?"

"Mary, of course I am afraid. I'm human just like you, but when I am afraid, I shift my gaze to look upon the face of God, and once again I know peace and if not peace, at least the silent resolve to keep moving forward. In God there is not only peace and the presence of love, but also the courage to endure."

"Jesus, you speak as if you have seen God's face. What does God look like?" I asked hungrily.

"Oh Mary," Jesus released an ecstatic sigh and with his arm around me, drew me closer. "The face of God is everything. It is the miracle of that star that just now blazed across the night sky. It is the brilliant purples and golds of the sun rising at dawn and the magenta and tangerines of the sun as it sets. It is the first drink of water after a long day of labor under a blazing sun. It is the sound of a newborn babe as it suckles at its mother's breast and the aroma of the earth just after the first spring rain. The face of God," he continued with a faraway look in

CHAPTER FIFTEEN

W e awoke the next morning to the sound of loud pounding on our garden gate and the clamor of someone impatiently ringing the courtyard bell. Martha, Salome and I quickly dressed and began proper meal preparations as Lazarus ran out to greet our impatient guests. Lazarus returned, bursting through the door with five stern looking men who were obviously high priests of the temple – proudly attired in the finest ritual wear. "Where is Jesus bar Joseph, called Nazarene?" one priest curtly inquired. Remembering proper Jewish custom, Martha, Salome and I remained in the background with downcast eyes. Lazarus offered an honest reply, "The man called Jesus bar Joseph, along with his Galilean companions departed before dawn for Capernaum by way of Samaria. A look of shocked disgust crossed the faces of the priests as a proper Jew would have avoided traveling through the Gentile territory of Samaria at any cost. One of the priests who had been standing toward the back of the group pushed his companions aside and took his place in the front of the group. At that moment, I heard a gasp escape Salome's lips. Was this the Asher who had enslaved her all those years? I looked deep into his eyes and saw that this was indeed the man.

Before I could avert my gaze he caught my eye and across his face spread the grimace of a wild cat that had just cornered his prey. A sly seductive smile crossed his lips and deep in his eyes I saw the image of his desire – sick twisted visions of submission and torture. He swallowed, his eyes rolled back in pleasure and he licked his lips in anticipated satisfaction. I saw the mask he assumed before his fellow priests and realized that he had seduced them as well, deceiving them into believing he was a God-fearing and righteous man. Apparently the other priests had fallen under his spell as they ignored the truth screaming in their hearts, "He is a liar and a deceiver – beware!"

As I gazed beyond the illusion of Asher to the deeper truth within, I became acutely aware of Salome's fear as she stood beside me – or was it indeed my fear – because beside me I felt no fear, only the steely determination of an animal who had no intention of being caught in this lion's trap. I felt Salome gather her energy about her as she stood tall and stared daggers into Asher's eyes. I quickly stole a glance and saw that as Salome stared at him, he nervously looked away.

With the silky manner of a keen serpent, Asher addressed my brother, Lazarus, "Brother, Lazarus, we come in peace." ("Liar!" I said to myself.) "We seek the rabbi Jesus bar Joseph for we hear he is a great teacher. We wish to learn of the good news he proclaims."

Lazarus, not fooled by Asher's seduction replied, "As I said, Jesus and his companions departed before dawn for Capernaum via Samaria. We do not know when they may return. The House of Lazarus would be honored if you would join us in breaking our fast." Lazarus offered his own seduction, "It is rare that we have the pleasure of serving such honored guests and from you we would have much to learn."

It would have been against custom to refuse an offer of hospitality, so speaking for the group, Asher replied, "House of Lazarus, we humbly accept your gracious and generous invitation and would be honored with what you can teach us about this Jesus." The nearly inaudible hiss in the way he said, "This Jesus" betrayed his true feelings about our beloved rabbi. Upon Asher's acceptance, Lazarus began the ceremonial washing and the men joined him at table.

Not to offend our "honored" guests, Salome, Martha and I assumed the traditional role of servant. A part of me felt terribly apprehensive about Salome's safety with Asher in our home, but at the same time something reminded me to trust. I half expected Salome to feign illness or to excuse herself to her private quarters, which she had every right to do. Instead, she bravely faced possible exposure. I also expected her to demonstrate some behavior that would reveal her fear, but instead, Salome boldly faced our guests.

About midway through the meal, Salome went around the table refilling our guests' water goblets. As Salome went to refill Asher's cup, I saw that she dared to look directly into his eyes with a look that seemed to say, "I know who you are and I know the truth about you." Asher returned her gaze with the startled expression of a child with his hand caught in the jar of sweets, but not for long; he quickly flew into a defensive rage, grabbing Salome's wrist with a menacing growl.

"Woman," he challenged, "do I know you?"

I held my breath waiting for the ax to fall while I uttered a prayer for Salome's safety and for the safety of our home. "Sir," she replied sweetly, like a spider setting a trap, "I have known but one man. Is it possible it is you – a high priest of the temple?" Then of all things, she winked at him! I feared she was treading in dangerous territory.

131

Asher nervously looked around at his brethren while they stared back at him with questioning eyes. "Woman, I'm not sure what you are getting at. As high priest, I have taken a vow. Perhaps I am mistaken."

Salome slyly smiled, "Perhaps sir, for the one man I have known had a weakness for young boys. This surely could not be you – high priest of the temple and our much esteemed and honored guest."

With feigned disgust, Asher threw down Salome's hand, "Woman, how dare you speak of such despicable things in my presence. Be gone from my sight as we continue our repose with our brother Lazarus."

Salome bowed deeply and with a broad look of triumph responded, "Yes sir, as you wish." Then she gaily skipped to her room.

For the remainder of the meal, Asher sat in silence while the other priests questioned Lazarus about Jesus.

With Asher thusly disarmed, the discussion about Jesus unfolded rather pleasantly. The priests asked about what Jesus taught and asked about the rumors of healings. "This man, dressed in leper's rags came to us and presented himself for the ceremonial cleansing. He claimed he was made clean by this man named Jesus," explained the priest who had introduced himself as Benjamin.

"It is true," replied Lazarus. "A group of lepers came here just yesterday and asked of Jesus that they be made clean. At his word, it was as they had asked."

A look of shock and wonder went about the faces of the priests. Asher broke in, "This cannot be. How does this man Jesus heal? By the power of Beelzebub?"

I felt a defensive anger rise in me as I desired to defend my Lord. But I heard Jesus' gentle voice, "Mary, have patience." I stepped back from my anger and looked more

132

closely at the men gathered at table. In their eyes I saw
a wide mixture of emotions. In some I saw the look of
doubt, indignation and blindness to anything outside their
tightly held beliefs. In others, I saw questions. And in
still others wonder and awe – bordering on hope. And in
a few, especially the priest named Benjamin, I saw a look
of excited anticipation. It was Benjamin who now spoke.

"Brother Asher, it is too soon to make such rash
accusations. We must learn more about this Jesus
– perhaps meet him personally so we can discern if he
comes from God or not." Turning to Lazarus, Benjamin
continued, "Brother Lazarus, we are grateful for your
generous hospitality. We are sorry we did not arrive in
time to meet Jesus bar Joseph, but I trust that through
Our Lord's divine providence, we may come to meet him
in the near future. Should Jesus pay you another visit,
would you please advise him that the house of Benjamin
would be most grateful to receive the blessing of his
presence?"

With that, Benjamin, Asher and the other priests arose
from table and bid us goodbye. I sensed this would not be
the last we would see of the priests, nor would this be the
last we would hear of their questions of Jesus.

133

PART TWO

Song of the Beloved — The Gospel According to Mary Magdalene

CHAPTER SIXTEEN

As the many months unfolded before us, Jesus continued his travels back and forth between Capernaum in Galilee and Bethany in Judea. The central focus of his ministry was in Capernaum and when he chose to visit us in Bethany it was in the company of only a few of his Galilean disciples. The remainder stayed behind to continue his work along the shores of the Galilean sea. When visiting the House of Lazarus, Jesus and I continued our daily prayer and worked together in ministering to the people who came to hear his message. During the times that Jesus was absent from me, I witnessed the healing experienced by those to whom I ministered and I grew in confidence of my own gifts. With each passing visit, I grew in my understanding of God's love within me and as this awareness of love grew, so too did the revelation of my own unique gifts. As I grew in my abilities and confidence and as Jesus and I worked together, our love continued to deepen. While Jesus would always be my teacher and Rabbi, we had become beloved companions, and Jesus treated me as if I were his honored equal. Our growing intimacy made his frequent absences that much more difficult to bear, but Jesus' words gave me some measure of comfort, "Mary, I am with you always, even until the end of time." While I still longed for his physical presence I did feel the closeness of his spirit, his heart resting in mine and could hear his whispered words of comfort that his spirit spoke to mine.

As Jesus' popularity increased and word of him spread beyond the districts of Judea and Galilee, the religious and political climate had grown increasingly tense. The scribes and Pharisees were divided in their opinion of Jesus, but to appease the fearful few, he was eventually forbidden from teaching in the temple. The straw that broke the camel's back occurred on that Sabbath day when Jesus healed a blind man within the temple precincts and stirred up an afternoon of theological debate. In siding with the fearful few, the temple priests and their Pharisaic supporters proved that fear was their true source of power.

The Romans, in turn, were increasingly wary about the crowds that Jesus attracted. It was one thing when his ministry was safely contained within people's homes, in synagogues or confined to the temple grounds, for in these places, the Romans could maintain some semblance of control. But, with Jesus' ministry pouring out into the streets, or held in an open field or along the hillsides, the Romans had little to no control. To add to the tension, there were always a few insurrectionists keen on the idea of a Davidic warrior Messiah standing in-wait for anything Jesus might say to incite them to revolution. Jesus continued to preach about compassion and peace, but these Zealots were bent on twisting Jesus' words to fit their own agenda. It was in the context of this tension that Jesus once again sought refuge in the House of Lazarus.

Jesus arrived just before sun up on the day after the Sabbath. This visit was accomplished in great secrecy as even I had not been forewarned of his arrival. I was sitting quietly in prayer as was my morning custom when I suddenly realized he was sitting beside me. This was not

136

the spiritual presence to which I had become accustomed. This was the actual physical body and blood of Jesus. I gasped in surprise and reached out my hand to touch his face, making sure it was real. He turned to look into my eyes while taking my hand from his cheek. He brought my hand to his lips and kissed my palm. Cradling my hand in his, he brought our hands to his cheek while a single tear escaped his eye and splashed onto our intertwined palms.

I acutely felt the deep sadness and concern that Jesus now carried within him. I reached over to embrace him as he allowed his tears to be shed. I held him in my arms and stroked his hair as he released the grief in his heart. I felt the love of Abwoon that dwelled within me reaching into Jesus' heart and searched his mind for the cause of this pain. In my mind's eye, I saw in images the things that pained him – Romans and their powerful empire built on fear and oppression – the hardened hearts of the Pharisees – all the people who had heard Jesus' message and had been unable to embrace it – those who had refused Jesus' healing. I saw the followers of Jesus and those of the house of Lazarus and the varying degrees at which they were not able to received Jesus' truth. These images began to spread out before me into future times and future worlds. I saw the wars that would devastate the earth – many fought "in the name of God." I saw the starving and hopeless people. I saw the multitudes of people who continued to live in darkness – hardened in mind and in heart.

Finally, in an image that shocked me to my core, I saw my beloved severely beaten and hanging on a cross – the most barbarous of the Roman methods of execution. My beloved was crying out in pain, "My God, my God, why have you forsaken me?" And then he was dead. My heart grew sorrowful at the troubled thoughts my beloved carried within his mind. As I held him, I too shed tears of grief for the burden my beloved bore and the burden that I now carried with him.

Jesus and I held each other in this sacred moment of raw vulnerability while the morning star began to fade and the dawn awakened. At cockcrow, Jesus placed his hands on my shoulders and looked deep into my eyes, "Mary, I am afraid my life here on this earth is coming to an end."

In panic, my mind began to race. How could his life be coming to an end? We had so much work yet to do and so much love yet to enjoy. How could God take him away from me so soon? My dreams of marriage and a family had not even come close to being fulfilled. There were so many people who were yet to embrace the Way of Love. There had to be another way. "But," I began to interrupt with pleading and desperate eyes.

Jesus placed a finger on my lips to silence my interruption. "Mary, I hate this as much as you do. I don't want these fears to be proven true, but I don't see any other possible outcome. The outside world is too afraid. Too many refuse to be open to the love of God within them. For three years I have shared the Way of Love and still most are deaf to the invitation to freedom. Those who are attached to their power – many of the Temple authorities and the Romans – grow more and more threatened by my presence and I have become an easy scapegoat for their own fears and insecurities. Abwoon has shown me the likely outcome and in this I am sad and scared. The only thing in this that gives me comfort is knowing that we will never be apart. I will remain with you, ever at your side, now and forever and you will remain with me."

"But Jesus, how can this be?"

"Mary, what was true before time began is true today and will be forever. We were one before time began, we are one now and we will always be one. It is through the gift of God's Holy Spirit – the Shekinah – that we are one. In this place of Divine Oneness neither physical proximity nor death can separate. What God has brought together, no man can tear asunder."

I wanted to believe his words, but even if it remained as it had in our times of separation that we could connect in mind, heart and spirit while in prayer, how would that cure the longing in my heart to feel his body close to mine, to know the touch of his hand in mine, to hear the rise and fall of his breath, to enjoy the honey-sweet sound of his voice, to gaze into his adoring eyes? How could I bear the knowledge that I would never again enjoy the physical presence of my beloved? Jesus' assurance of our infinite oneness was simply not enough to assuage the pain of the sword that began to pierce my heart at the thought of his death. A tear escaped my eye which Jesus gently kissed away. And we embraced.

"Mary, I too am afraid. I cannot bear the thought of putting you through the pain of my death or the unfulfilled longing that will result. I can't even go into what it might be for me. While I know death is simply a doorway, it feels very final. My dreams for our life together will be for naught as will be the dreams of the ministry I had hoped to continue to build with you at my side. Abwoon's work is not yet accomplished and I am saddened by humanity's blindness and hardness of heart. While I would like to continue to believe that the world will turn around and God's message of love will be able to be received, I cannot deny that the tensions in

139

Jerusalem are rising and that I have been made the target of these tensions. Part of me wants to quit the ministry all together and return to the simple life of a carpenter with you as my wife and the mother of our children, but I fear that is not what God deems as the path of the highest good. Besides, how can I compromise on the truth that God has revealed when I know it to be the remedy to the suffering and violence of the human condition? I know this to be the road to compassion and peace. How can I not continue to share this?

"Jesus, this is not something to be taken lightly or a decision to be entered into in haste. Let us take this time together to pray and to discern where God is calling us. Perhaps God will show us a path that neither of us can yet perceive. Take this time away from the crowds, accept the hospitality of my brother's house and let us support you in this prayer. I sense that you pray not only for yourself or for me, but for the world. Let me pray with you and together we will find God's answer."

Jesus accepted my invitation as together we entered into a time of deep prayer and discernment. For the next several days, Jesus remained in the house of Lazarus and together we prayed. It was a time of deep intensity as I accompanied Jesus in his prayer for clarity of discernment. We prayed and we discussed. We turned to scripture and we prayed some more.

Over time, the truth that Jesus was called to uphold and the likely consequence of standing in this truth became more clear. Jesus came to understand that he was being called to be steadfast in his understanding of our Oneness with God and to adhere to this truth, whatever the cost. The Pharisees and many of the high priests were already threatened by Jesus' message of love, and if people

140

believed in their Oneness with God, what need would they have of the religious laws and rituals that promised to bridge the gap between themselves and God? Many of the religious authorities had profited through the culture of fear that they had propagated. Fear and intimidation had created blindly obedient masses, but what many of the religious authorities did not yet understand was that in teaching the truth of Oneness and God's law of love, they would empower their members who would generously support those who brought them to love while freely giving service to the world through their own unique gifts for the benefit of all humankind. Those who benefitted from the culture of separation and fear would believe they had too much to lose and Jesus would be perceived as a threat – not only to their power and control – but to the very lives that they had come to know. As we realized the dire nature of these consequences – the possibility of Jesus' own death, Jesus' fears began to surface, and mine along with him.

I remained with Jesus as he battled the demons of fear that waged a war within his mind. Along with the fear of death came the grief of loss and Jesus paced the garden in determined anger shaking his fist at God for allowing the death of his hopes, his dreams and his visions. I prayed to Abwoon to help me be strong as I struggled with my own grief and fears so that I could be the source of support that Jesus needed. I found my prayers to be unnecessary as Jesus and I supported each other through the rising and falling emotions that presented themselves during this discernment. I held him when he needed to be held and he held me when I was feeling weak or afraid. I paced with him when he needed to move and he paced with me. Together we shook our fists at God in support of our

141

mutual grief and we gave each other space when we knew we needed to be alone.

All the while that Jesus and I prayed, Martha, Lazarus, Salome, Rabbi Nicodemus and his wife, Joanna also kept a silent vigil. Martha and Joanna held Jesus in prayer while preparing nourishing meals and herbed wines strictly suited for bringing peace to the spirit. Salome retreated to her room from which came the tell-tale click, click, click of the prayer beads which were her one possession and reminder of her native land, traditions and peoples. Between the click, click, click, she was heard murmuring the ancient mantras to the names of her own El-Shaddai. Lazarus kept at the long-neglected maintenance and repairs to our home and gardens as this was his own form of prayer. And from Rabbi Nicodemus, we heard the ancient tones of the Kaddish.

Yis'ga'dal v'yis'kadash sh'may ra'bbo, b'olmo dee'vro
chir'usay v'yamlich malchu'say, b'chayaychon
uv'yomay'chon uv'chayay d'chol bais Yisroel, ba'agolo
u'viz'man koriv; v'imru Omein.
Y'hay shmay rabbo m'vorach l'olam ul'olmay
olmayo.
Yisborach v'yishtabach v'yispoar v'yisromam
v'yismasay, v'yishador v'yis'aleh v'yisalal, shmay
d'kudsho, brich hu, l'aylo min kl birchoso v'sheeroso,
tush'bechoso v'nechemoso, da,ameeran b'olmo;
vimru Omein.
Y'hay shlomo rabbo min sh'mayo, v'chayim
alaynu v'al kol Yisroel; v'imru Omein.
Oseh sholom bimromov, hu ya'aseh sholom
olaynu, v'al kol yisroel; vimru Omein.

After several days in prayerful discernment, coming to clarity about his mission while wrestling the demons that would be obstacles to that mission, Jesus arrived at a place of peace within himself. "Mary, I am ready – or at least as ready as I will ever be. I will send word to the Galilean disciples who camp near Jerusalem and together we will go into the city and to the temple and allow fate to take its course." In unison, we released a sigh if not of relief, at least of resignation. "But first I must tell my mother and my brother John about what God has revealed and what must now come to pass," he added.

While we sat in silence contemplating this path, I heard a light rap on the door that lead from the interior hallway to the garden. I rose to see who it might be, wondering why Lazarus, Martha or Salome would not just enter. I slowly opened the wooden door to see who it might be and was startled to behold the face of a stranger.

There stood a woman, dressed in humble linen robes with a mantle of the most brilliant indigo I had ever seen. The depth of the color and the weave of the cloth were reminiscent of the crimson mantle Jesus so often wore. These were precious woolens from the land beyond Persia. While I sensed her to be a woman much past childbearing, there was a look about her that seemed ageless; but, it was in her eyes that the depth of her extraordinary inner beauty was revealed. Her eyes drew me in, bringing peace to my heart. And the color – her eyes beheld the same chameleon-like quality as Jesus'. Of course! Her eyes were the very eyes of my beloved. This was surely his blessed mother, Mary!

I stepped toward her and embraced her. Mary leaned into my embrace and offered me the kiss of peace. As we exchanged the kiss of peace, I had the feeling of being showered with a thousand rose petals of the most brilliant

white and a quiet peacefulness came forth from her embrace. I felt surrounded and held in peace. She spoke, "Sister Mary, now called Magdalene, I bid you thanks for tending to my son in his hour of need and for being his chosen beloved. I am Mary daughter of Joachim and Anna and widow of Joseph the carpenter, and this is Jesus' brother and my son, John."

Alongside Mary stood a young man, barely past betrothal age, sixteen or seventeen perhaps. I looked hard upon John. I saw beyond the youthful excitement in his eyes, the mask of innocence and naiveté, past the hint of worry on his brow, and beheld a wisdom that seemed to come from ages past. This one was sure to catch the world unaware with his visionary insights and depth of understanding. As John stepped forward and offered me the kiss of peace, a brilliant light exploded in my mind. I immediately saw that *he could see*. No fear or illusion clouded the vision of this young man. He saw clearly in mystical dream visions of symbol and metaphor. This was a man who experienced truth deeply and who spoke in the mystical language of the prophets. His presence drew forth images of the great Hebrew visionaries – Joseph of Egypt, Nathan and Daniel – men who saw in symbol and dream. I immediately felt an affinity with this young man and knew he spoke only truth.

Jesus rose from the garden bench that had been our place of prayer and held his arms out in joyful welcome toward his Galilean family. I quietly stole from the garden so that Jesus could share with them the results of his discernment.

As I left Jesus to be alone with his family, I was drawn to memories of the stories Jesus had told me about his family. As a young girl, Mary had been betrothed to

144

Joseph, a man who had been widowed and left to raise two young sons. Upon the completion of her first menarche and after the prescribed ritual cleansings, Mary and Joseph were married. His two sons, Joseph and James were five and two years old respectively and Mary raised them as if they were her own. Jesus was born within nine months of Mary and Joseph's wedding, closely followed by his two sisters, Joanna and Susanna. Sixteen years after Jesus' birth, John was born and sadly, Joseph died shortly thereafter. Jesus' eldest brother Joseph took over the family business of carpentry and remained in the family home in Nazareth. James and Jesus had entered into religious study, both training to become Rabbis – Jesus in the tradition of the Essenes as his cousin John had done before him and James in the company of the Sadducees. With no man to raise her newborn son, Mary moved to Capernaum to live with her brother, also named Joseph, a wealthy merchant who had recently been widowed himself. Joanna and Susanna, not yet of the age of betrothal, accompanied Mary to Capernaum. Mary's brother, Joseph, raised Joanna, Susanna and John as if they were his own.

Jesus had always described his mother with great love in his eyes – a woman of gentle patience with the ability, through a simple glance, to bring peace into a room. This trait proved to be invaluable in raising three sons who were hell-bent on competition. Joseph and James focused their attention on gaining their father's love and acceptance. James and Jesus competed for spiritual knowledge. As the middle son, James proved to be the greatest challenge, always in conflict with one or the other of his brothers. Mary was the only one who could calm his impatient and frustrated spirit.

145

That evening we ushered in the Sabbath with Jesus' mother and brother joining us. Mother Mary was given the honor of lighting the Sabbath candles and reciting the blessing while Jesus invited John to take the highly coveted seat at his right. After the blessings were said and we partook of the meal, Jesus prayed, "Loving Abwoon, I give thee thanks for these of the House of Lazarus, the gift of my blessed Mother and my beloved brother in Spirit, John. I ask your blessing on this house of peace as I prepare to depart. I place these loved ones in your hands, knowing that they shall continue your work in the world. Give them courage during times of challenge and peace in the awareness of their oneness with you. I ask this in the name of all the holy men and women, prophets and teachers who have found the path of truth."

As Jesus uttered the words, "As I prepare to depart," a sigh of resignation exhaled from all at table and we looked to each other with quiet concern. We knew the path that had been laid out for Jesus and we knew our respective roles along that path – to be a source of love and support for Jesus and for each other as we accepted our path of fate. We blinked back silent tears as we grieved the certain losses that lay ahead.

John, still not ready to let his brother go, began to bargain, "Brother and Teacher," John inquired, "Must you really embark upon this path of certain death?"

Jesus took John's hand, looked into his eyes and answered, "John, my time has come. It is time to go into Jerusalem to reclaim the temple for Abwoon."

"But my Lord," John argued, "This is exactly the excuse they need to try you for treason and put you to death. Brother, you will be walking to your own execution."

Jesus turned to John and placing his hands on either side of his face, looked into his eyes and whispered, "Yes John, this is how it shall come to pass. It is the path laid out for me and I cannot refuse it and continue to stand in God's truth."

A groan of profound grief escaped John's lips and he collapsed into Jesus' arms. Jesus – eyes moist with tears – tenderly held his younger brother. "Brothers and Sisters, for this is what you are, I know that the path we are about to tread is fearful, yet I have come to testify to the truth that we, along with all of creation, are one with God. I have come to open the eyes of the blind and to proclaim the kingdom of God – a kingdom of peace and love that is in our very midst. I will not refrain from delivering this message or standing in this truth, even if it means my own physical death. But worry not about those who destroy the body, for the body is merely a shell for the Spirit that lives within. In physical death, our Spirits are released to live in the fullness of remembering our Oneness with God. In this way, death is only an illusion."

More than anything I wanted to believe Jesus' words, but anger stormed within me at the reality that death appeared the only likely path. Wanting to support Jesus' truth, I choked back the protests that were warring in my mind. Death is still death and something significant would have to happen to prove this otherwise. Death meant I would never see Jesus again or feel his body next to mine and that was just not acceptable. Jesus' instructions interrupted my angry thoughts.

"On the morning after the Sabbath, we ride into Jerusalem. Judas is making preparations. And so it begins, and so it shall end."

In silence, the death knell sounded as quiet tears of

mourning glistened in the eyes of all gathered – beloved
John, Mother Mary, Martha, Salome, Lazarus and me. As
we sat in silence, I felt Jesus' hand reach for mine as he
choked back his own tears of grief. I looked into his eyes
and there lay the deep sadness of loss in the knowledge of
what was too soon to be. From beneath the sadness arose
a longing that I had seen many a time in his eyes, but
in this moment, they held a new sense of urgency. This
longing tugged at my own unfulfilled heart and I knew
we needed at once to be alone. I arose from the table and
took Jesus' hand while we retreated down the hallway
leading to my private quarters. Together we crossed the
threshold and into the bridal chamber.

Chapter Seventeen

As we crossed the threshold and closed the door behind us, Jesus took me into his arms, with one hand woven into my dark, curling hair, the other wrapped around my waist, he drew me to him. For what seemed like a lifetime we held each other in silence, breathing in this sacred moment as our hearts joined in their beating. Taking in the enormity of what we had been through and what we were soon to face, I became acutely aware of the rising and falling of Jesus' chest next to mine, the soft brush of his breath as it tickled my cheek, the warmth of his arms as they enfolded me and the play of his fingers in my hair. As we stood there in love's embrace, I could feel a rising sensation of resolve and courage as we gathered this energy around us.

As I felt his breath shift within our embrace, I looked up to see that he was looking down at me with a mixture of wonder and longing in his eyes. "Mary, I love you. If this was a normal life and if we were under normal circumstances, I would ask Lazarus for your hand in marriage. The most difficult part of accepting the path that Abwoon has laid out for us is that we will not be able to share our lives together as husband and wife. And in this awareness, my heart is breaking. You are my beloved. I know this to be true and I know you feel the same. I want nothing more than to share my life with you and for us to continue to share in God's work. I could not face possible death without you knowing the depth of my love for you."

Struck silent by his words and by the enormity of what lay before us all I could do was nod back in silent assent. Jesus looked deeply into my eyes, took my face into his hands and kissed me on the lips. As his lips brushed mine, the longing and passion that we had until that moment held at bay, suddenly exploded between us and we became husband and wife, in body and spirit, if not by law and I soon understood why the rites of the marriage bed were held as sacred and carefully guarded within the hearts of those who met there. For in the marriage rite, I found a place of quiet stillness in my mind, and I knew the Oneness of which Jesus so often spoke in a way that was even more profound than what I had found in prayer. I too will hold the details of the marriage bed close within my heart, but what I experienced in Spirit, I will gladly share here for it is for this that the rite of marriage was truly made.

As Jesus and I came together in body, I saw our spirits also joining as one. No longer two, we became one. I was tempted to linger in the bliss of this oneness, but as the consummation of our marriage become complete, even this oneness was not enough. Something new seemed to be coming forth between us, through us and beyond us. I felt this *something new* as the sensation of fire igniting in the center of the oneness that we had become then coming forth in shudders that rose between us and burst forth out of us. As this fiery energy moved through us, I felt our spirits lifting out of our bodies as they joined with the energy of all that is. In that moment, we became one with the stars, the earth, the universe and all of creation. I was no longer Mary, the Magdalene, sister of Lazarus, I was

no longer Mary, the sister of Martha. I was no longer the beloved of Jesus. And Jesus was no longer Jesus. All that seemed to make us separate and unique was melting away. There was no *I*. There was no *we*. There was only that which *is*. I became aware that this must be the rapture that the apocalyptic writers had spoken of. In this state of oneness, I now understood what Jesus meant when he promised that we could never be parted.

I surrendered to this blissful state of ecstasy for what seemed like an eternity and was content to remain there until I was suddenly brought back to consciousness by Jesus' gentle kiss on my lips. I opened my eyes and smiled back at him with stars in my eyes. As I gazed into his chameleon colored eyes which now reflected the deep greens of pleasure, I knew the depth of his love for me and my love for him. Jesus brought his hand up and placed it along the side of my face, "Mary, I love you. I have always loved you." And he kissed me again. We collapsed then into each other's arms and fell into a deep and dream-filled sleep.

As we slept on the wings of bliss, we dreamed, and in our dreams our souls spoke to each other. We dreamed of all the desires, longing, hopes and wishes that would not find their fulfillment in this lifetime. We dreamed of the life that could have been – marriage, a family – a long life of joy and happiness. We saw in vivid detail our home in the country, our barefooted children playing among the groves. We regarded our extended family and their joy in our coming together. I beheld Jesus and myself growing old together surrounded by loving family and friends. While such images should have deepened my grief, instead, I felt only contentment and joy. It was as if this life existed in the here and now, but on some parallel plane. I knew that what we dreamed was the truth of our life together – not the death that would soon come between us.

As we briefly woke from that place of pure fulfillment, Jesus reached over, his eyes dreamy, and took my hand in his and gently kissed the inside of my palm, "Mary, I love you and this love will never die." With that he gently kissed the tears of joy that now fell from my eyes and we held each other as we fell back into a deep and now dreamless sleep.

I awoke before dawn filled with a sense of deep contentment. I turned and there beside me lay my beloved, Jesus. I gazed in silent adoration as I absorbed the fullness of this man. He lay there peaceful and at ease in his sleep, his eyelids fluttering lightly as if dreaming deeply. A slight curve of a smile graced his lips, lips I desperately wanted to bend down and kiss, but I dared not for fear of waking him. Instead, I enjoyed this moment before he awakened to appreciate my husband's beauty: I took in the broad shape of his forehead, the straight line of his nose, the gentle arch of his eyebrows, his pronounced cheekbones and the strong line of his jaw. Framing all of this were the gentle curls of his chestnut hair. I dared to reach out my hand to gently finger the halo of curls of this perfect man, my beloved. I now understood the sacred and erotic poetry of Solomon as the ancient words rang in my mind: "I am my beloved, and my beloved is mine." I breathed a sigh of contentment as I sat in rapt adoration.

I was suddenly startled out of my reverie by the sound of preparations being made for the early morning meal. I shook my head clear of the dreamy state I was in and looked up to see Jesus smiling down at me. He tenderly brushed my hair from my face and gently kissed me on the lips, "Come my beloved, the day is upon us and we can delay no longer." He took my hand and led me toward the day.

CHAPTER EIGHTEEN

Exiting my room we found Martha, Jesus' mother, John, Lazarus and Salome enjoying a simple meal. We joined them – Jesus at the head of the table and me at his left. "My son," Mary inquired, "should we expect our Galilean brothers and sisters today?"

"Yes, they will be arriving for the evening meal," Jesus replied.

My heart sank for a moment with the weight of all that this day would bring. Jesus reached for my hand, brought it to his lips, and leaned in close to whisper, "Mary, I too am afraid. Let us not indulge in this fear. Instead, let us allow the memories of last night to carry us through our fear." A warm blush rose to my cheeks and I felt hot at the recollection of last night's intimacies. I turned to catch Jesus' playful grin and kissed him on the lips. At once, the peace in my heart was restored and I enjoyed our simple breakfast.

After breaking fast, Jesus and Lazarus returned to the garden to discuss Jesus' impending plans. The other women and I cleared the morning meal and began to prepare our home for our guests. As I reached for a broom to sweep the floor, Martha approached and placed her hand over mine. "Not yet sister, I have something important to share with you." A twinge of guilt arose within me as I feared she may not approve of the intimacy

153

I now shared with Jesus. Martha, ever able to read my mind, offered a broad, approving smile while she gently kissed my cheek. She silently led me to her quarters. She approached her bed and knelt to reach for the trunk sheltered beneath. To my knowledge, the chest had not been touched since the day when Martha had retrieved the sacred objects of our Hebrew childhood. I could not imagine what else this chest might contain. She gestured for me to sit beside her as she opened the chest. At the top of the chest lay beautiful hand-embroidered linens of the most brilliant white. These were the linens to catch the virgin's blood on her wedding night – the final test of a bride's worth. My heart sank in the knowledge that these linens would never be for me. Martha removed the linens to reveal the bridal gown which lay beneath. This was the most magnificent bridal gown I had ever seen. A brilliant silken robe of the most brilliant azure – it was the color of the sea, embroidered in gold and bejeweled in carnelian, tiger's eye and topaz. This was the perfect gown for my golden sister.

She gently removed the gown to reveal another layer of linens. These she removed to reveal yet another gown. This was more beautiful than the first. The sight of it took my breath away – luxurious silk from the orient in the deepest and most spectacular crimson I had ever seen. Instead of jewels, this robe was embroidered throughout in sparkling gold and crimson – elegant in its simplicity. Accompanying the robe was a matching crimson veil. But why would Martha have need of two bridal robes? I looked at her with questioning eyes.

"Mary, this bridal robe and veil are yours. Mother hid this away in my wedding chest just before Lazarus brought us here." Completely overwhelmed by this demonstration

154

of mercy and generosity, I burst into tears.

"Mary, we all know that when Jesus goes into Jerusalem, he shall face certain death. Even though you have no marriage contract, we all know that you are his beloved wife. You must now wear this in honor of the sacred role you have accepted as our teacher's beloved." My heart burst in the profound wisdom and awareness of my loving sister. I embraced her in thanksgiving. Martha reached her hands further into the depths of the chest. The sudden change of her expression showed she had reached her mark. Up through the other contents of the chest, she pulled up her prize – an earthenware covered jar. This jar, I knew, held the sacred nard, both cherished and feared by every Hebrew woman. With this nard, we were called to anoint our husbands and our children in their deaths. My hands shook as Martha placed the sacred contents into my hands. I shook my head at the irony. Today I would don the robes of the bride, while anointing my beloved for his death. Together Martha and I sat in sacred silence, overcome with the enormity of it all.

Upon Martha's insistence, I remained in my room so that I could prepare my heart and mind for what lay ahead. Around three in the afternoon, I heard a gentle knock on my door. Salome peeked her head in, "The Galilean brothers are soon to arrive. May I help you dress?" She gave me a quick and knowing smile which I returned with gratitude. Salome entered and proceeded to dress me in my bridal attire. From deep within her own robes she pulled out a carefully wrapped package. She offered me the package and invited me to open it. Within were a pair of golden earrings, jeweled hair wraps and ribbons; golden bangles and an ankle bracelet. "I want you to have these," she looked at me lovingly. "Lady

155

Chuza presented these to me as a gift at the awakening of my womanhood. I now know I shall never again need these adornments and I'd love for you to wear them on your sacred day." Speechless, I gratefully accepted her gifts. After she wove the ribbons and hair wraps into my hair and attached the veil upon my head, I was ready.

Just as we were finishing, I heard the clamor of arriving guests. Salome gestured for me to wait while she went to greet them. I turned my ears to listen to the voices and conversations in the other room. I heard Lazarus greeting our guests and introductions being made. I heard the group settling at table to await the ceremonial washing. I dared to peek out the door and could glimpse Lazarus preparing to wash our visitors' feet. Just as he was about to proceed, Jesus approached him, took the basin and towel and moved toward the tables. They were now outside my line of vision, but I could hear the stunned silence as Jesus approached to offer the ceremonial washing. A few moments passed while Jesus moved around the table. Interrupting this solemn ritual Simon's gruff voice burst forth, "You shall not wash my feet Lord, it is I who should wash your feet!"

"Simon, I will say it again, if you are unable to allow me to wash your feet, you have not yet been purified of your false self and will receive no inheritance through me."

"Then Lord, wash my hands and head as well," was Simon's reply.

"Simon, you ask me to provide the ritual washing of one fully purged of the illusion of separation. By your request, yet again you have shown me that you remain in the world of illusion and imprisoned by your pride. Your feet alone shall I wash."

"As you wish it Lord," Simon replied in humbled tones.

After washing Simon's feet, Jesus continued with the other guests. Just as I heard the sound of Jesus reclining at table, Martha gently knocked and peeked in at me. "Mary, it is time." Martha opened the door and along with Salome and Jesus' mother, Mary, began to sing the bridal hymn. I felt strangely self-conscious – all this ceremony for a "marriage" that I knew would most likely never truly come to pass. I entered the center room as the women – the others now joining in, offered the hymn. With the veil covering my face, I looked around at our guests and saw a mixture of surprise, disgust and enthusiastic welcome. I was tempted to give into my own fears of unworthiness and sinfulness, but heard Jesus' voice in my mind, "Mary look not to those who would judge. Look to me, who loves you beyond all measure." I lifted my eyes to meet Jesus' gaze and was comforted by his passionate smile and the twinkle of joyful regard in his eyes. I approached my beloved, now seated at table, bowed to him, and kneeling before him, removed the lid from the jar of blessed nard, poured a generous amount into my hands and anointed his head, his face, his hands and his feet. I gently kissed the feet of my beloved. I rose my head to face him and just as he was about to raise my veil to offer the marriage kiss, there was a pounding on the table. Jesus and I looked up, startled, toward the explosion and beheld Simon, red-faced and standing. "What is the meaning of this!?" he shouted. "Why has there been this waste of expensive oil. It could have sold for more than a hundred days' wages and the money given to the poor."

Jesus responded, "Simon. Leave her alone. Why do you feel compelled to constantly make trouble with Mary? She has done a good thing for me. First she has become my wife, now she has anointed my body for burial. Amen,

157

I say to you, wherever the gospel is proclaimed to the world, what she has done will be told in memory of her." Jesus gently lifted my veil and kissed me on the mouth. With the exception of Simon, who sulked in the corner, all offered the marriage blessing:

Baruch Ata HaShem Elokainu Melech HaOlam,
SheHakol Barah Lichvodo
Baruch Ata HaShem Elokainu Melech HaOlam, Yotzer
Ha'Adam
Baruch Ata HaShem Elokainu Melech HaOlam, Asher
Yatzar Et Ha'Adam Betzalmo, b'Tzelem Dmut
Tavnito, VeHitkon Lo Mimenu Binyan Adei Ad.
Baruch Ata HaShem Yotzer Ha'Adam
Sos Tasis VeTagel HaAkarah, BeKibbutz Bane'ha
Letocha BeSimchaa. Baruch Ata HaShem,
Mesame'ach Tzion BeVaneha
Sameach TeSamach Re'im Ahuvim, KeSamechacha
Yetzircha BeGan Eden MiKedem. Baruch Ata
HaShem, MeSame'ach Chatan VeKalah
Baruch Ata HaShem Elokainu Melech HaOlam, Asher
Barah Sasson VeSimcha, Chatan VeKalah, Gila
Rina, Ditza VeChedva, Ahava VeAchava, VeShalom
VeRe'ut. MeHera HaShem Elokeinu Yishama
BeArei Yehudah U'Vchutzot Yerushalayim, Kol
Sasson V'eKol Simcha, Kol Chatan V'eKol Kalah,
Kol Mitzhalot Chatanim MeChupatam, U'Nearim
Mimishte Neginatam. Baruch Ata HaShem
MeSame'ach Chatan Im Hakalah.
Baruch Ata HaShem Elokainu Melech HaOlam, Boreh
Pri HaGafen.

Blessed art Thou, Lord our God, King of the universe
who created all things for his glory.

158

Blessed art Thou, Lord our God, King of the universe
Fashioner of the man.
Blessed art Thou, Lord our God, the sovereign of
the world, who created man in His image, in the
pattern of His own likeness, and provided for the
perpetuation of his kind. You are blessed, Lord, the
creator of man.
Let the barren city be jubilantly happy and joyful at her
joyous reunion with her children. You are blessed,
Lord, who makes Zion rejoice with her children.
Let the loving couple be very happy, just as You made
Your creation happy in the garden of Eden, so
long ago. You are blessed, Lord, who makes the
bridegroom and the bride happy.
Blessed art Thou, Lord our God, King of the Universe,
who created joy and celebration, bridegroom and
bride, rejoicing, jubilation, pleasure and delight, love
and brotherhood, peace and friendship. May there
soon be heard, Lord our God, in the cities of Judea
and in the streets of Jerusalem, the sound of joy and
the sound of celebration, the voice of a bridegroom
and the voice of a bride, the happy shouting of
bridegrooms from their weddings and of young men
from their feasts of song.
Blessed art Thou, Lord, who makes the bridegroom and
the bride rejoice together
Blessed art Thou, Lord our God, King of the Universe,
creator of the fruit of the vine.

After the marriage blessing was proclaimed, I joined
Jesus at table as the marriage feast was set before us. I
gazed in wonder at the feast Martha and Salome had
prepared in secret as I had kept to my room in prayer. My

heart swelled at their generous acceptance of our marriage. I looked up at Jesus whose eyes met mine. We leaned toward each other and kissed. Those who had joined us at table met our kiss with a round of supportive applause. I noticed out of the corner of my eye that Simon alone refused to join in the support and instead sat with arms crossed firmly across his chest. My heart sank in sorrow for Simon's inability to accept that even greater than the Law of Moses was the Law of Love. I felt Jesus' hand reach for mine beneath the table and he squeezed my hand in reassurance. He wrapped his arm around me and held me close to him as we began to share what would be our first and final meal as husband and wife. As we feasted with our family and friends, Jesus and I held each other close, squeezing out every last drop of joy, knowing that even as we celebrated, death stood waiting at the door.

CHAPTER NINETEEN

On the morning of the following day, Jesus and the Galilean men, including John, made the two mile journey from Bethany to Jerusalem to partake in the Passover festival. Jesus had asked that the house of Lazarus, including his mother, Mary, remain in Bethany so that we could offer prayer and support from a distance. While we waited, Mary sent word to her brother Joseph in Capernaum to join us in anticipation of what we all sensed would soon transpire in Jerusalem. While I wanted to accompany my beloved to Jerusalem and walk beside him on this path, we agreed it would not be so. If things went in the direction we feared, someone would need to carry out Jesus' mission. We also agreed that what Jesus needed most as he took back the temple for Abwoon, were my prayers. Because of the bond we now shared, I would be able to witness the events as they were unfolding through Jesus' eyes. So, while I could not be there in body, knowing that I could see in spirit gave me the comfort I needed to accept this distant task.

Word had gone out ahead of Jesus and a mob of people awaited his entrance into Jerusalem. They were all there – people who had found hope in his words, the simply curious, the skeptical and even those who despised him – all there to greet Jesus and the company of men at the city gates. Judas had procured an ass for Jesus who desired to depart this world on the back of an ass – a symbol of poverty of spirit and humility. Jesus wanted the people to understand that he was not the warrior king they awaited, but a humble servant. Sadly, the crowd missed Jesus' meaning in this gesture.

The people thronged around him at the gates and it took all the strength of those well-weathered fishermen to keep the crowds at bay. The crowds waved palm fronds and chanted Hosannas as they welcomed their "King." Jesus bore all this humbly and with a fair bit of cynicism, knowing how quickly his adoring fans would exchange their praise for spite. Jesus and the men made their way slowly through the city streets on their journey toward their ultimate destination – the temple – which Jesus had been forbidden to enter. Jesus and the men approached the guards at the temple gates and Judas handed over the agreed-upon bribe – thirty pieces of silver. The guards quickly stepped aside and let them pass.

Once inside the temple grounds, the men came upon the market – the place where money changers and breeders had set up their stalls to sell livestock and to exchange currency for the prescribed temple sacrifice. Jesus had frequently preached against these prescribed sacrifices, as they served no other purpose than to burden those who already struggled to provide for the daily needs of their families or as an obstacle to the rich, who only used the sacrifice to show off their means. It was here that Jesus stood in defiance over the Pharisees' prohibition of his preaching. In the middle of the marketplace, Jesus began to preach:

"Woe to you who lay burdens on the people's shoulders but will not lift a finger to move them. Woe to you whose works are performed to be seen. They widen their phylacteries

162

and lengthen their tassels. They love the places of honor at banquets and seat of honor in synagogues. Woe to you blind guides. Woe to you scribes and Pharisees, hypocrites and blind fools!"

As Jesus preached, the crowd began paying attention to his words, and protesting the temple-sacrifice. As Jesus preached, a newfound zeal overtook him and his eyes were lit with the power of the spirit. In fact, although I had never met the man, I thought I could see the spirit of John the Baptizer enter into Jesus as his preaching became more and more urgent. As the zeal within Jesus increased, so, too, did the enthusiasm of the crowd. Jesus' preaching had stirred their unspoken anger and resentment at the prescribed sacrifice. The crowd's unspoken gall turned to angry protest as they began to turn over the tables of the money-changers, spilling their coins onto the ground, and releasing the animals from their cages. Soon, an all-out riot ensued. As the crowd proceeded to destroy the marketplace, Jesus and the men quietly slipped from their midst and made their retreat to the room procured for them by Rabbi Nicodemus in the center of the city – that which has now come to be known as *The Upper Room.*

For the next several days, Jesus, and the Galilean men remained in the Upper Room in prayer while Nicodemus sent word from the temple. The Pharisees, Sadducees, Scribes and High Priests were in hot debate over what to do about Jesus. Those whose hearts were open heard the truth in Jesus' words and sought to learn more. Some were afraid because of the Romans. Some saw Jesus as a threat to their own power and some, just simply, could not see past their own limiting beliefs to the truths that lay hidden within their own hearts. In the end, fear and power won the debate and it was decided that Jesus would

163

be brought to trial on charges of blasphemy, handed over to the Romans as a traitor. The people were calling him *King of the Jews* – something the temple officials claimed Jesus had never denied. The Romans would not stand for a threat to Caesar's reign. Nicodemus got word to Jesus that the temple guards would be sent to arrest him before dawn of the fourth day.

On the evening of the third day of the week, Jesus shared the Passover meal with the Galilean men. We had already celebrated our final meal together and as Jesus had communicated to me in prayer, Jerusalem had become too dangerous for us to join them for the Passover observance. "Mary, I have called you Magdalene for a reason. As the great tower, you must remain as a beacon of truth for those who have eyes to see and hearts open to enjoying the fullness of God's love, and a mirror for all who long for that which they cannot name. Should I perish, you will need to carry out my mission of love – one that they will never expect from a woman – and the House of Lazarus must be protected so that it may support you in this mission." While I wanted nothing more than to be by his side, I remained in Bethany where Martha, Mother Mary, Salome, Lazarus and I gathered in prayer. Mary's brother Joseph was expected to join us the following day. In Bethany we held prayerful vigil as the events in Jerusalem took form.

After finishing their Passover meal, Jesus sought time for his own prayer and preparation. Feeling imprisoned in the Upper Room, Jesus invited John and James to accompany him to the Garden of Gethsemane, Jesus' favorite site within the city walls. Simon stood up in protest, "John is but a boy and James will not be enough to keep you safe. Let me go along with you." Jesus accepted his offer in hopes that Simon, too, could join

him in prayer and that in these final moments he might find the softness of heart that had, at this point, eluded him. So under the cover of darkness, Jesus, John, James and Simon stole from the Upper Room and found their way to Gethsemane.

For the first time, Jesus' companions saw the vulnerability of the man they called *Master* – the kind of vulnerability that up to this time, Jesus had only shared with me. From my place of prayer, I felt within me the moment that my beloved Jesus fell to his knees in earnest supplication to God. As if sitting beside my beloved – or rather, within him, I felt his pain and saw his companions' response. As Jesus' heart tore open and he uttered his first plea to Abwoon, "Take this cup away from me." Simon turned away. He could not bear the sight of his teacher in this desperate and weakened state. Confused by a mixture of revulsion and the tug of his own fears, Simon began to walk away. Just as he turned, Jesus called out to him, "Simon, you will deny me. I tell you, before the cock crows on the fifth day, three times you will deny me." With this proclamation, my beloved looked deep into Simon's eyes, deep into his soul and I felt Simon look away in shame as he realized the truth of Jesus' words. Simon stumbled through the dusk and sank to his knees beneath an ancient olive tree, where he shed his own tears of grief and shame.

Jesus began to beg and plead with Our Lord, "Abwoon, I've done everything you've asked of me. This is a hard-hearted people and many refuse to see the light of truth. Must I be punished for the sake of a few? Am I a worthy sacrifice for their blindness? Are you so cruel – crueler to me than you were to Isaac? You spared Isaac, now prove your love and spare me!"

165

James looked on as his younger brother groveled before our Lord. A proud and haughty man, filled with vanity over his own faith and adherence to Hebrew law, he could not tolerate his brother's lack of faith. He strode over, slapped Jesus hard across the face, "Snap out of it brother. Show some dignity. If you are as special as mother always said you were, God will rescue you from the hands of your accusers."

Jesus looked back with fire in his eyes – the kind of fire known only between siblings. "Oh you would love for me to die on the cross – to show the world that you have always been the favored one, and to take your role as leader, wouldn't you? I'll tell you what James, take the role as leader, I don't want it. It is yours!" James turned his back on his brother and walked away in a huff.

All that remained was John – soft-spoken and gentle John, with the depth of kindness in his eyes. He gingerly approached his brother Jesus, knelt down beside him and placed his hand gently on his shoulder. "I am here brother. I will not leave you alone in this. Do not despair. God will somehow work the good in all this." With tears streaming down his face, Jesus looked deeply into John's eyes and saw in his light-filled irises, the depth of his compassion and love.

For what seemed like hours, Jesus poured out his fear, bargaining with God, pleading and begging, screaming and ranting with God for his cruelty. Finally, just before dawn when he had emptied himself of all that lay within him, he sighed and said, "Not my will but your own. Let it be done to me as you will." A sense of peaceful surrender, if not resignation, took over his countenance.

At the moment of Jesus' surrender, James began shouting from somewhere near the entrance to the garden,

166

"Soldiers – Roman soldiers and temple guards – brother." In haste Jesus and John rose to their feet as the sound of soldiers' boots echoed across the garden. Simon was startled out of his sleep and drew his sword. He took his place of defense in front of Jesus and was ready to strike. "Simon, put down your sword," Jesus pleaded, "or they will kill you too." I saw the soldiers enter the clearing dragging Judas by the nape of the neck. The soldiers held their grip on the struggling Judas, and he was no match for their weapons or their strength. The soldiers threw Judas at Jesus' feet. "Show us the one they call *King of the Jews,*" they sneered. Judas slowly pulled himself up, shaking in fear and hanging his head in shame. The soldiers who had taken the bribe at the temple gates knew Judas to be one of Jesus' followers and fingered him as one to follow if Jesus was to be found. He had been discovered at the market while procuring provisions for the disciples who remained hidden in the Upper Room. The soldiers captured him, and upon threat of death, forced him to lead them to Jesus. Judas approached Jesus, kissed him on the cheek and with tear soaked eyes whispered, "Forgive me Lord. I had no choice." Jesus embraced him, "Judas, there is nothing to forgive. All is as it should be. Remember that you are love." Without ceremony, the soldiers wrenched Jesus from Judas' embrace, quickly bound his hands behind him and marched him out of the garden to the streets of Jerusalem.

I startled out of my reverie and rushed to the places where my loved ones either slept or prayed. "Quickly, our Lord, Jesus has been arrested. We must leave for Jerusalem now!"

We quickly gathered what we could and made hast to Jerusalem by way of the main road. As God would have it, we met Joseph on the road as he was making his way to our home. Mary ran forward and embraced her brother with tears in her eyes. "Thank God you are here! You have arrived just in time. Jesus has just been arrested by the Roman guard and we are hastening to Jerusalem to offer our prayers and support." Joseph quickly fell in step beside us. I listened as Mary shared in hushed tones all that had transpired in the past several days and what we anticipated upon arrival in Jerusalem.

By the time we reached the ancient city, the place was in an uproar. "Jesus has been arrested. So much for the *King of the Jews*. Let's see if his Abwoon will save him now!" Jesus' adoring fans from just a few days before had turned hostile and violent. We pushed our way through the crowds and listened for where they may have taken Jesus. We heard in murmurs and shouts, "He stands before the Sanhedrin." We adjusted our course and began to make our way toward the temple. We knew we'd never gain access to the Sanhedrin's council chambers where our beloved was being questioned, but we wanted to get as close as possible. We made it to just outside the temple gates – now closely guarded by a regiment of Roman soldiers. We found a place near the wall, grasped each other's hands and began to pray. Overcome with fear and worry, we turned to the version of the Kaddish our Lord had taught us – the prayer Jesus revealed as a powerful tool for healing, and began to chant the ancient Aramaic phrases:

Abwoon d'bwashmaya
Nethqadash shmakh
Teytey malkuthakh
Nehwey tzevyanach aykanna
d'bwashmaya aph b'arha
Hawvlan lachma d'sunqanan yaomana.

168

Washboqlan khauabyn (wakhtahayn)
Aykana daph khnan shbwoqan l'khayyabayn.
Wela tahlan l'nesyuna
Ela patzan min bisha
Metol dilakhie malhutha wahayla wateshbukhta
l'ahlam almin.
Ameyn.

As we continued our prayer, we heard a voice rise above the crowd, "Brother Lazarus. Sister Magdalene." We looked up and there was John pushing his way through. He had dared the crowds, fighting his way to the Upper Room where he had tried in vain to encourage the other disciples to come to the temple to support their teacher and friend. But, the Galilean disciples refused, fearing that they too would be brought to trial for having known and followed Jesus.

John entered our intimate circle, embraced his uncle, Joseph, and joined us in prayer. After what seemed like hours, we heard a commotion near the gate. The Roman guards stepped away from the gate and formed a protective barrier between us and the doorway. The gate was opened. We moved to get a glimpse and in between the wall of soldiers we saw our beloved, with hands bound behind him as he was roughly shoved through the gateway with a soldier on either side of him. The crowd pushed forward as Jesus came into view and standing behind him on the other side of the gate – Ciaphas and Annas, the High Priests of the temple, "Take this blasphemer and traitor to Pilate." They spit on the ground, shook the dust from their feet, turned and walked away as the temple gate was closed and locked behind them. It was three in the afternoon on the fourth day of the week.

Finished with their work at the temple, the Roman guards gathered around Jesus and formed a protective barrier between him and the crowd. We tried to get closer to get a glimpse, perhaps to touch or at least give Jesus a comforting glance – but to no avail. Instead, I reached forth with my spirit toward my beloved. "Jesus, I'm here. We are all here. You are not alone." As I offered up this prayer, Nicodemus emerged from the temple gates with his head hung low and face streaked with tears. "Brothers and sisters, I did everything I could do. The Pharisees and the High Priests had already decided Jesus' fate. They brought him up on charges of blasphemy for which he was found guilty in spite of my protests and those of my brother rabbis. The High Priests could not see past their positions of power and the Pharisees could not see the light shining in the darkness of their literalistic interpretation of the Law."

"Jesus is being sent to Pilate on charges of being a traitor for proclaiming himself to be king over Caesar. When asked by the High Priest if he were the Messiah, the one who was prophesied, the new David, Jesus replied, 'I am that I am.' We know what Jesus meant by this but to the High Priests, that was all they needed to trump up charges of treason, thereby placing jurisdiction in the hands of Rome. He will be charged and tried before Pilate at the Praetorium tomorrow morning," Nicodemus explained. We hung our heads in resignation knowing this would be the end of our beloved and that our greatest fears would indeed come to pass. The Roman law was clear – if you challenged Caesar's rule, you would be put to death. And in Rome, there would be no mercy.

Together, we found our way through the streets of Jerusalem to the Upper Room where the other disciples remained in hiding. When we arrived, we found a tired and battered crew. They had spent the past twenty-four hours debating Jesus' authenticity. Some clung to their own illusions of a messiah-king who would liberate the Jews from Roman rule – they had clearly missed the point of Jesus' teachings. Simon and James had spent the day arguing over who would carry out Jesus' teachings in his stead and who of them best understood his teachings. It was a curious discourse as I listened to both present their own view of Jesus' words. I thought to correct them when I heard Jesus' voice, "Mary, it is as it will be. Leave them to their debate. Remember – 'darkness and light are but one.'"

Away from the chaos in the center of the room, in the furthest corner, all alone, with his knees tucked up close and his head hung low, sat Judas. I drew closer to him, knelt beside him and placed my hand on his shoulder as he wept. I felt my heart cleave in two as a heart-wrenching sob escaped his lips. "Mary, I meant no harm. I had no choice. The soldiers forced me to take them to the garden. It is all because of the morning at the temple and the bribe. Why had Jesus entrusted me with the money? Why me? Why me? If I had not gone, they would not have recognized me as Jesus' follower."

Judas had a point. With the exception of him and John, the other disciples looked quite similar and a Roman would not have been able to distinguish one from the other. As a Jew of Egyptian descent, Judas bore a strikingly unique appearance. In contrast to the ruddy, weather beaten, bearded complexion of the Galileans, Judas' skin was as smooth as marble, clean shaven and a light, milky-brown. Unlike the working men who let their hair grow to shoulder length, Judas kept his tightly cropped, and rather than the deep chocolate brown and sometimes black of the Judean's eyes, Judas' were a clear sea green— obviously his most distinguishing characteristic. To put it mildly, Judas stood out from the rest of this surly mob. I, too, wondered why Jesus had chosen Judas when he would be so easily recognized.

As Judas wept, I reached out to embrace him and instead, felt compelled to place my hands on either side of his face. Covering his ears as my thumbs reached out to lightly touch the place on his forehead between his eyebrows, I experienced the most curious vision. Following a burst of turquoise and indigo light, I witnessed Judas, a small group of people and myself traveling through the desert sands in the land of the Pharaohs with the ancient pyramids, built on the sweat of our ancestors, rising in the background. Judas was leading the way. I felt a peace come over Judas as he looked into my eyes and quietly acknowledged that he too had seen the vision. Through my compassionate presence and healing touch, he had been released of the blocks to hearing, knowing and believing in the truth of what would be. We embraced in our mutual knowing, grateful for the gifts that Jesus had given us to be open to God's healing of the fears the kept us from knowing and living in the peace of God's love. We turned our attention to the heated debate going on around us. It was finally Lazarus who interrupted the angry discourse, "Brothers, our teacher and friend will stand before Pilate tomorrow morn. We cannot abandon him in his time of need."

"Lazarus," quipped Simon, "It will be sure death if we show our faces at the Praetorium."

"That may be," responded Lazarus, "but better to die by the sword than to betray the truth."

172

"What truth?" asked Simon, "That Jesus is the son of God, the messiah-king, John the Baptizer, Elijah, the new Moses, or God himself? For which truth do we sacrifice our own lives?"

At this point, Mother Mary stepped into the center of the group. The room grew quiet as her peaceful, compassionate presence embraced the crowd. "My son has always honored each of us for our own truth, judging none as right or wrong or better than another. For some, he will be king, for others Lord, Beloved to some, rabbi, teacher, prophet, friend, healer to others. Let those who feel called to accompany him on this stage of his journey do so, and for those who are not so-called, let us give them honor and love. While as a woman I will not be allowed within the Praetorium gates, outside I shall stand in prayer and support of my son."

"As will I," said Lazarus.

"And I," said John.

"So shall I," responded Martha and Salome in unison.

"And I," said Judas as he rose from his place on the floor.

To these Joseph and I added our own assent. The other disciples remained silent as I expected they would.

Just before dawn, we departed our shelter in the Upper Room and made our way through the streets of Jerusalem. As we got closer to the Praetorium, we could hear the noise of the gathering crowds. Human beings are always up for a spectacle, especially when it might be at another's expense and doubly so if there might be the possibility of viewing a public execution – and the Judeans were no different on this account. We arrived at the Praetorium just as the guards opened the gates. We gathered more closely and paused for a moment of prayer. It had been decided that

Lazarus and Joseph would serve as our witnesses within the Praetorium, while Judas and John served as our escorts outside. I felt my heart clench and tears rose in my eyes as I watched my brother join the rabble.

We stationed ourselves as near the gate as was possible. As I felt God's peace rise within me, I imagined reaching out to Jesus and wrapping him in it. I felt his presence and, for but a moment, felt the fear, the exhaustion and the frustration that he was feeling – but it left as quickly as it came. "Mary, I love you, and I know and I feel your loving support – but I must be alone with myself in this. Forgive me, but the feeling of your love will tempt me to stray from this path." I knew the truth of these words and released my beloved to his own counsel while still holding him in prayer. Still one in our bond as beloved, however, I was able to witness the events as they unfolded, only now from a place of detached observation.

The energy within the Roman court was tense. I felt flashes of violent anger tinged with desires for revenge. It felt as if Jesus' fate had already been decided and that this entire scene was merely an exercise in formalities. As I searched the faces in the crowd, I saw a wide range of responses to the proceedings that lay ahead. To those who had found comfort in Jesus' words or experienced one of his healings, I saw the face of confused grief. In the face of others, I saw a sense of having been betrayed. And in others, I beheld outright hatred. Finally, there were the slithering snake-like eyes of those we later learned had been paid by the temple priests to incite the crowd against Jesus, thereby ensuring his fate. Past the crowd, I regarded the stage at the far end of the Praetorium that served as Pilate's seat of judgment. Six Roman guards stood at attention across the front of the stage with swords drawn

174

and ready. In silent procession, two Roman trumpeters made their way across the stage and took their place at its center. They raised their horns and heralded the beginning of the proceedings. First a murmur, then a hush, fell over the crowds. One-by-one, the accusers and those who would pass judgment filed in, each accompanied by a Roman guard. Annas and Ciaphas, High Priests of the temple stood as Jesus' accusers. Following the High Priests, entered Pontius Pilate, Roman governor of Judea. Pilate took the center chair – the one meant for a Caesar or a king. Annas and Ciaphas were made to stand down stage to Pilate's right. Pilate gave the guard to his right a look and a slight nod at which the guard picked up a mallet and struck the gong behind Pilate's chair signaling the beginning of the proceedings. Pilate silently nodded toward Ciaphas and Annas who straightened their postures as Annas began to speak, "Pontius Pilate, governor of Judea, province of Rome, we come before you today on the matter of Jesus bar Joseph of Nazareth." Annas paused while awaiting Pilate's response. Instead, Pilate sat in stone-faced silence. Annas, visibly shaken by his show of disinterest and disrespect shivered, straightened his shoulders and cleared his voice before continuing, "Yesterday Jesus bar Joseph was tried before a jury of his peers, accused and found guilty of blasphemy." Before Annas could continue, Pilate with impatience in his voice broke in "Blasphemy?! How are your ridiculous religious laws any concern of mine or of this court? You waste my time and try my patience, priest." Pilate made to rise and depart the proceedings. Ciaphas, with his serpent-like voice broke in, "Wait my Lord; it is not for the blasphemy that we recommend Jesus to your court. It is what he said during our questioning of him that caused us even greater

175

concern than the blasphemy he spoke against our God. It was the treason that he spoke against your Lord, Caesar."

Pilate's eyes, remaining veiled in suspicion, brightened slightly and he returned to his chair. "Go on priest," Pilate urged with a flick of his wrist. "Jesus proclaimed himself to be King of the Jews – a direct act of treason against Caesar," announced Annas. A gasp fell over the crowd. Pilate rubbed his chin in thought. "Hmmmmm…. King of the Jews you say? I know of this Jesus bar Joseph of Nazareth and he seems mostly harmless – hardly a king or a threat to Rome, but I will entertain this game that you wish to make of him. What is he to you anyway? I thought you Jews stuck together."

"There is no tolerance among us for those who threaten Caesar," Ciaphas hissed.

"Ciaphas, you are a liar. I know you care only for your own position of power. But let's see what the accused has to say for himself." Pilate clapped his hands and a door was opened at the side of the stage. Still bound, Jesus was led in with a Roman guard at each shoulder in escort. A groan of shock leaped from my lips. My beloved was not the man I had seen just one day earlier. His face drawn. His eyes encircled by dark shadows. His lips dried and cracked from dehydration. He looked as if he hadn't slept in days. The guards shoved Jesus toward Pilate and made him stand to Pilate's left, facing the High Priests.

"Jesus bar Joseph, of Nazareth, is this your name?" asked Pilate.

"It is," Jesus replied.

"Are you the one who has been found guilty by the High Priests of blasphemy?"

"I am that I am," Jesus replied.

Upon hearing Jesus utter those words – words

forbidden by the high priests, the crowd went wild. "Blasphemy! Heresy! He is possessed of Beelzebub," shouted the crowd while some merely hung their heads in shame. How could this man they thought to be holy speak such atrocities? What they did not understand was the deeper meaning of this phrase. Jesus had taught us that "I Am" is not only the unutterable name of the Lord, it is also a phrase which empowers us to return to our awareness of Oneness with God – to let go of the fears that keep us trapped in the world of perceived separation and to remember that we are One with God in love. Jesus used this phrase to help us remember our Oneness with God – not to proclaim himself as equal with God. To explain this truth of Oneness, Jesus had used the image of a drop of water in the ocean – like the drop of water, we are seemingly separate, but that when we return to Oneness with God, we are like the drop of water returned to the ocean….no longer separate, but indistinguishable from the whole. Jesus knew of the great power in the utterance of YHWH. He knew that the utterance of this sacred phrase would awaken some from the state of stupor in which they remained.

Pilate held up his hand to silence the crowd, "I have no mind for your silly religious beliefs. The High Priests can do with you what they will over this ridiculous squabble."

"But Lord," interrupted Ciaphas, "this man called himself king – a direct threat against Caesar."

"Ah yes," acknowledged Pilate, "What do you say to this accusation Jesus bar Joseph? Are you King of the Jews?"

Again, Jesus uttered the sacred name, "I am that I am."

Another uproar erupted from the crowd, "Blasphemy!

Heresy. Remove him from our sight! Smite him down."

Pilate turned to the crowd, "Is this man your king?"

"We have no king but Caesar!" screamed the crowd.

"Jesus bar Joseph, are you proclaiming yourself to be king?" Pilate asked again.

"I am that I am," was Jesus' final reply.

Pilate shook his head, reached out and grabbed Jesus' shoulder, leaning in to whisper in his ear, "You are either mad or an idiot Jesus bar Joseph. Why do you respond to me in these riddles? Do you not know I have your life in my hands? If you persist in this, I will have no choice but to find you guilty of treason, the sentence of which is death."

Jesus whispered back to him, "Pontius Pilate, you have nothing in your hands. I answer only to the truth."

"And what is this truth of which you speak?" Pilate inquired.

"Come and see," Jesus offered.

In that moment, I felt something stir in Pilate – a doubt, followed by a brief moment of longing. Something in Pilate opened in that exchange – the desire to know more, a hunger for truth, a longing for peace. But just as the light of truth ignited in Pilate's heart, Ciaphas again interrupted, "You have a duty to Caesar."

Ciaphas' arrow of fear met its intended mark and in a single instant, snuffed out the spark of truth that had been lit within Pilate. If he began the journey toward truth, everything he had ever known would slip from his fingers – his livelihood, his financial security, the home he had made for his family and, most importantly, the meager power he wielded as governor of this God-forsaken land and its thick-necked people. "Perhaps a flogging will get the truth out of you Jesus bar Joseph." Pilate pounded his fist on the table

178

next to him and ordered the soldiers, "Flog him."

The soldiers grabbed Jesus by the shoulders and roughly dragged him from the stage, pushing and shoving him down the stairs and through the crowd to the flogging pole that stood in the center of the courtyard – ever ready for its next victim. As they dragged Jesus to the center of the crowd, a regiment of soldiers poured into the courtyard, making their way through the crowd to the center of the courtyard, forming a barrier between the flogging pole, the whip-bearers and the crowd. The soldiers positioned Jesus facing the pole and grabbing the neck of his garment, tore his tunic in two revealing his naked back. The tunic fell off his shoulders to his waist where it was belted. The guards untied Jesus' wrists from behind his back and roughly drew them around the flogging pole, where they were secured. The flogging began. Two Roman soldiers with braided leather whips stationed themselves a few paces behind Jesus and in practiced strokes took one turn after another at his naked back.

They flogged my beloved thirty-nine times. I watched in horrified anguish as the force of each whip strike threw him back and tore at his flesh. Blood splashed and oozed down his back soaking the tunic which hung limply at his waist. He screamed out in agony as tears of pain stung his eyes and cheeks. He braced himself for each new blow as the sweat from exertion mixed with his blood, pouring salt into his wounds. As I witnessed this assault on my beloved, all I could do was weep. I wanted to rush to him, untie the ropes that held him and hold him in my arms where he would once again be safe and unharmed; but, I knew it must not be so. He had clearly told me, "Mary, this is my path to walk and you must not attempt to interfere. Your life must not be put at risk. There is too

much at stake." There was nothing I could do but gather
Abwoon's love around me and send it forth toward my
beloved to strengthen and assist him through his pain.

As the thirty-ninth lash was complete, I saw Pilate
hold up his hand. "Enough. Bring the prisoner to me."

The guard closest to Jesus moved forward and with
his sword; and severed the rope that bound Jesus' wrists
to the pole. He collapsed onto the ground, the sand
and dust filling his open wounds. Jesus screamed out in
agony – a blood curdling scream that sailed over the noisy
crowd. Sick with horror and weak with shock, I felt my
knees buckle under me as I fell to the ground – at one in
tortured anguish with my beloved. My companions rushed
to my side and held me as I wept for his pain. I felt the
canyon of separation that seemed to be widening in Jesus'
soul. The God my beloved had come to know and with
whom he had grown in Oneness seemed to be slipping
from his grasp. Instead, what was growing within him
was the darkness of fear and perceived separation. Jesus
was beginning to doubt. The suffering and pain of the
flogging had weakened his resolve and he now wrestled
with the fear of death. I could sense that more than
death itself, Jesus had grown fearful of the pain. He lay
there in the dust, paralyzed, immobile, and bereft of spirit
and hope. I used this opportunity to turn the love that
was being shown to me by my companions into further
strength for our Lord.

"Bring the prisoner to me," Pilate more sternly ordered
again.

Into that space in Jesus' mind where I knew he still
remembered Oneness, I whispered, "Jesus, my beloved.
You are not alone. I am here as are Lazarus, Martha,
Salome, Judas, John and your blessed Mother. We are

here. We are holding you in God's love. Remember this love. Remember that you are One with God in this love. You are not alone. You are not alone. You are not alone." I felt a shift in Jesus' energy as he opened his eyes, rolled painfully over to his side and pushed himself up off the ground. In an unusual act of mercy, both guards reached down, helped Jesus to his feet and braced him as he struggled up the stairs to face Pilate. Pilate gestured toward Jesus to come closer. Unable to stand or lean towards Pilate's ear, Jesus fell, barely managing to claw his way to his knees. Pilate leaned toward him and gently placed his hand on Jesus' shoulder and whispered into his ear, "I know of the High Priests' jealousy and of their evil intentions. You seem a reasonable and harmless man – certainly not a threat to Rome. I can help you if you will let me. Just tell me you are not who they accuse you of saying you are. I will ask again, 'Are you the king of the Jews,' to which you will reply, 'I am not.' And we will cease these silly proceedings."

Buoyed by the knowledge of our love and support, a new-found sense of confidence and resolve filled Jesus. "Pilate," Jesus responded, "It is already done. It is finished. I have no place in this world. Only in Abwoon's kingdom is there a place for me."

"All you need to do is to deny those words," Pilate pleaded, "Deny that you are who the High priests said you say you are and I will set you free."

"There's no freedom here. The only freedom available to us is in love – this is where YHWH resides, in love," Jesus explained.

"So you will not recant?"

"If I am to stand in the truth of love, I cannot deny who I am in YHWH."

181

"Your words confuse me and your attitude confounds me," Pilate said in exasperation, "but if this is your chosen path – your own demise – far be it from me to interfere. Jesus bar Joseph, you are either a fool or a prophet and for neither do I wish to waste anymore time. But if you are the prophet they say you are, forgive me for what I am now forced to do."

At this, Pilate rose from his place beside Jesus' ear. "Jesus bar Joseph, please stand." Pilate gestured toward the guards to help him. "Jesus you stand accused of being a traitor against Rome in claiming yourself to be king of the Jews. How do you respond to these charges?"

"I am that I am."

Again the crowd shouted their offense at Jesus' utterance of the forbidden name. My hands flew to cover the anguished cry escaping my throat.

Pilate raised his hand to silence the crowd, "Jesus bar Joseph, I find you guilty of being a traitor to Rome. The sentence is death – death by crucifixion. The sentence will be carried out at noon tomorrow – the sixth day of the week."

While Jesus and I had come to an understanding that this would be the likely verdict, nothing can prepare you for the moment a death sentence is issued. At the proclamation of this sentence, I had the sensation of being torn in two. "No," I silently pleaded, "Not crucifixion." Crucifixion was the most horrific, heinous and torturous methods of Roman execution. He would be tied and nailed to a cross beam, hoisted by rope and pulley to a supporting vertical beam then left to slowly die of suffocation as the weight of his body collapsed into itself. It sometimes took up to three days before a victim of crucifixion might enjoy the reprieve of death. Crucifixion was a slow and agonizing death usually reserved for only the worst criminals. For a Jew, this would be the most humiliating death – in crucifixion, there was no chance of honor.

At Pilate's signal, the guards came toward Jesus, raised the shredded portions of his tunic around his shoulders. Jesus winced as the rough-hewn linen brushed his torn and bleeding flesh. When the soldiers went to bind Jesus' arms, Pilate reached out his hand and shook his head. The guards led Jesus from the stage unbound, presumably to the prisoners' cells below. The other two guards came forward as Pilate rose. They headed toward the exit, but Pilate stopped and turned back. He went to stand before Annas and Ciaphas who held their hands out in thanks. Instead of reaching out to accept their gratitude, Pilate spit on the ground at their feet, shook the dust from his feet, turned his back and walked off the stage. Ciaphas and Annas stood there in shock which they quickly masked with prideful indignation.

While all this was unfolding, the crowd continued to shout in victorious celebration over the impending torture and death of the man who, just days ago, they had welcomed into the city with "Hosanna" and "All Hail, Messiah, King of the Jews." I felt the bitter taste of bile fill my mouth as disgust and revulsion filled my being. How could the people turn so quickly when many here had been healed and cured by Jesus and many more had found comfort in his teachings? It all felt so pointless. Why had Jesus even bothered with the likes of these stiff-necked people? His gifts had been wasted and his generosity squandered. I was sick and disgusted by this show of fickleness. I wept first for Jesus, then for the people, for they had rejected the freedom of truth and love that Jesus had offered.

183

After a time, the gates to the Praetorium were opened and a rowdy and blood thirsty throng erupted from the gates and spilled out into the streets. We held our ground as the flood of people passed by us. Lazarus and Joseph were the last to depart the Praetorium as the guards swiftly closed and barred the gates behind them. We gathered to embrace them and listened in rapt attention, "We spoke with the guards and Jesus will be held tonight in the prisoners' cells below the Praetorium. He will be allowed one visitor and we think it should be mother Mary. What do you say?" We all agreed with his choice. Joseph and John encircled Mary with their arms and escorted her around the back of the Praetorium to the visitor's gate. John remained with Mary as Joseph went to make arrangements for Jesus' burial.

We agreed that we would return to the Upper Room to inform the disciples of what had transpired and to try once more to convince them to join us at dawn in love and support for Jesus as he went to face his death. John and Mother Mary would meet us there.

When we arrived at the Upper Room, the tension in the air was palpable. If I could name the tension, it would be an insidious mixture of guilt and shame. Exhausted from debate, finger pointing and blame, the men sat in separate corners of the room, each trapped in the wasteland of his own mind. As we entered, Simon rushed toward us, sword in hand, "Why have you come here? Can you not leave us in peace? How can we be sure you weren't followed?" Lazarus held up his hand, "Simon, it is finished. Jesus has been found guilty of being a traitor and will be crucified tomorrow at noon."

A collective gasp came forth from the men who had been hiding in the Upper Room. James began, "I told

Jesus it would lead to this. I told him his truth would lead to him getting killed."

Thomas broke in, "I don't believe it. He never made such claims. He never said he was a king."

Philip cried, "Oh no. Not my Lord. Please forgive me for not being with you in your time of need. I knew some of the high priests, if I'd been there, maybe I could have convinced them not to pursue this."

Simon listened to their words and was suddenly overcome with zeal. He pushed past Lazarus and ran out the door, "I will stop this outrage." He had no idea how fruitless his efforts would be. With Simon out of the room, we were able to explain the events of the day to a rapt audience of terrified men. Within the hour, however, Simon burst back into the room breathless, his eyes filled with terror. "No one may leave this room! "

"Simon, what happened?" Philip inquired.

Simon told us of what he found in the streets of Jerusalem – a mass of people stirred up in anticipation of an execution, blood thirsty and hungry for more – in Simon's words, "To seek out and find all of Jesus' followers and put them to death with him." What I heard instead was the truth behind Simon's words. On his way to the Praetorium, three separate people had asked him if he knew Jesus bar Joseph and what he thought of his upcoming execution. These were the natural inquiries of curiosity and had nothing to do with some sort of blood thirst. Simon's own fears and sense of self-importance had colored the way he heard these inquiries, leading him to jump to illogical and dangerous conclusions. I wanted to ask Simon if it wasn't his own shame speaking over the way he had just brought Jesus' prediction to pass. Instead, I softened my inquiry.

"Simon, is this indeed how it is or simply your perception of things?"

In fury, Simon stepped forward, raised his hand and slapped me hard across the face, "Shut up whore!"

Lazarus stepped between us and in my defense, went to strike Simon in return. I stilled his hand, "Lazarus, stop. He doesn't know what he is doing."

Without a word of discussion, Lazarus, Judas, Martha, Salome and I turned to leave. Knowing the disciples' fear had won over the truth of love, we intended to journey home to Bethany, planning to return at dawn to offer our love and support to Jesus, our teacher, friend and beloved. Just as we exited the front door of the home which housed the Upper Room, we were met by Nicodemus. "Are you leaving?" he inquired.

"The disciples have given into their fears. We journey toward Bethany and shall return tomorrow before dawn," replied Lazarus.

"You will do no such thing," argued Nicodemus. "You will come and stay at my home in the city."

"Aren't you afraid of the High Priests?" Lazarus asked.

"I wash my hands of them. Their jealousy and thirst for power has closed their eyes, their ears and their hearts to the truth. In killing Jesus, they deny the very scripture that tells us the law of God is in our hearts – not buried in their rigid interpretation of the Law. They seek to manipulate and control while Jesus seeks to empower. If my support of Jesus means my banishment, so be it." Nicodemus proclaimed.

We followed Nicodemus to his humble home deep within the labyrinth that was Jerusalem. Joanna, had already prepared a meal; clearly attuned to what Nicodemus would discover in the Upper Room. None of us had much of an appetite, but knew we must eat if we were to be of any use the following day.

After dinner, I fell into a deep and fitful sleep. Two hours past midnight, I awoke with a start, fear coursing through my veins, my heart pounding and bedclothes drenched in sweat. And the strands of the dream began to reveal themselves:

I saw the life that Jesus and I were meant to have lived – the life that began with the day he had sat beside my bed and brought me back to life and continued with Jesus teaching at my brother's home and the natural unfolding of our love – first as teacher to student, then as equals and peers. Eventually, Jesus came to Lazarus to offer the betrothal contract which was then followed by our courtship. After an appropriate courtship period, we were wed and a wedding feast was held in our honor in the home of Joseph, Mother Mary's elder brother. During our wedding feast, the wine ran out and Jesus performed the miracle of turning water into wine.

As our life as husband and wife unfolded, so did our ministry, becoming priest and priestess within a new world order. Jesus' teachings were able to be heard by many and because of this, fear and intolerance were released from our world. Because of the release of fear, people were now empowered to discover the law of God in their hearts – the simple law of love. The awareness of this love forever altered people and empowered them to be healed of the spiritual fears that prevented them from becoming the unique expression of God that they were born to be, and in the living out of this gift, people became fulfilled, content and whole. Jesus' teachings (and now mine) breathed new life into temple belief and practice. The prohibitive postures of the Pharisees were replaced with the open attitudes previously associated with the Essenes and the people came to worship not because they were obliged, but because they sought to give praise within a community to the God who had blessed them with love. The impact of this transformation reached far beyond the boundaries of Judaism, beyond Judah and beyond our little corner of the world. Religious, cultural, tribal and racial separation fell away as all that was "of love" from every culture and belief system came together in sharing, learning and discovery. People were no longer divided by their differences, but came together in their similarities.

And then I saw Jesus and myself as we came together in the sacred marriage rites and the children that came forth from that bond. Little Miriam, Joseph our first born son, Johann and Judas named after our closest companions and Martha – the eldest and more like my dear sister than even her name could portray. Jesus and I grew old together – enjoying a long and fruitful life. It must have been the conclusion of this vision that had startled me awake. As the dream replayed in my mind, my heart sank, surrendering to the grief of a life not lived, a purpose unfulfilled and a mission thwarted. I wept bitter tears of sorrow over the loss of the life Jesus and I could have had together – but even more than this loss, I grieved the death of the vision – the vision of a new world rooted in love and harmony, no longer imprisoned by the illusion of separation and fear.

As I began to calm down, I remembered all Jesus had taught me about grief and about prayer. I allowed myself to grieve the loss of what could have been and opened my heart and my mind to Abwoon. As I allowed myself to let go of what could have been, Abwoon showed me another vision – not of the life we could have had, but a life with

Jesus lived in eternity. God showed me that Jesus would be with me always….in this life and in the next….and every life after that. We would never truly be separate and over the millennia, we would come together to bring forth the fulfillment of all I had seen revealed in this dream. Not in this epoch perhaps, but in a time to come. God promised a new life in this loss – a resurrection in the face of death. God was working all of this for the good. I just didn't see it yet and it might not come to fruition in this lifetime.

While I still felt an acute sense of loss, I was uplifted by this new vision for in some deep place within, it all felt true. Perhaps not in this lifetime, but maybe in the next, the illusion of separation would fall away and all would live by the simple law of love. Then the world would know peace. Comforted by these thoughts, I fell back into a restful sleep and was met with another vision. In this third vision, I saw the holy city of Jerusalem part – like the Red Sea had parted for Moses and the Israelites in their exodus from Egypt. Out of the center of this newly opened path through the city of Jerusalem, came a heart shining like the sun – a heart crowned with thorns and pierced by a sword, but shining as if on fire. This heart glowed with the light of a million suns, bathing the earth in glorious illumination. What was dark had become light, and the world was made new. I saw all separation fall away and a world that lived in love. Just as the vision came to its natural conclusion, I heard the cock crow. Dawn was upon us. I arose quickly and joined the others in the kitchen where we broke fast in haste and then Lazarus, Martha, Salome, Judas, Nicodemus and I made for the city gates.

CHAPTER TWENTY

We arrived just in time to position ourselves inside the gates of the city before the crush of the crowd was upon us. From deep within the heart of the city we heard the shouts signaling that Jesus had recently departed the prison gates. We stood prayerfully waiting for Jesus to reach us. From across the city we could hear the shouts and jeers. We were unable to make out the specific words, but the tone said it all – stirred to hatred and spite, people felt the burden of betrayal upon them. Whether out of revenge or merely out of the effect of group think, it sounded like the entire populace of Judea had turned against Jesus. My heart broke with this awareness – not for Jesus, but for the people who could have benefitted from receiving his message into their hearts.

As the shouting grew louder, we knew Jesus was drawing near. The crowds pushed hard upon us, as they too felt his proximity. They could not wait to indulge their inner voyeur – one that thrived on the witness of another's pain and suffering. About 100 yards from where we stood, the road took a sharp left toward the center of the city. We saw the crowd pushing forward, signaling Jesus' arrival. We craned our necks to see past the crowds and to catch a glimpse of our beloved. My heart skipped a beat as I caught a peek of Jesus' scarlet cloak – the cloak

190

that had become my own intimate symbol of the man
I loved. Mother Mary had retrieved his red cloak along
with a fresh linen tunic to replace the one destroyed in
the lashing. I breathed a sigh of relief for the restoration
of some shred of dignity, but as Jesus came fully into
view that breath quickly flew from my chest. I felt as if
someone had punched me in the stomach as I beheld what
had been done to my beloved.

There was no dignity here. Instead, Jesus had been
marked with shame. Upon his head, the soldiers had
placed a woven wreath of hawthorn – a veritable crown
of thorns. He wore the fresh tunic, but it was soiled and
stained from the blood that dripped from the puncture
wounds made when they forced the crown upon his head
and the fresh wounds from yesterday's flogging soaked
through the back and sides of the tunic. What had once
been an ecru colored linen was now stained blood red.
Across his shoulders they had bound a six inch square
crossbeam that was roughly six feet in length. He bore
this crossbeam as an ox does its yoke. His scarlet cloak
was draped across his shoulders in the fashion of the
priests in the temple – clearly intended to make a mockery
of both Jesus and of those who had brought these charges
against him.

As I beheld the mockery of my beloved, I reached
out with both my heart and my mind to offer comfort. I
waited and watched as Jesus painfully struggled to make
it through the crowd with Roman soldiers pushing and
shoving him along the way. I wondered how he could
walk at all with that crossbeam tied to his shoulders – it
must have weighed fifty pounds or more. As they came
within fifty yards of us, I saw two figures break through
the crowd – Mother Mary and John. After visiting Jesus

in the prisoner's cell, they had found their way back to the Upper Room and had spent the night there. On seeing her son, Mary rushed forward and wrapped her arms around her him. I saw them lock eyes as they exchanged silent words, tears flowing down their faces. The soldiers burst forth and wrestled them apart as John came forward and escorted Mother Mary back into the crowd. I caught Mother Mary's eyes and beckoned for her to join us. She gestured to John and pointed us out in the crowd. John took Mother Mary's arm and led her toward us.

The crowd continued to press upon us as we waited for Jesus. Finally, he drew near and just as I caught his eyes, Martha broke through the crowd and with the cloth that had been intended for my marriage bed, she wiped Jesus' face clean of the sweat, blood and tears that streaked his face and blurred his vision. I could not help but see the irony in this – the cloth that was intended to catch the marital blood now caught the blood of my beloved's death. Jesus looked clearly and deeply into my eyes and in that moment, I felt the depth of all he felt – resolution and fear, shame and disgust, frustration and surrender, hatred and love. Jesus' spirit was wracked with the fullest experience of human emotion. Understandably, part of him sought vengeance on his accusers and on all who had abandoned him and another part of him dwelled in the deep well of compassion, wanting to offer forgiveness. I was almost knocked off my feet by the impact of all that Jesus held within him. I took a deep breath and blinked my eyes as I allowed myself to be present to all that Jesus was feeling so that I could continue to hold him in loving support. Jesus held my gaze and our hearts met at the intersection of unfulfilled longing and knowing resolve. My breath caught in my throat and my heart ceased beating as the guards pushed him past.

Our little group, which now included Mother Mary and John, gathered together and with the force of our numbers, we pushed ourselves through the gates of the city and past the crowds. Once on the other side of the city wall, the way opened up for us. The path which led toward the hill at Golgotha moved through a barren and rocky land, past refuse heaps and the smoldering fires of Gehenna where Jerusalem deposited its waste. It was a stark and stinking place near the tented community of lepers. Most of Jerusalem would be too repulsed to venture along this part of the path, but there would be those whose curiosity would get the best of them. It was not curiosity, however, that urged us on. It was our love for Jesus. We could not let our beloved face his death alone.

While we would have preferred to walk beside Jesus for this final leg of his journey, the guards kept us at bay. Jesus walked fifty feet in front of us as we followed in prayerful pursuit. As we approached the hill and Jesus was urged toward the final ascent, the guards closed rank, "No one but immediate family on the hill." Lazarus quickly strode forward, "This is my sister, Mary called Magdalene, she is Jesus' bride, this is his mother Mary and John her son. This is Jesus' immediate family." "They may come forth," responded the guard. I came forward and embraced my brother in gratitude for this great gesture of love.

Lazarus, Martha, Salome, Nicodemus and Judas remained at the bottom of the hill where Joseph later met up with them, while the Roman guards stood in rank to hold back what remained of the curious on-lookers. We followed behind Jesus, his two guards and the soldier who would lead us to where we could stand in prayerful watch. It was painful to see my beloved slip and stumble up the uneven path under the weight of the cross. He stumbled and fell three times as we proceeded up the path, the soldiers offering only a small measure of assistance. Once we met the crest of the hill where it evened off onto a flat surface, the guard stopped and held up his hand, "This is as close as you may approach." My heart sank in disappointment, but I could see the compassion in his orders. We stopped and took in the scene. At the crest of the hill stood three upright wooden supports. On the two outside beams hung criminals who had already been crucified, waiting the reprieve of death. The center beam, the tallest of the three, stood empty, obviously in wait for its next victim – my beloved.

Mother Mary, John and I moved close together and stood in anxious anticipation of what was about to unfold. We watched as the soldiers led Jesus to the foot of the center support where they struck him behind the knees, forcing him to fall into a kneeling position on the stony ground. The soldier nearest Jesus tore the red cloak from across his shoulders and threw it toward us. John rushed past the guard to retrieve Jesus' cloak which he brought to me. As I reached for the garment, a heart-wrenching wail escaped my lips. I fell to my knees as the shields of strength fell from my shoulders and I grieved the loss of my beloved. John and Mother Mary knelt beside me as they shed their own tears of loss.

I looked up as the soldiers tore Jesus' tunic from his body, leaving him naked but for his loincloth. They pushed him down onto his back with the beam still tied to his wrists and shoulders. As Jesus lay prostrate, his shoulders and arms stretched out across the beam, the

soldiers knelt beside him, one on each side, and held
his arms against the cross as a third approached with a
hammer and iron spikes six inches long and three quarters
of an inch square in width. I held my breath as I watched
the executioner kneel down at Jesus' right hand, placing
the spike over his wrist and in one stroke, he brought the
hammer down. I will never forget the scream of pain that
escaped my beloved's lips. It seemed in that utterance,
that the very rock upon which we knelt was split in two.
The hammer came down two more times, each followed
by Jesus' screams of agony. The executioner turned to
Jesus' left wrist and did the same. I knelt transfixed and
paralyzed by my beloved's agony and it was only because
of John's gentle nudge that I remembered to breathe. I
was torn between simply getting up and running as far
away as I could from this violence and rushing forward
to still the executioner's blows. Instead, I clutched Jesus'
scarlet cloak even tighter to me. If I could not hold my
beloved in his pain, I would clutch his cloak, mustering
for both of us, the courage we needed to move through
this pain.

After his arms were securely nailed to the cross, the
soldiers forced Jesus to his feet, and dragged him, tripping
and stumbling to the upright support. A rope and pulley
system had been put in place, which was secured to the
cross. A group of soldiers heaved and pulled, dragging
Jesus off the ground while Jesus cried out in agony,
gagging and choking as the air was slowly squeezed from
his lungs. After Jesus was raised to a height, roughly ten
feet off the ground, the executioner again came forward
and nailed a wooden support at Jesus' feet. In the same
fashion as his wrists, the executioner nailed Jesus' feet to
the cross – first one, and then the other. After he was

finished, another soldier approached with a ladder and a sack across his chest. He propped the ladder against the support beam, climbed to reach Jesus' head and pulled a hammer, a single nail and a wooden plaque from his pouch. He nailed the plaque above Jesus' head and on it was written the charges against him: "Here is Jesus, 'the Christ' King of the Jews."

The soldier replaced the hammer into his sack, and pulled from his pouch a small clay bottle and a reed. He uncorked the bottle, inserted the reed and held it toward Jesus' lips. Surely this was an apothecary's blend of herbs to aid unconsciousness – intended to alleviate some of the suffering of death. Grateful for this act of compassion shown toward my beloved, I looked on in sadness as Jesus shook his head in refusal. The soldier shrugged his shoulders in resignation and descended the ladder. After this was all accomplished, another soldier stepped forward with trumpet in hand. He blew the trumpet and proclaimed loudly, "Here hangs Jesus bar Joseph, found guilty of being a traitor for proclaiming himself to be king – a crime against Caesar, against Rome and punishable by death." He blew the trumpet again. The time was twelve o'clock noon.

As the last note of the trumpet rang, the sky darkened, thunder cracked and the earth began to shake. The "gods" were not pleased with this act of treachery. The Romans, who still worshipped the gods of earth and sky were visibly shaken by the elements' response. They shifted their feet and whispered to each other in questioning tones. All the while, I smiled in silent knowing of Abwoon's displeasure. The guard who held us at bay now invited us to approach, "You may go nearer to the cross." We ran to the foot of the cross and stood in prayerful support for our beloved.

The soldiers prevented us from getting close enough to touch Jesus, but we stood within an arm's length.

"Jesus, my son, we are here." offered Mother Mary.

"My mother is that my mother? I want my mother." Jesus pleaded in plaintive whispers, barely able to get the words out from his suffering and pain.

"Yes my son, I am here and John and Mary, your bride, are here with me," she responded.

"John, my brother, here is our mother. Take her into your home and care for her," Jesus implored.

John stepped dutifully to Mary's side and placed his arm around her shoulders protectively. Mother Mary began to weep and bowed her head toward his shoulder as he wrapped his arms around her in comfort.

"My beloved," I whispered, "You are not alone. We shall be here praying with you until you draw your final breath." As I uttered these words, I felt Jesus' heart open in search of mine and when our hearts met, I felt his heart tear in two as mine had when John had given me Jesus' scarlet cloak. "My God, my God. Why have you forsaken me?" my beloved begged in heart breaking agony. At that moment, the impact of Jesus' pain reached the hearts of the Romans, the others criminals who hung on either side of him, and any of the curious onlookers who remained. In unison, they fell to their knees in sorrowful penitence.

The soldier nearest us shouted, "We have killed a prophet, a Son of God, we are doomed." In the midst of his own pain, Jesus uttered a prayer of absolution, "Abwoon, forgive them they know not what they do." I wept in wonder over Jesus' compassion as I began to chant the Aramaic formula of forgiveness:

"Washboqlan khauabyn wakhtahayn aykana daph khnan shbwoqan l'khayyabayn."

197

For three hours we stood and wept, kneeling or lying prostrate in prayer as our beloved's life breath was slowly squeezed from him under the weight of his body as it hung on the cross. We listened to his pain. He wept tears of loss, moaned in agony and in moments of fear, yelled out in anger toward his god. We rode the waves of Jesus' final spiritual journey as he moved from pain and fear, remorse and loss, doubt and rage to resolution, compassion, surrender, peace and back again. For three hours this went on as the Romans stood in their own form of prayer beside us. As time went on other curious on-lookers began to join us in our prayer. At three o'clock in the afternoon, one of the Roman guards came forward with spear in hand and in one swift and final act of mercy, plunged the spear into Jesus' side. Jesus' head flew back in the face of this new-found pain, but instead of the grimace of agony, a peaceful smile played upon his lips and he whispered, "Abwoon, into your hands I commend my Spirit. It is finished," and his head fell forward and released his final breath as blood and water poured out of his side.

As Jesus released his final breath, my resolve gave way and the grief and horror that I had contained erupted into wailing and screaming. I tore at my hair and at my garments wanting to be freed of anything that might stand in the way of release. It was finished. Jesus was dead. As we poured out our grief, some of the Roman soldiers who had been moved by Jesus' love drew toward us, knelt on the ground and offered their own prayers. I, in turn, was moved by their compassion and in awe over the ability of Jesus' love to transcend even the perceived separations of culture, belief and rank. Lazarus, Martha, Judas, Nicodemus, Joanna and Mary's brother Joseph who had joined them after the noon hour soon joined us at the top of the hill. After a time, the commanding officer came and said, "We must take him down from the cross so you have time to entomb him before the sun sets." We nodded in our assent.

We stood in silence as the soldiers worked together to remove Jesus from the instrument of his torture and death. They removed the spikes from his feet, and then lowered the crossbar as Joseph, Lazarus, Nicodemus, Judas and John bore the weight of his lifeless body. They laid him out on the ground as they removed the spikes from his wrists and the crown of thorns from his head. The men gathered about Jesus' lifeless body as Mother Mary and I laid out the red cloak – the only thing we had in which to wrap his body. As they laid his body upon the cloak, I fell upon him, wrapping myself around his lifeless body. I held him to my heart as I cried and I rocked him as I would a child. My heart was broken, my soul torn in two. But as I held him to me, I was more and more certain that this body had been just a shell and that my beloved, no longer dwelled within it. And I heard my beloved's voice as I had all those many times before, "Mary, do not be afraid. I am with you always, even to the end of time." These words gave me the strength I needed to release his body. I stepped back and allowed the men to gather him up to be carried to the place of his entombment.

During the evening and into the morning, Joseph had accomplished the preparations for Jesus' burial. First he returned to Bethany to retrieve the burial nard that had been set aside for Martha's dowry, along with the burial cloths that were all housed in the wedding chest beneath her bed. He located a humble tomb near Jerusalem since their family tomb was several days' journey to Capernaum.

The tomb he had procured was in the potter's field just outside the city walls in the hillside caves usually reserved for the poor. We took up Jesus' beaten, broken and lifeless body and walked in procession the short distance to the potter's field intoning the Kaddish, the Hebrew song of mourning. Three Roman soldiers followed us at a respectful distance, having been ordered to see that Jesus was properly buried and to stand guard at the tomb until three days had passed. The High Priests wanted to make sure that no one was able to fake a resurrection, thereby confirming Jesus' prediction that he would be raised from the dead. We arrived at the tomb, a small cave hollowed out in the limestone. The space was large enough for us to enter and stand upright. The men lay Jesus upon the floor of the cave while Mother Mary and I prepared the burial cloths. The burial cloths were strips of linen which we first covered in the burial nard – a mixture of resin, oils and spices which were to mask the stench of death while deterring insects, vermin and other animals from feasting on our dead. We soaked each strip and carefully bound his body from foot to head. A separate cloth was used for the head which we first covered in nard, then draped over his face from neck to crown, then over the back of his head to his shoulders. This was wrapped in strips of linen as the rest of the body had been. After his body was anointed and bound, we said our final prayers, our individual goodbyes and departed the tomb.

I waited outside the tomb as John, Lazarus, Nicodemus, Joseph and Judas, along with three of the Roman soldiers rolled the stone in front of the tomb. Mary, Martha, Salome and I held each other as we waited. After the tomb was safely sealed, the men returned to us, John holding in his arms, Jesus' scarlet cloak. He came toward me and gently laid it into my arms. I wept at his thoughtful generosity. We said our goodbyes as Mary, Judas, Joseph and John turned toward Jerusalem to deliver the news to the Galilean disciples waiting in the Upper Room. Lazarus, Salome, Martha and I turned toward the road to Bethany. As we turned toward home, I heard my beloved's voice for what I was sure would be the final time, "Mary I am with you always, even unto the end of time." This time, I found no comfort in these words, only the finality of death.

PART THREE

CHAPTER TWENTY-ONE

While Jesus had done his best to prepare me for what lay ahead, seeing his broken, beaten body hanging on the cross cleaved my heart in two. The man I loved beyond all else lay dead. He was gone. As the stone fell before the entrance to the tomb, a strange sense of finality filled my being. It is finished. Never again would I see my beloved. Never would I hear his strong, loving voice. Never again would I behold the curl of his hair, nor the twinkle in his chameleon eyes that seemed to carry within them the entire world. Never again would I feel the tremor of my heart when his skin brushed against mine or the peaceful calm of his serene presence as he sat beside me in prayer. The terror and inexplicable grief that had pierced my heart was replaced by a cold nothingness. I felt neither joy, nor sorrow, anger nor contentment. I felt nothing but the cold, stark barrenness of the tomb where my beloved's dead body now lay.

After the final refrain of the Kaddish, we returned the two miles to Bethany, to the house of Lazarus, in silence. Too aggrieved to partake of the Sabbath meal, we retreated to our separate quarters in silence.

On the morning after the Sabbath, I awoke before dawn in the same way that I had every day after Jesus healed me and raised me from the death in which I had existed. Upon waking, I expected to feel nothing but the numbness of the days past. I expected to desire nothing but to roll over and return to the world of sleep. Instead, I felt the urge to resume my ordinary routine of morning meditation in the garden. I arose and proceeded into the garden to the bench I had shared with Jesus every morning for the past three years. I approached the bench and lovingly ran my hand over its marble seat recalling what Jesus and I had shared in this sacred space. The grief of this loss suddenly overtook me and I collapsed on the ground as my tears splattered over our bench.

As I knelt beside the bench weeping with head in hands, I felt a faint shift in the air around me. I lifted my head slightly to see if perhaps Lazarus had come out to join me. As I looked up, my heart leaped into my throat and ceased beating. My beloved Jesus stood there before me. I rubbed my eyes to make sure it was not some trick of the rising sun, but there he was as real as he had been all those past times in prayer and even more so, he stood before me in flesh and blood.

I stood and reached out to embrace him, to feel his skin on my cheek, and he opened his arms to return my embrace. We had held each other for but a moment, when Jesus gently pulled away. He took my face in his hands, lightly kissed me on the lips and said, "Mary, I am with you always, even until the end of time and it is time for you to come into your own power, to embrace your own Christhood. In this, I must ascend. And, you must not cling to me so that you too may rise. You must go to my brothers in Jerusalem to let them know I have risen and you must explain to them its meaning." With that he kissed me again on the mouth. "Mary, be empowered in the flame of the Shekinah, God's Holy Spirit." He departed from my sight as quickly and as silently as he had arrived.

I stood there in silent wonder. Even death had no power over my beloved. As sure as he had been here just one week ago, he stood before me again. I felt his touch, the brush of his lips on mine, the comfort of his embrace. Just as suddenly, he was gone. I inhaled deeply in the hopes of comprehending this experience and the cock crowed. I remembered Simon's denial of Jesus and was provoked by Jesus' words, "Go to my brothers in Jerusalem." I ran into the house to be greeted by Martha, Salome and Lazarus' sleepy faces. "I have seen the Lord. He is risen just as he said he would." I ran to each of them in turn, took their hands in mine, and looked into their eyes, "It is true. He has conquered death. He came to me in the garden. He is risen!" As I relayed the message to their open minds and hearts, they were able to see the truth as I had witnessed it. As a group we embraced in celebration. "We must go to Jerusalem! Jesus instructed me to tell his brothers there that he has been raised from the dead." We immediately departed for Jerusalem where we knew the Galilean disciples stayed in hiding.

CHAPTER TWENTY-TWO

We hastened toward Jerusalem with a newfound zeal. Freed of the depression of loss, we were now filled with a new hope, a new purpose. Jesus had conquered death. We did not yet fully understand the implications of this accomplishment, but we knew we were now witnesses to the truth Jesus had prophesied. A new openness of heart had settled upon us and our eyes were open in a different way. The sun shone brighter, the colors of the earth glowed in vivid shades of vermillion, ochre and umber. The sky expanded into an endless cerulean clarity and music danced in the air. I personally felt awakened as currents of energy pulsated through my body. Every nerve of my body was charged and alive with excitement.

We arrived at the gates of the city and easily passed the guard's inspection. Lazarus, who knew the twists and turns of the city streets, acted as our guide to the Upper Room. We came to the building which housed the Upper Room, entered the lower foyer, ascended the stairs and knocked on the door. At that we heard the tentative steps of someone coming down the hall. Philip cautiously opened the door. His gentle voice interrupted my thoughts. "Thank goodness," he exclaimed, "We were afraid the soldiers had discovered us after all. Family of Lazarus, what brings you here?"

"Jesus has conquered death. He is risen from the dead. He came to me to announce the good news as I arose for prayer the morning!" I excitedly replied.

A new look of hopefulness lit up Philip's eyes. "Is it true? Is this really how you saw it Mary? Was he there with you in flesh and blood?"

"Yes Philip, Jesus came to me in the garden. I was able to touch him, to feel his skin, to stroke his hair. He spoke with me as he had for these past three years. He embraced me and healed me of my grief. He is alive."

"Where is he now?" Philip inquired.

"As much as he suddenly appeared to me in body and blood, he just as quickly departed from my sight. It seems the constraints of the natural world no longer apply to him. I do not understand it myself, but that is how I experienced it."

"We must tell the others," Philip invited.

Philip stepped aside and bid us enter. We entered the room to be greeted by the terrified and grief stricken faces of our Galilean brothers. The light that I had been feeling after being visited by our Lord began to dim as I surveyed the faces of these men. I took a moment to receive the thoughts and feelings of our brothers. They feared for their own lives as known followers of Jesus. They felt shame for having abandoned our Lord to die – too afraid for their own lives to accompany him to his trial or on the journey to his death. They felt betrayed. The man they had called their Messiah had been tried and executed as a common criminal. Most importantly, they were filled with grief. The man they had come to love and to whom they had given their lives was now dead. I felt sadness for our brothers and uttered a silent prayer of healing for their broken hearts and battered spirits.

Simon pushed his way through the group and was the first to speak, "What are you doing here woman? Do you come to taunt us for our cowardice?"

"Brother Simon, fear not our judgment or reproach. We come to share with you the great news. Jesus lives and has conquered death."

Simon shook his head and crossed his arms. He waved us off, "Away from us with your lies. Jesus is dead and our hopes along with him. Be gone from here and leave us to mourn."

"Simon. Cephas," I gently added as I reached out to touch his shoulder, "It is true, Jesus lives. He is risen from the dead. He tasted death and conquered its grip and has been as present to me, as you are to me this moment. Allow your heart to be opened so that you too can receive the good news."

He shot back. "I will not believe that our Lord lives until I see his empty tomb."

"Then let us go to the tomb and witness the miracle that has taken place in our midst!" I enthusiastically invited.

The Galilean disciples looked at each other with doubtful and questioning eyes. Who would dare to leave the perceived safety of the Upper Room and venture to Jesus' tomb to see if what we told them was true? Boldly indignant, Simon threw down his arms in disgust, "Fine, I will go."

With that, our small group, Simon, Lazarus, Martha, Salome and I departed the Upper Room and wound our way back through the labyrinth of the Jerusalem streets, outside the city gates, down to the limestone caves and to the tomb Joseph had secured for Jesus' broken body. As we approached the hillside, we came upon two sleeping soldiers. Startled at our approach, and with spears held aloft, they inquired about our business.

"We come to pay our respects at the tomb of Jesus our brother who was killed three days ago," Lazarus replied.

The soldiers looked to each other and nodded their consent. Lowering their spears, they allowed us to pass. They turned to watch us approach the tomb as the entire group, including the soldiers, uttered a collective gasp. The stone that had been placed with great difficulty in front of the tomb had now been rolled away. The soldiers ran to the tomb to look inside. "There is nobody there!" they exclaimed. Too shocked to adhere to their duties, the soldiers allowed us to pass. We rushed into the tomb and discovered it to be as the soldiers had said. The body of Jesus was no longer in the place where we had laid him. All that remained were the cloths with which we had covered his body. The face cloth had been neatly folded and set over to the side. I went over to the burial cloths and gently lifted the facial cloth and tucked it inside my robes. As we stood there in silent shock, the soldiers argued in the corner about who had fallen asleep and who let someone come by to open the tomb and steal the body. Of course I knew better and simply allowed their arguing to keep them from noticing our presence. Simon began pacing and stomping around. "How could this have happened? That stone could not have been moved by a single man. Where is Jesus' body?"

"Simon, it is as I told you. Jesus is risen. He is no longer here. He has conquered death," I explained.

Simon shook his head in refusal and walked over to the soldiers accusingly. "How could you let someone steal the body of this man? How did you let someone inside?"

"Sir, we did nothing of the sort. We were here

209

all night. Even if we had fallen asleep, no one would have been able to get by us, roll away the stone and steal the body without us knowing. We simply do not understand," was the guards' reply.

I took this as an opportunity to share our Lord's love. "This was the tomb of Jesus bar Joseph," I instructed the guards. "He came to teach us of love and to remind us of the powerlessness of death. He was crucified on a cross yet now he lives. I have seen him with my own eyes and felt him with my own hands. He has conquered death." The soldiers simply shrugged their shoulders in confusion.

Simon still shook his head in confused resistance. Lazarus broke in with compassion, "Simon, we will not figure this out standing here. Let us return to Jerusalem where we can share this with the other disciples and see what they might make of it all."

We returned to Jerusalem. With Simon and his doubt leading the way, the journey was slow and less hopeful than the journey we had begun that morning. We returned to the Upper Room and shared the news with those who awaited our return. Upon hearing of the empty tomb, the room broke out into heated discussion and disagreement, with the house of Lazarus, Judas, Joseph, Mary and John determined believers, Philip, Nathaniel and James were undecided and the rest simply refused to believe. Thomas stated the sentiments of this group, "I will not believe that the Lord lives until he stands before me and I can place my hands into his wounds." At that proclamation of doubt, Jesus suddenly appeared in the midst of the arguing group. "Oh ye of little faith. I send Mary, the one with eyes to see and a heart fully open to the love of God within her, to tell you of the resurrection, and still you doubt. You see the empty tomb and still you refuse to believe." Jesus held out his hands, his wrists still marred by the wounds of his crucifixion. "Go ahead Thomas place your hands into my wounds and into my side as well." Thomas fell prostrate on the ground sobbing. "Forgive me Lord for my unbelief." The rest of the disciples followed suit. All, that is, except for Simon. He retreated to the back of the room and fell hard against a chair. He bowed down his head in shame and let loose tears of regret. Jesus approached Simon, gently placed his hand on his shoulder, "Simon, there is nothing to forgive. It is your stony heart that prevented your belief. Will you allow the love of God to heal you, restoring your heart to a heart of flesh?" Simon nodded his silent assent. Jesus placed both hands on Simon's shoulders and thus allowed God's healing love to move through him, relieving Simon of his stony heart. I wept in gratitude for Simon's openness to God's love. Sadly, it would not last.

Jesus invited us to recline as he sat among us and began to reiterate all he had taught about his death and the promise of resurrection. He reminded us that death is merely an illusion and that our physical death frees our Spirit, our true nature, to return to the full awareness of its Oneness with God. Death is a door to freedom, but not at the expense of the human journey. The purpose of this journey is to be human and with that comes suffering, but God promised a remedy to that suffering through remembrance of the love of God, and the love that is our true nature. If we can attain recollection of this truth while still in the body, we are able to transcend the suffering of the human condition – not to eradicate this suffering, but to move through it to God's eternal promise of new life. Jesus had accomplished this goal. It was his firm belief in this truth that allowed him to bring healing

211

into the world and it was this belief that allowed him to transcend physical death. "What I have done, you also shall do. And even more than this," was his expectation of us all.

I found myself in a state of wonder as I observed the transformation that was beginning to take place in the Galilean disciples. Their attachment to the idea of Jesus as savior from Rome had clouded their ability to see the truth. They had interpreted Jesus' teachings through this distorted lens and were therefore unable to see the deeper truth in his parables and lessons. But, the miracle of the resurrection had opened their eyes. The fear, shame and grief that had previously permeated the room were now transformed to a hopeful excitement. As the sun began to set on this momentous day, Jesus stood to bid his adieu. "No Master, do not go," was Simon's desperate plea. "Simon, do not cling to me. I must return to Abwoon and you must continue the work that I have begun." With that Jesus departed from our sight. The house of Lazarus then bid our Galilean brothers, Mother Mary, Joseph and John a good night as we made our way home.

Chapter
Twenty-three

The immediate weeks following the resurrection of our Lord became for us a time of retreat and contemplation. The house of Lazarus settled into a reflective, quiet routine. I awoke each day for my morning meditation and discovered that Martha, Lazarus and Salome too had embraced a morning discipline. Respectful of our individual needs for private time with Abwoon, we carved out our own meditative sanctuaries. I maintained my garden retreat, Martha retired to a cushion near the hearth, Salome carved out a rooftop sanctuary and Lazarus, always a man of the outdoors, took to walking the land surrounding our property. In addition to our private meditation time, we gathered as a group for meditation, reflection and discussion. We shared with each other personal experiences of Jesus and our memories of his teachings and how we now understood them. This time of group meditation was always followed by a simple, nourishing meal. We remembered the way in which Jesus had fed the multitude and we recalled the many wondrous meals we shared with our Lord.

Rabbi Nicodemus was the first of our companions that Lazarus told about the resurrection of Jesus upon our return from Jerusalem. He and Joanna soon joined our small family group as we gathered in prayer. The men and women who had gathered with us while Jesus still lived also began to join our daily gatherings. This was a dynamic group with some able to accept the truth of the resurrection while others, those who had been attached to the interpretation of Jesus as their warrior king, flat out refused and ceased visiting.

On the second morning after the physical appearance of our Lord before the Galilean disciples, I arose from sleep and entered the garden for my daily meditation. As I intoned the sacred name of Abwoon and began to settle into the Divine Presence, the air around me took on a sudden change. My closed eyes filled with a warm and brilliant light and the air was charged with energy. A sweet aroma surrounded me – a mixture of sandalwood, frankincense and myrrh. I slowly opened my eyes and standing before me was my beloved – in flesh and blood as he had appeared two days before. I leaped up to embrace him. Jesus returned the embrace and passionately kissed me on the lips. As we kissed, I found myself drawn to thoughts of our marriage bed and for just a moment desired to continue where we had left off, but at the same time, there was something inside of me that suggested this could not be so. While Jesus had transcended death and now stood before me, presumably in physical form, the intimacies that we had shared were somehow no longer possible. I thought I might feel regret or longing in this awareness, but instead, I felt only an acceptance of it. I wondered at the truth of the resurrection, what it might mean and how it was possible.

"Jesus, how is it that you can be with me today, in this way? I saw your lifeless, broken and battered body. I was there when we lay you in the tomb. You were dead and

214

yet now you are here as you were with us twice on the day of resurrection. How is it that you can now stand before me, presumably exactly as you had stood before me before your death?"

"Mary, this mystery cannot be explained in human terms. It is by your faith that you are able to perceive me in this way. The truth of the universe lies beyond physical form and perceived structure. It is light and love that we are made of, momentarily gathered together in the form of flesh and blood. When the fullness of these truths is realized, the power of flesh is no longer superior to the power of light. In this state, physical death is but an illusion, a change in form. In my death, the fullness of my Spirit was released from physical confinement. It is my Spirit that temporarily gathers together as form so as to be seen. Thus it is that I may be present to you in body and blood. But Mary, do not cling to me in this form for this is but temporary and I must eventually return to Abwoon in wholeness."

"Lord, I am grateful for whatever time you may be present to me in body and blood. For I now understand your words, 'I shall be with you always, even until the end of time.'"

"Mary, in the next several weeks, I would like to join you in your morning prayer. I have much to teach you that could not be taught until your eyes were open to see the resurrection."

"Oh Jesus, I would be honored and grateful to learn. My hunger to learn has only grown stronger with your passing."

In the coming days, Jesus came to me during my morning prayer and broke open a whole new layer of truths that I had been previously unable to receive. He

215

began by helping me to more fully understand the truth of our Oneness with God – that the purpose of the human experience is for God to express and to experience God's self in all the infinite ways that are possible not only through the human condition, but through all acts and expressions of creation. Jesus taught me that our origin is in God and that before the human experience, all we knew was the love, joy and bliss of Oneness with God. In order to know God even more fully and for God to experience even more of God's infinite nature, the temporary perception of separation from God was created and became the human condition. In this perceived separation from God, we experience fear and this fear manifests itself in seven identifiable fears:

- The fear of lack – that there is not enough and that our needs will not be met.
- The fear that we are not uniquely gifted to reveal God in the world.
- The fear that we are not free to be who God has created us to be.
- The fear that we are not loved.
- The fear that we are not free to express our truth.
- The fear that we do not know our truth, our path, or destination.
- The fear that we were alone or have been abandoned by God.

I learned that these seven fears were acted out through seven behavioral compulsions – what has now come to be known as the seven deadly sins:

- Gluttony
- Lust
- Wrath
- Envy

216

- Greed
- Sloth
- Pride

As I came to understand the connection between our deeper spiritual fears and their resulting compulsions, I asked how these could be healed. Jesus answered by revealing to me how all of the parables, stories, healings that he had shared and facilitated somehow revealed the ways in which we could transcend these fears through what Jesus referred to as the seven sacred truths:

- All of our needs are abundantly met in this moment by our loving Abwoon.
- Each of us is uniquely gifted to reveal God's love in the world and are called to do so.
- There is nothing outside of us that can keep us from living and being the person that God has made us to be and wishes to be through us.
- We are one with God in love, and therefore our very nature is love. Love is not something to be earned, neither can it be taken away.
- Expressing our truth shall set us free.
- We are one with the mind of God which seeks to reveal our truth, our purpose and our path in the way and the time that is in our highest good.
- We are one with God.

Each of these truths leads to the ultimate healing which comes about through the recollection of our Oneness with God. Jesus showed me the many pathways through which we could come to be healed of this perception of separation from God and be restored to the awareness of Oneness and love. He showed me the energy healing practices of the East that help to facilitate this healing, he demonstrated how the seven phrases

217

of the prayer that has come to be known as "the Lord's Prayer" can be used as a tool for healing. Jesus also reminded me of how the forbidden name, YHWH, is, in fact, a profound tool for healing and that in uttering the forbidden sounds, darkness gives way to light. He taught me that it was never Abwoon's intent that this name be forbidden, but that it be revealed to all so that they could remember the freedom of God's love. It was the priests who had forbidden the utterance of God's Holy name so that they could keep the people in fear and remain in their own place of power.

Jesus showed me how every human journey eventually leads to the healing of this perceived separation from God and that all of humanity would one day embrace the full recollection of their Oneness with God – if not in this life, perhaps the next. Jesus showed me that the psalmist was right in saying that in God "darkness and light are but one," for what we perceive as evil and darkness is simply that which has not yet remembered the love that is their truest nature. Jesus taught me that it is in this moment, when that remembrance has not yet occurred for someone, that we are called to exercise patience and compassion while they struggle to remember this truth. And now I understood for the first time the truth that Jesus promised would set us free – the truth of our Oneness with God.

During these weeks of private instruction, I withdrew from my communal time with Lazarus, Salome, Martha and the people of the village so that I could receive these teachings and fully absorb them into my consciousness. After the sixth week, I began to feel as if my time with Jesus was drawing to an end, a feeling confirmed when Jesus revealed that it was time for him to ascend to Abwoon and return fully to the Oneness so that he could be even more present to me and to others who longed to receive these teachings.

Although I knew this imminent departure and full return to Abwoon must be so, my heart sank at the thought of losing him again. And even though I had come to enjoy this time of instruction, it was his physical presence I would miss the most.

As tears began to flow from my eyes, Jesus reached out to touch my cheek and reminded me, "Mary, do not be sorrowful, I will be with you always, even until the end of time." The energy of comforting love flowed from Jesus' hand into me, enveloping me in peace and restoring my hope. I sighed in resignation and acceptance of what must be. I wrapped my arms around Jesus and held him until we both surrendered even more completely than I thought possible to the path that Abwoon knew to be in our highest good. We slowly released our embrace and in a moment's breath, Jesus was gone and I stood alone in the garden.

I reclined upon the bench that Jesus and I had shared so many times and pondered all that had been and all that was yet to be. I offered a silent prayer of gratitude along with my own request to Abwoon for the strength and courage I would need to bear the absence of my beloved and to carry on his mission in his stead.

CHAPTER
TWENTY-FOUR

It was the fiftieth day since Jesus had been raised from the dead and our household was preparing to celebrate the Jewish feast of Shavu'ot, commemorating the day the Lord gave Moses the Law on Mount Sinai. As was customary, we were preparing milk and cheeses for the evening meal. The sun was just beginning to set and Martha had begun to light the candles for Shavu'ot. As the first candle took flame, I felt a shift in the air around me. I had the sensation of the earth vibrating beneath my feet and I felt an energy like that of fire moving up through my legs, into my belly, up through my solar plexus, heart, throat and finally, forehead, where the force of its gathering strength and power suddenly exploded into flames of light out of the top of my head. This energy coursed through my body, purifying and empowering me. It emboldened me with a love greater than I had ever known, and it radiated from my being in all directions. The sensation of this energy continued for several minutes and slowly calmed. What remained was an overwhelming and overpowering love that opened my eyes to see the world through an entirely new light. Everything around me glowed with the power of this love and I suddenly saw the Presence of the Divine in everything. The earth had

220

been made new….and I along with it.

As I took in the miracle of this experience, Lazarus and Salome burst into the kitchen.

"Martha, Mary, did you feel that? What happened? Everything has been transformed!"

I paused in silence and trying to grasp what had just taken place. It was then that I heard my beloved's voice, "Mary, you have all just received the gift of my Holy Spirit. From this point forward, we are One. What man has separated, Abwoon has restored to Oneness." I repeated these words to Lazarus, Martha and Salome. We sat in stunned silence, each of us coming to grips with the power and potential in this precious gift and what it might mean for our mission. So deep in thought were we that we ate our Shavu'ot meal in silence and after cleaning up, retired to our respective private quarters, as we allowed what would later come to be known as the Pentecost experience, to take root within us.

The next morning, I returned to my morning prayer, renewed, refreshed and restored in my belief in Oneness with my beloved and his message. We were one and there was nothing that could change that. Through the miracle of the Pentecost, Jesus was not only One with me, but with all those open to their own Christed presence.

While I remained in prayer, the bell at the garden gate rang. I heard Martha get up from her place of prayer near the hearth to see who it might be. A few moments later, I heard her re-enter and I heard the voices of Mother Mary, John and Judas with her. I raced from my bench in the garden, and joined them in the kitchen, where I found Lazarus and Salome, Mother Mary, Judas and John, who had all come to tell us that in Jerusalem, while hiding in the Upper Room, a strange occurrence had taken place.

They went on to describe exactly what Lazarus, Martha, Salome and I had experienced, except that Simon seemed to have an experience that was unique to all of us.

Immediately after the disciples received the gift of Jesus' Holy Spirit, Simon had gone mad, proclaiming in the streets of Jerusalem that Jesus had been the Messiah, and that the Jews had killed him, and that he, Simon, had been appointed as the conduit through which they could receive the forgiveness of their sins. He also claimed that they needed to be baptized by him and that if they were baptized, they would receive not only forgiveness, but the gift of Jesus' Holy Spirit, as well. I was confused by what Simon was proclaiming in the streets of Jerusalem because this was not the message that Jesus had revealed to us. Jesus had told us time and time again not to get hung up on the idea of him as a Messiah to be worshipped, and certainly not as the warrior king to which some of the Jews had become attached. Instead, he wanted us to be attentive to the truth that he knew so well – that our original state is that of love through our Oneness with God. Simon's message seemed a distortion of what we had learned from Jesus.

Not wanting to be tempted by judgment, I brought this quandary to my heart. After a few moments of silent prayer, I heard Jesus' voice in my mind, "Mary, some will find their Oneness with God through the path that you and the House of Lazarus have embraced – a path of contemplation and prayer. Others will experience Oneness with God through baptism and other rituals. Some will find it through active worship. And still others through acts of service. All paths lead to God. Simon has his own unique gifts and will lead people in his own way." With that, I let go of my confusion and of the temptation

222

to believing there was only one path to God.

As we continued our ministry in Bethany, Judas travelled back and forth with news from Jerusalem. As Mother Mary, Judas and John shared their version of Jesus' message, and Simon proclaimed the forgiveness of sin and the coming of Jesus' Holy Spirit through baptism, Jesus' brother, James, began to preach another message all together. I heard he had been struck by an experience had by one of the other disciples, Cleopas, on the day that Jesus had been resurrected. Cleopas reported that he and his wife had encountered a man, while journeying toward Emmaus, who was similar in appearance to Jesus – so similar, in fact, that they proclaimed him to be Jesus – and that this was confirmed when they sat down to break bread with him. When they returned to the Galilean disciples with this tale, James became convinced that it was in the Passover meal, specifically, the breaking of the bread and the sharing of the third cup that one was able to receive Jesus' Spirit. As I reflected on this, I realized the profound truth that Jesus could be experienced in any way that we were open to receiving him – in the breaking of the bread, the sharing of the cup, in the waters of baptism and the oils of anointing (as I had poignantly experienced with my beloved).

As time went on, however, division grew among the Galilean disciples. Simon gathered around himself those disciples who had already been pre-disposed to placing Jesus in the role of a Messiah to be worshipped, eventually forgetting the very human journey that allowed Jesus to transcend the false perception of separation from God and to rediscover his original nature as love. As a result, those who found themselves drawn to Simon tended to put Jesus on a pedestal – seeing him as only Divine and

223

never human – and thereby unattainable. As such, in their own personal journeys, they were often not interested in taking responsibility for their own spiritual growth and development and became vulnerable to their own unhealed wounds, specifically the shame they carried, like Simon, for having denied Jesus at the time of his trial and crucifixion. Unable to forgive themselves for their betrayal, they instead projected their guilt onto the Jewish and Roman authorities, becoming increasingly anti-Roman and anti-Semitic.

Simon, in turn, had projected his personal guilt upon Judas and began spreading a distortion of the truth of the events that transpired in the Garden of Gethsemane. In Simon's version, Judas was the one who had betrayed Jesus by bringing the temple guards to the garden, pointing Jesus out to them and getting paid thirty pieces of silver for his betrayal. I was deeply saddened when I heard of these lies, as Judas had never been anything other than a good and faithful servant of Jesus' message. As these stories spread about Judas, he drew further and further away from the Jerusalem brothers and spent more and more time in the house of Lazarus, until he eventually came to live with us as one of our own.

James, filled with shame over his own betrayal of his brother, could not bear to maintain a personal relationship with Jesus as the Christ; at the same time, however, he could not deny that his brother had died and been raised from the dead. James found that in the celebration of the paschal meal, he was able to keep an arm's length distance between himself and Christ while still honoring the truth of Jesus' crucifixion and the miracle of the resurrection. James initiated the ritual of the sacred meal and began to preach to those who gathered for the meal as they broke bread and shared the cup among them. Many came to know Jesus in the breaking of the bread and the sharing of the cup, but sadly, many maintained the same arm's length distance modeled by James.

Mother Mary, Judas and John reported that only a few were open to contemplation as a path through which they could receive Jesus' teachings.

As the three separate groups in Jerusalem grew in their division, our community in Bethany grew in wholeness. We gathered daily for meditation and prayer and to explore and integrate Jesus' teachings – especially those he had imparted to me during those times of private instruction. We discovered a peaceful ease within the routine of prayer, learning, reflection and sharing. Even the day-to-day tasks of running a business and a home took on a whole new light of joyful fulfillment. Those drawn to our home found within it a model of contentment and joy that Jesus had promised would come to those who placed Abwoon at the center of their hearts. Even in moments of conflict, we found an ease and effortlessness in their peaceful resolution. When it came to big decisions – how to deal with the increasing numbers, how to care for those in the community suffering from sickness or lack of resources – we found decisions most effective when first brought to prayer and arrived at through a process of discussion. No decisions were made until a consensus had been reached within the group. Unlike the Jewish and Roman hierarchical and patriarchal models to which we had grown accustomed, we found that our group organically became collaborative and supportive, and that women and men worked best together when regarded as unique, but equal. And, while Lazarus, Martha and I might have been looked upon as leaders, we found that when empowered to do so, all within our community eventually discovered their own unique giftedness and offered these gifts freely and generously for the good of the whole group. Some were called to teach, others to heal; some to complete the day-to-day tasks of planting, nurturing and harvesting, others to feed the community; and some to manage the financial resources. Each and every person within the community shared their gifts in common and for the good of the whole. Our existence became filled with joy; peaceful and contented.

CHAPTER TWENTY-FIVE

We spent many months living in the peace and harmony of "the new world" as Jesus had described it to me. The love that my brother, sisters (for I now considered Salome to be my sister) and I had come to know through Jesus spilled out of us and drew people toward us. The joyful delight we found deepening within us seemed to radiate out of us, reminding others of what they too longed for in their lives. Our home quickly grew to overflowing in the number of men, women and children that found their way to our table and the word quickly spread to neighboring villages of the love that people would find in our home. We discovered that when one lives in the love that they are in God, the purpose of their life becomes effortless. Our mission in continuing Jesus' work of compassionate healing and teaching was a joy and was accomplished without striving. We found profound contentment in being and living the law of love.

One afternoon while enjoying a time set aside for our own family prayer while gathered around the outside dining table, our peace was interrupted by an urgent knocking at the garden gate. Lazarus went to investigate who sought our attention with such urgency. He quickly returned with Mother Mary, John and the Galilean disciple, Philip.

227

Mother Mary made the introduction, "Blessings house of Lazarus and community of Bethany. We bring greetings from Jerusalem and a request for your assistance. Here with us is brother, Philip, who wishes to share with you his concerns about how things are transpiring in Jerusalem among the Galilean community." Philip bowed toward each of us in a greeting of peace and began to speak.

"I have listened intently to the teachings of Simon, James and John along with Mother Mary and Judas. I have observed a growing gap of alliances and an increasing tension between these three markedly different interpretations of Jesus' teachings. And until now, I have encouraged my brothers to be of open mind and open heart and to seek the common message between the three. Instead, Simon grows more and more antagonistic and James increasingly withdrawn. In fact, James has taken to worshipping the bread he now proclaims to be the very body of his dead brother and is all but unreachable. Simon, on the other hand, with his antagonistic views against Rome and the Temple, is stirring up the people to avenge the death of their Lord. Their hunger for bloodshed is becoming a threat to the safety of any who claim to honor the teachings of Jesus – even those of us who seek harmony and peace among all people. I see a measure of truth in all three perspectives, but find myself resonating more and more clearly with the approach that Mother Mary, John and Judas have shared with us. Regretfully, it seems the other Galilean brothers have begun to close their minds to any perspective that had been supported by Judas due to Simon's conviction that Judas betrayed Jesus to the Roman soldiers. Thanks to Simon's poisonous tongue and denial of his own betrayal of our Lord, it seems these words cannot be fully received. I have heard from Mother Mary and John that you of the house of Lazarus, the community in Bethany, have found a way to live in peaceful harmony and have cultivated a community rooted in the love of Christ and empowered to give up its own selfish concerns for the good of the many. I am in awe over what they have reported to me, especially in light of what I have witnessed in Jerusalem – everything but harmony and peace. Would you believe women are not even welcome in Simon's community and James just ignores them all together?"

My brother Lazarus was the first to speak to Philip's concerns. "Brother Philip, we have heard of the conflicts in Jerusalem from your companions. We have held these conflicts in prayer in the hopes that Abwoon would illuminate a middle path. Your words suggest to me that you are instead seeking a more direct path of intervention?"

"What I was hoping," said Philip, "was that the Magdalene would honor the Jerusalem community with her presence – that she might share with the Galilean brethren the hidden teachings she has received directly from our Lord. Mother Mary and John have done their best to bring us these words, but as you can imagine, Simon and James are resistant at best and downright condemning at worst. I was hoping that if they could hear these words directly from the Magdalene, perhaps they might have a change of heart and hear the truth of these words."

"I am happy to accompany you to Jerusalem," I offered, "but I cannot promise that my words will have any effect on Simon or James. It seems they are called along a different path, but I am certainly willing to try if it helps to support peace among the divergent paths of the Jerusalem community."

Philips's shoulders relaxed and he breathed a sigh of relief as I assented to his request. "Mary," he inquired, "before we depart for Jerusalem, would you mind sharing with me these hidden teachings so that I may hear them first with my own heart before standing before the accusatory faces of Simon and James. I would like to hear the teachings for myself, unfettered by the distraction of their hostility." I nodded my consent and invited Philip to join us at table as I repeated for the sake of all those present the private teachings that Jesus had imparted on me in those weeks prior to his ascension.

After I finished sharing these teachings, I looked hard upon Philip and saw that as tears flowed down his cheeks, a new light of hope shone in his eyes. Philip took my hands in his and looked deeply into my eyes. "Thank you Mary. I now understand fully why you have been called Magdalene, the great tower, for you have not only the eyes to see and the ears to hear but a heart open to receive the fullness of Jesus' truth. We are truly blessed to have one such as you to carry on Jesus' teaching and healing. I believe that you will have the power to bring cohesion and unity to the Jerusalem brothers and that through this, we will have peace in Jerusalem." I listened to his words, but doubted that this would be so. I loved Simon and James and I knew that neither had yet found the fullness of their Oneness with God; that both still operated out of fear. I would not, however, deprive Philip of his hope for reconciliation among the Jerusalem brethren. And for his sake and for the sake of the others, I hoped that his faith would be rewarded.

The following morning, I departed with Philip and

journeyed by foot the two miles to Jerusalem. As we walked, I asked Philip to tell me his story and how he had come to be in Jesus' company among the Galilean brothers. Philip shared with me that he had grown up in the house of a scribe in the town of Bethsaida. As the son of a learned man, he had been taught to read and write from the time he was a young boy and had been schooled in Hebrew, Aramaic and Greek as well as Coptic, the written language of the Egyptians. He had been groomed to take over his father's business as scribe for the local synagogue and for the local merchants, businessmen, and peasants who might be in need of a written contract. It was through his father's business that he had come to know Simon and Andrew, fishermen who frequently utilized the services of Philip and his father in securing contracts with the Romans for fishing rights in the Sea of Galilee. One day, Simon and Andrew arrived at Philip and his father's shop with word of a preacher who had recently come into the area. It was John the Baptizer, who had come to preach of the repentance of sin and to offer baptism. Simon and Andrew had invited Philip to accompany them to the shore of the sea where John was preaching that evening Philip accompanied Simon and Andrew to the Sea of Galilee to hear John preach.

Philip was immediately struck by the power of this man. John, known as *the Baptizer,* was a rugged man who had spent the majority of his days in the desert in prayer and meditation. Unlike the quiet mystics that Philip had encountered in his work, John the Baptizer possessed an irresistible zeal. Philip recounted the awe he had felt as John stirred up the crowd into a repentant frenzy which drove them all to seek baptism. Although Philip watched as Andrew and Simon willingly complied with John's

231

invitation, he was somewhat reticent. A thoughtful and reasoning man, groomed for patience and attention to detail, he was not one to make rash or hasty decisions. He waited, watched and took in John's words, but was never called to accept John's baptism for the forgiveness of sins.

Philip remained content in this decision until one morning when Andrew and Simon burst into his shop and proclaimed, "We have seen the son of God." Again, Philip was skeptical. Son of God? What did that even mean? Simon and Andrew relayed to Philip what they had seen in their journey with the Baptizer. They had come to follow John's path along the Sea of Galilee and along the river Jordan, continuing their fishing trade along the way. They had been with John along the Jordan, south of the Galilean sea and had witnessed a miracle. A man called Jesus bar Joseph had come to be baptized by John. The entire crowd saw and heard the miracle that occurred as this man came forward to be bathed in water, as a voice from the heavens proclaimed, "You are my beloved son, with you I am well pleased." Jesus had arisen, visibly shaken, embraced John, and quickly departed. Forty-some days had passed and Jesus bar Joseph was now in Capernaum, preaching the word of God. "You must come and see him," urged Andrew. "This one is even more powerful than John the Baptizer. We think he may be the Messiah, the one who was foretold." Again, Philip was cautious, but he agreed to accompany the brothers to see this man Jesus. They arrived in the center of the village of Capernum and found a man preaching. Philip stood and listened to his words and found them inspiring to be sure, but weren't all preachers' words inspiring?

Just as Philip was about to turn to leave the crowd and return to his home, Jesus turned and looked straight at him. Something in Jesus' gaze held Philip transfixed. He stood in his place while Jesus began to speak, "thus says the Lord, I will remove from them their hearts of stone and I will place a new heart within them – a heart of flesh and in their hearts I will place my law. No longer will one have to be taught the law, for they will know it in their very hearts." Something in these words and in the way that Jesus continued to speak directly into Philip's eyes moved him. Philip felt something within him shift as if a veil of apathy that had kept him from discerning truth had been pierced through with a blinding white light and the solid boulder that had been resting in his chest was cracking open and his chest was filling with light; and, accompanying that light, an overwhelming feeling of love and peace. Philip felt every part of his being relax into this state of peace-filled love and he found himself smiling in joy and gazing at the world through a new set of eyes. Jesus approached him, placed his right index finger in the center of Philip's brow and the palm of his left hand on his chest and speaking to him directly said, "Philip, I see that you have not only ears to hear and eyes to see, but a heart open to love. Come with me."   Philip did not understand Jesus' words, but through the light in his mind and the trust in his heart, he knew that he had to follow this man. "I will gladly follow you if you can accept the gift of my service as scribe," Philip offered Jesus. To which Jesus replied an enthusiastic, "Yes." With an exchange of service agreed upon, Philip followed Jesus to his home in Capernaum where he studied and learned from this man who spoke of love.

Philip, unlike Simon or Andrew was not drawn to Jesus because he might be the Messiah who would rescue Israel from the clutches of Rome. Philip and his

233

father had found a comfortable existence under Roman occupation and as long as they could continue to put food on the table of their families, they were content to leave things alone. Instead, Philip found himself drawn to Jesus' message of love. He had found within Jesus' teachings a confirmation of the harmony that he and his father had found in the midst of Roman occupation. Philip heard Jesus teach about tolerance, acceptance and oneness. The Romans were not the enemy. The enemy, Philip now understood, were the inner fears that kept people from knowing the love that Jesus came to proclaim.

As Philip unfolded his story before me, I found in him a man of quiet resolve who had found peace and contentment in a world wrought with conflict. Even before meeting Jesus, he had found a way to live in peaceful contentment in the midst of Roman occupation, something that most Jews had failed to accomplish.

Philip escorted me through the city gates as my heart skipped a beat recalling the days of Jesus' trial and death. He led me through the meandering streets of Jerusalem until we arrived once again at the home that had been provided to the Galilean brothers through the generosity of Nicodemus. Philip led me up the stairs to the Upper Room, opened the door and ushered me in. As I entered the room, Simon, who had been sitting at table pondering his next street sermon, stood up in anger, "Why have you brought her here?" Simon sneered. "I have brought the Magdalene to us so that she may share with the Galilean brothers the secret teachings that Jesus imparted to her." "Secret teachings?" Simon stormed. "Why would Jesus, the Son of God and King of Heaven, impart secret teachings to a woman, especially this one, a whore?" I was saddened by the fear that had overtaken Simon to

234

cause him to respond in such a harsh and negative way. Levi (also called Matthew) stood up. "Simon, that was uncalled for. Just because Jesus loved her more than us, does not make her a whore. Set aside your petty jealousies and let the Magdalene speak." The other disciples echoed Levi's request. Outnumbered, Simon relented and invited Philip and me to sit and share with them Jesus' secret teachings.

I shared with the Galilean disciples all that Jesus had taught me in the time between the resurrection and his ascension. I spoke of the truth of Oneness and the love that we, are in Oneness with God. I spoke of the seven truths that reflect this Oneness. I also spoke of the false perception of separation that causes us to forget this Oneness and how this perceived separation causes us to know fear along with the seven compulsions that arise out of this fear; that it is this fear and its resulting compulsions that are the cause of disharmony, conflict and war within us and between human beings. I shared with them the remedies to these fears as Jesus had instructed me. Many of the disciples nodded their heads in agreement and understanding as I shared these teachings. Simon, however, sat with arms firmly clenched across his chest with a look of refusal on his face. James, on the other hand, sat with bread in hand, presumably in prayer, silent and oblivious to all that was going on around him. Inwardly, I shook my head in confusion over this strange change that had come over Jesus' own brother.

"These are strange and bizarre thoughts that you share with us Magdalene," Simon interrupted. "How did you receive these teachings?" "I received them through our Lord, Jesus, in the silent places in my heart while resting with him in prayer," I responded. "When did you receive

235

these teachings?" Simon inquired. "Between the days of Jesus' resurrection and ascension." I explained. Simon's face became smug. "Well, that explains it – hysterical ramblings of imagined visitations. I would imagine as much from a woman who allowed herself to be taken by a group of drunken men." I felt Simon's words like a dagger in my belly and I felt tears of not only personal shock and hurt but also of sadness for Simon's jealousy. When Philip looked over and saw my tears, he stood up and pounded his fist on the table in protest and in defense of me. "Simon that is enough! Mary was but a child when that happened and it was through no fault of her own. How dare you use that to hurt her or to taint her reputation! Jesus chose her to be his closest disciple for a reason and that reason is her openness of heart. Your heart is closed to Mary as a bearer of Jesus' message and your refusal of her insights will end up being your demise." With that, Philip took my hand, "Mary, we are leaving, it is obvious that we are not welcome here." The disciples sat in stunned silence as we departed.

As we left the Upper Room and made our way through the streets of Jerusalem, I wept. I wept for the hardness of heart of the Galilean brothers, especially for Simon and James. Jesus had been correct in giving Simon the name of Cephas – rock, I thought, – for that is what he was, an immovable boulder, firmly rooted in his own ideas of Jesus, and there was nothing that was going to convince him otherwise. As for James, he was sure to gather around himself others also marked with great zeal, but inclined to the worshipping of idols, for that is the relationship he had developed in his devotion of the bread. As judgment and condemnation gathered around me, Jesus' voice interrupted my thoughts, "Mary, do not

236

judge Simon and James or their disciples. Trust that
God is working the higher good in even that which you
perceive as idol worship or empty ritual. Everyone finds
their Oneness with God in their own way. Remember, all
paths lead to God." Humbled my own self-righteousness,
I continued the journey to Bethany in silence.

Chapter Twenty-six

When we returned to Bethany, we settled once again into the peaceful and harmonious lifestyle we had cultivated before Philip had come knocking at our door. We returned to our routine of daily personal and communal prayer and welcomed anyone that would come to join us. We also found our own rhythm of daily service. Lazarus continued the business of his vineyards and orchards and in the cultivating and selling of his precious oils. He resumed the travel that he had forsaken after Jesus' death. Martha, as before, took over the supervision of the household, orchards and vineyards in Lazarus' absence. Between these tasks, she took to the care and feeding of the sick and the hungry who found their way to our home. It seemed there was never an end to the sustenance at Martha's table. Many found healing and comfort through the loving nourishment that Martha so readily provided. No longer was she plagued by the fears that there would not be enough. I, on the other hand, found myself not only tending to my own prayer, but called upon to teach and counsel. Women and men from the community found their way into our home, seeking to know more about the teachings of Jesus and how to know the love that Jesus preached. Some came in groups and some came as individuals, seeking healing and comfort of their fears and from the wounds of their past. Judas and Salome found themselves drawn to the work of the earth. Between times of personal and communal prayer, they could be found tending the olive trees or pruning the grape vines. They fell into the work of the land and found in this an even greater depth of peace than what they had found even in silent contemplation. Mother Mary and John remained with us for several months, but eventually, Mary longed to return to her brother's home in Capernaum where she could enjoy the quiet of solitude. John, her youngest son and designated guardian returned to Capernaum with her.

Philip chose to remain with us and set about recording his recollections of Jesus' words. A man drawn to simplicity and concise thought, he condensed his recollections of Jesus' teachings into a series of short statements.

- For those who have eyes to see.
- Judge not, lest ye be judged.
- Love one another as I have loved you.
- Get up and walk.
- The truth shall set you free.
- Where the Spirit of the Lord is, there is freedom.
- Before pointing out the splinter in your brother's eye, remove the beam from your own eye.
- You need do nothing.
- Seek ye first the kingdom of God.
- When you pray, go into your inner room and pray in secret.

These were the statements that Philip began to embrace as his own spiritual path and in compiling this list, developed a moral code, not only for himself, but for others to follow. During this time, Philip also began to write his understanding of the teachings that I had shared

239

with him and began to develop his own understanding of Jesus' teachings. Philip frequently sought my company and counsel as he synthesized these teachings and allowed them to be integrated within him.

Our lives and our ministry continued to unfold and expand as those with ears to hear found our home. Those from the village whose hearts were moved by Jesus' message became our constant companions and travelers frequently found their way to our table. Lazarus shared the truth of love with the merchants and farmers with whom he did business when the Lord led him to do so. Martha continued to serve God at table, Judas and Salome through the earth and Philip through his writing. I continued to serve in the way that God had called me to: through attentive listening, teaching and counseling and through the laying on of hands. I came to understand that Abwoon had gifted me with the ability to hear the truth beyond the words and through this gift was able to lead many toward the healing of those hidden wounds within them so that they could more fully embrace the true self that sought to be made known. It was a busy, yet fruitful and fulfilling life. Two full years passed since the death and resurrection of our beloved and while I greatly missed his physical presence, he continued to be present with me in prayer as he promised he would be. While I had gained a measure of acceptance of this, I still longed to feel his arms around me and to rest in his embrace. Although I had fully embraced my Christed self, I was still human after all.

240

CHAPTER
TWENTY-SEVEN

While the life we led at the house of Lazarus unfolded in a harmonious and effortless way, the world outside of us grew more turbulent. Tensions between the Romans and the Judeans increased with the Zealots leading the charge. Riots both within the city of Jerusalem and in the surrounding territory became more common and travel became increasingly dangerous. As the tensions increased, the Pharisees' voices grew louder and their power increased as the people gravitated toward the message of perceived security in their literal interpretation of the law. As the Pharisees grew in power, the followers of Jesus who remained in Jerusalem found in them a worthy reflection of their own fears. To James and Simon, the Pharisees became the enemy. Simon, James and their respective followers spoke openly and sometimes violently against the Pharisees. As these tensions escalated, we sensed it would not bode well for the Jerusalem disciples. Confirmation of this came to me first in a dream and was validated by an unexpected night visitor.

It had been a fulfilling day of prayer, teaching, healing and sharing Jesus' message of love. As was typically the case after a rewarding day of ministry, I had easily fallen into a deep and peaceful sleep. Two hours past midnight, I was awakened out of a dead sleep with my heart pounding, fear coursing through my veins and sweat dripping from my brow. I breathed into the fear and eased my pounding heart with thoughts of love. As my mind and my body began to relax, the dream came back to me.

Stephen, one of Simon's followers was preaching in the temple courtyard. He was boldly proclaiming Jesus to have been the Messiah that the prophets had foretold and who had become the fulfillment of the Law. "The Law of Moses," Stephen proclaimed, "is null and void and the Pharisees now speak in vain." Stephen went on to make threats against the Pharisees for the way they had denied the Messiah and murdered the Son of God. Stephen attempted to incite a riot against the Pharisees and charged the audience to take the temple back for the chosen one, the Messiah who the Pharisees had murdered. The crowd, already filled with fear as a result of the rising tensions between the Romans and the Jews found Stephen's message to be the final straw. Stirred up in fear and frustrated by their feelings of powerlessness, the crowd turned on Stephen, picked up stones and killed him. As I recalled the dream image of Stephens bloody and lifeless body, I heard an urgent knocking at my bedroom door.

Lazarus burst through the door visibly shaken, with fear and worry on his face. "Come quickly, Nicodemus arrives with terrible news from Jerusalem. Brother Stephen has been stoned." I jumped up from my bed, quickly pulled a robe over my sleeping tunic and ran with Lazarus to the central dining room where everyone was gathered – Martha, Salome, Judas, Philip and now Nicodemus. "Is it true?" I asked. Nicodemus nodded a slow and grief-filled yes. "How did it happen and why?" Lazarus asked. Through frustrated tears, Nicodemus explained to my brothers and sisters, exactly what I had seen in my dream. Nicodemus went on to say that as a result of Stephen's stoning, all followers of Jesus were now in grave danger. Stephen's death had been the final straw for the Pharisees who saw Simon, James and their followers as an unnecessary distraction in an already tense political situation. As one of Nicodemus' friends in the temple had confided, a prohibition had been issued against anyone teaching or preaching the Jesus message, and that anyone caught doing so would be tried for blasphemy and would suffer the same fate as Stephen. "Jerusalem is no longer safe, and I suspect Bethany may not be safe for much longer," Nicodemus explained. "I also know," Nicodemus continued, "that Annas and Ciaphas will do everything in their power to make sure the Jesus movement is squashed. You have become too much of a threat to their power. Many of the other priests remain neutral on the subject, but with the Pharisees on one side of the debate and Jesus' followers on the other, they will side with the perceived security the Pharisees offer."

We all took our seat at table in stunned silence. We looked around the room that had become our home and our temple and wondered what this could mean. Martha broke our silence, "We must bring this to prayer and allow our Lord to comfort our fears and bring us guidance." Of course, this was what we must do. Philip immediately took her cue and began to intone the Aramaic prayer that Jesus had taught us. The gentle strains of his voice, combined with the power of those ancient phrases immediately drew me into a state of peace. As the peace of God enfolded me, I saw before me a vision. I saw Mother Mary and John on their journey to Capernaum and going on from there to a place unknown aboard one of Joseph's trading vessels. "Ephesus" is what I heard as their destination.

Next, I saw the Galilean disciples. After Stephen's stoning, it was decided that Simon, for his own safety should return to Galilee and make that the center of his ministry. James remained in Jerusalem as head of the community there and tried his best to placate the temple authorities, suggesting that it was Simon who was the problem and with Simon safely off in Galilee the temple had nothing to worry about. Trouble was always stirred up, however, when Simon returned from Galilee to confer with the Jerusalem community, so much so that Simon was eventually imprisoned. He somehow managed to escape and became something of a fugitive, traveling from village to village in the further reaches of the Roman Empire, preaching his own version of Jesus' message in opposition to the Judaism that Jesus had so devotedly practiced. The Jerusalem community would have been safe from temple scrutiny if it hadn't been for Simon's frequent return visits where he did nothing but stir up the people to anger and revolt. James became more and more frustrated with Simon's refusal to be of peace and eventually asked him not to return to Jerusalem.

Finally, I saw the course of my own life unfolding. As in the vision that Judas and I had previously shared, I saw Judas, myself, Lazarus, Martha, Salome and Philip as we journeyed along the desert road on our way to Egypt. We travelled through the vast expanse of the desert wilderness through which Moses had led his people and through which my own beloved, Jesus had traveled as a child with his parents and siblings. Passing the holy mountain on which Abwoon delivered the Law to Moses, we encountered the nomadic camps of the desert shepherds and found comfort. Finally, like beacons from the desert sands, rose the pyramids near the banks of the fertile landscape of the Nile river basin which marked the path of our journey. We continued our travels through the lush and fertile territory of the Nile delta, arriving in the rich and abundant, cosmopolitan city of Alexandria where we would establish a home. My vision stopped as we reached a low and humble home of whitewashed limestone with a strange symbol over the door that looked like a full moon held in between what could be hands or horns. As I looked upon this symbol, an ancient knowing entered my being as tears began to fall from my eyes.

I slowly opened my eyes and looked around our circle to see that all had tears in their eyes. We shared what we had seen in the midst of our prayer and as I expected, we had all experienced the same vision. After all had been shared, I sat in silence and pondered the ramifications of what we had seen. On one hand, it broke my heart to even consider departing my brother's home, the place where I had found refuge and healing and where I had found my first love in Jesus. I also knew, at least for the time being, that we would not be safe here, more importantly, we would not be free to continue Jesus' mission. My greater concern, however, was for Lazarus. How could he bear to leave behind the business that he had so carefully built; the relationships he had cultivated and the success that he had made for himself? As if in answer to my quandaries, I felt Lazarus reach over and lay his hand on mine. "Mary, it will be ok. I will leave the estate in the care of the men and women who have worked here and trust that Abwoon has more important things in store for the house of Lazarus. In truth, it has become a burden doing Jesus' work while still running a business. I will be relieved to be free of the business and pass it on to other capable hands. Besides, I've always wanted to visit the pyramids." And he winked at me.

We spent the next three days in prayerful preparation. Lazarus chose from among his workers, Benjamin, a kind and capable man. Lazarus invited Benjamin, along with his family to move into and care for the home, the vineyards and the olive groves. Lazarus chose from among the men who had traveled with him in his trading, Reuben, who would continue in Lazarus' stead. Both men were grateful for Lazarus' generosity and promised to find a way to share their abundance with us in our travels. Lazarus worked with Philip and Judas to prepare the provisions and the animals for travel. We would go by foot with an ass or two, a few goats and a cart to carry food and water for the journey. Judas, having made this journey before, determined that it would take us a full turning of the moon to reach his home city of Alexandria.

On the night before we were to leave, we shared our final meal in the house of Lazarus. While it was not the Sabbath, we treated it as if it were. Martha lit the candles and recited the requisite prayers. We enjoyed a hearty and nourishing meal in preparation for the journey ahead. There was a bittersweet feeling as we shared the meal. We grieved over having to leave our home and the life we had come to know. We grieved the hardness of heart that prevented those in power from being open to Jesus' message of love. We grieved for our Galilean brothers and the scrutiny they had called upon not only themselves but upon us as well. Mixed in with the grief, however, was a sense of anxious anticipation. We would be journeying to new lands and new people; a cosmopolitan city that Judas informed us was a melting pot of Greeks, Romans,

246

Jews and Egyptians. Judas' own father was Egyptian and I looked forward to learning more about their unique culture, religious beliefs and practices. As the light outside grew dim and night fell upon us, we reluctantly cleared the table, swept up the last of the crumbs and for the final time put away the dishes that would now be used by Benjamin and his family. Before retiring to our mutual rooms, we held hands and chanted the Aramaic prayer that Jesus had taught us:

Abwoon d'bwashmaya
Nethqadash shmakh
Teytey malkuthakh
Nehwey tzevyanach aykanna
d'bwashmaya aph b'arha
Hawvlan lachma d'sunqanan yaomana.
Washboqlan khauabyn (wakhtahayn)
Aykana daph khnan shbwoqan l'khayyabayn.
Wela tahlan l'nesyuna
Ela patzan min bisha
Metol dilakhie malhutha wahayla wateshbukhta
l'ahlam almin.
Ameyn.

O thou from whom the breath of life flows, and is present in all forms of vibration and light.
Your Divine presence lives within us.
Your counsel rules our lives, opening our intention for co-creation.
Your one desire then acts with ours, as it is in all light, so shall it be in all forms.
You grant what we need each day in bread and insight, sustenance and support for our growing lives.
You untie us from our own limiting actions as we untie

others from the strands we hold of theirs.
You free us from what holds us back from our true purpose,
ensuring that surface things do not delude us,
From you is born all ruling will, the power and life to do,
the song that beautifies all –
from age to age it renews.
These statements are the ground
from which all my actions grow.
Amen. *

We embraced with tears in our eyes, bid our final
farewells to the home we loved and retired to our rooms.
Before climbing into my bed for my final sleep, I sat in
prayerful meditation before Abwoon. "Abwoon," I prayed,
"I know that this is the path that you have ordained to
be in our highest good and for this I am grateful. Help
to keep us safe, and provide for all of us the ears to hear
and the eyes to see your truth as it is revealed before us.
We humbly offer ourselves as vessels through which your
love may be revealed in the world through the gift of our
beloved Jesus and his Holy Spirit. I trust that you will
bring to us those in search of this love and those called to
the path that you have revealed to us, and that the Spirit
of Jesus will accompany us all the days of our lives. Amen."

I slipped into bed, drew the cover over my shoulders
and quickly fell asleep. It was in dreaming that I
discovered the answer to my prayer. I saw myself walking
along a processional to a great and glorious temple that
stood before me. The temple was of hand-hewn marble
and stood far taller than even the temple of Jerusalem had
stood. I came to the temple and stood before the entrance
to its outer courtyard. I walked across the threshold into

* Douglas-Klotz, 1990

the outer courtyard. I felt drawn to continue through the courtyard to the temple gates. I walked up the twelve stairs that led from the courtyard to the gate of the inner temple. I came to the ornate doorway, gilded in gold and bedecked with jewels and reached out my hand to grasp the handle. Just as I was about to take the handle into my hand and open the door, it opened toward me. I stepped back and standing just inside was a tall and stately man – his head and face cleanly shaven with skin the same milky brown as Judas. He bore the white robes of a temple priest, for that is what he was. He reached out his hand toward me and as I looked into his eyes, I saw the eyes of my beloved, my Jesus, smiling back at me. "Yes Mary, I am with you always, even until the end of time."

Resources

It has been my most humble honor to be the vessel through which this narrative has come forth. I would be remiss if I did not give credit to the mountain of texts which influenced this writing, some unconsciously and some directly. I want to offer a special thank you to Cynthia Bourgeault and her scholarly work, **The Meaning of Mary Magdalene,** *which was released after I began crafting this novel and which I avoided, not wanting it to unduly influence this work. I waited to read her book until this novel was complete. Reading her book gave me the affirmation I needed to know I was on the right track and the validation and motivation I needed to move forward with publication. Thank you Cynthia!*

Bourgeault, Cynthia, *The Meaning of Mary Magdalene – Discovering the Woman at the Heart of Christianity,* Shambhala Publications, 2010.

Douglas-Klotz, Neil, *The Hidden Gospel: Decoding the Spiritual Message of the Aramaic Jesus,* Quest Books, 1999.

Douglas-Klotz, Neil, *Prayers of the Cosmos,* Harper One 1993.

Eisler, Riane, *The Chalice and the Blade,* Harper Collins, 1987.

Eisler, Riane, *Sacred Pleasure,* Harper Collins, 1995.

Ericco, Rocco A. *Setting a Trap for God: The Aramaic Prayer of Jesus,* Unity Books, 1997.

Ferrini, Paul, *Love Without Conditions – Reflections of the Christ Mind,* Heartways Press, 1994.

Ferrini, Paul, *Silence of the Heart - Reflections of the Christ Mind Part II,* Heartways Press, 1996.

Ferrini, Paul, *Return to the Garden - Reflections of the Christ Mind Part IV,* Heartways Press, 1998.

Ferrini, Paul, *Creating a Spiritual Relationship,* Heartways Press, 1998.

Ferrini, Paul, *Dancing with the Beloved,* Heartways Press, 2001.

Ferrini, Paul, *I Am the Door,* Heartways Press, 2011.

Harvey, Andrew, *Son of Man – The Mystical Path to Christ,* Jeremy P. Tarcher, 1998.

Haskins, Susan, *Mary Magdalene – Myth and Metaphor,* Harcourt Brace & Company, 1993.

Hoeller, Stephan, *Gnosticism – New Light on the Ancient Tradition of Inner Knowing,* Quest Books, 2002.

Johnston, William (Ed.), *The Cloud of Unknowing,* Image Books, 1973.

Judith, Anodea, *Wheels of Life: A User's Guide to the Chakra System,* Llewellyn Publications, 1987.

King, Karen, L., *The Gospel of Mary of Magdala – Jesus and the First Woman Apostle,* Polebridge Press, 2003.

Leloup, Jean-Yves, *Judas and Jesus – Two Faces of a Single Revelation,* Inner Traditions, 2006.

Leloup, Jean-Yves, *The Gospel of Mary Magdalene*, Inner Traditions, 2002.

Leloup, Jean-Yves, *The Gospel of Philip,* Inner Traditions, 2003.

Leloup, Jean-Yves, *The Gospel of Thomas,* Inner Traditions, 2005.

Leloup, Jean-Yves, *The Sacred Embrace of Jesus and Mary – The Sexual Mystery at the Heart of the Christian Tradition,* Inner Traditions, 2005.

Levine, Peter A., *Waking the Tiger: Healing Trauma,* North Atlantic Books, 1997.

MacDermot, Violet, *The Fall of Sophia – A Gnostic Text on the Redemption of Universal Consciousness,* Lindisfarne Books, 2001.

Malachi, Tau, *The Gnostic Gospel of St. Thomas – Meditations on the Mystical Teachings,* Llewellyn Worldwide, 2004.

Malachi, Tau, *Gnosis of the Cosmic Christ – a Gnostic Christian Kabbalah,* Llewellyn Worldwide, 2005.

Malachi, Tau, *Living Gnosis – A Practical Guide to Gnostic Christianity,* Llewellyn Worldwide, 2005.

Malachi, Tau, *St. Mary Magdalene – The Gnostic Tradition of the Holy Bride,* Llewellyn Worldwide, 2006.

Marion, Jim, *Putting on the Mind of Christ – The Inner Work of Christian Spirituality,* Hampton Roads, 2000.

Mirdad, Michael, *The Seven Initiations of the Spiritual Path,* A.R.E. Press, 2004.

Myss, Caroline, *Anatomy of the Spirit: The Seven Stages of Power and Healing,* Three Rivers Press, 1997.

Pagels, Elaine, *Beyond Belief – The Secret Gospel of Thomas,* Random House, 2003.

Prakash, Prem, *The Yoga of Spiritual Devotion – A Modern Translation of the Narada Bhakti Sutras,* Inner Traditions, 1998.

Ramsay, Jay, *The Crucible of Love: The Path to Passionate and True Relationships,* O Books, 2005.

Schwan, Marie, Syrup-Bergin, Jacqueline, *Take and Receive Series – Love, Forgiveness, Birth, Surrender, Freedom,* Word Among Us Press, 2004.

Vivekananda, Swami, *Bhakti Yoga – The Yoga of Love and Devotion,* Advaita Ashram, 1922.

Yogananda, Paramahansa, *The Yoga of Jesus – Understanding the Hidden Teachings of the Gospels,* Self-Realization Fellowship, 2007.

Biography

Lauri Ann Lumby is an ordained interfaith minister, spiritual director and Reiki Master Practitioner. She is the pastor of the *Authentic Freedom Virtual Church* and spiritual director of the *Superhero Academy*™. Lauri offers one-on-one spiritual mentoring, classes, workshops and retreats. She is the author of several books including, *Authentic Freedom, Christouch* and *Returning*. You can learn more about Lauri, her writing and professional services at www.yourspiritualtruth.com.

OTHER BOOKS BY LAURI ANN LUMBY

Returning – a woman's midlife journey to herself

Christouch – a Christ-centered approach to energy medicine through hands-on healing

Authentic Freedom – claiming a life of contentment and joy

Lauri Ann Lumby is the owner of Authentic Freedom Ministries, Authentic Freedom Press, and is the creator of Authentic Freedom™ an interdisciplinary approach to the psychological and spiritual formation of adults. You can contact Lauri at:

Authentic Freedom Ministries
Oshkosh, WI
www.yourspiritualtruth.com

www.ingramcontent.com/pod-product-compliance
Lightning Source LLC
Chambersburg PA
CBHW052026020726
47501CB00004B/1265